SEA DJINN

by

LINDA DAVIES

Published by **JERBOA BOOKS**
PO BOX 333838 Dubai UAE
www.jerboabooks.com
First Edition printed in 2007
Second Edition printed in 2009
ISBN 978-9948-431-62-6
Approved by the National Information Council UAE:
No 803 6 February 2008

Text © LINDA DAVIES
Cover Design: CLAIRE BOND

This book is for

Hughie, Tommy and Lara,

adventurers three,

my inspiration

and my delight,

with all my love.

Novels in the Djinn Quintet by Linda Davies:

SEA DJINN

FIRE DJINN

Look out for Storm Djinn, coming soon

Adult novels by Linds Davies

NEST OF VIPERS

WILDERNESS OF MIRRORS

INTO THE FIRE

SOMETHING WILD

FINAL SETTLEMENT

These books are for adults,
and your parents might enjoy them!

You can read more about Linda Davies on her website:

www.ex.ac.uk/~RDavies/arian/linda.html
or simply type in Lindadavies.com

PRAISE FOR SEA DJINN BY LINDA DAVIES

Media Comments

'Dubai's Harry Potter' Emirates Today

'A joyful fantasy.. steeped in the heritage of the region. Wonderful.' Time Out Dubai

Time Out Dubai chose Sea Djinn as the only children's book in its Books of the Year 2007

'A fine piece of prose.' Friday Magazine

'A fast-paced, beautifully descriptive adventure with just the right mixture of compelling characters, well-obserevd humour and page-turning excitement. The Arabian flavour is perfectly balanced so that the book will appeal to children in Dubai, Arabia and far beyond.' Julia Wheeler

'The author has an amazing feel for words and puts it to effective use.' Khaleej Times

'A romping fantasy. Readers can effortlessly transport themselves into Sea Djinn's adventurous world.' Time Out Kids

'Five star. Thrilling, beautifully written book for children with local relevance and international punch. (Adults will secretly read it too!)' You

Reader comments

'This exciting and innovative story opens the door to a new world. I loved it and look forward to reading Fire Djinn.' Pauline, 14, English College

'Sea Djinn is the best book ever! The characters are hysterical and it was fun reading about the same sea that we swim in. Can't wait for Fire Djinn.' Jay, 8, Dubai American Academy

'This book is extremely creative and uses a lot of description so you can actually picture the setting in your head as well as what is happening. It made me want to read more and more of it because of the action. I can't wait for Fire Djinn!' Jack, 11, Repton

'I think Sea Dijnn is a fantastic book with lots of action and adventure. My Mum and I read this together and we couldn't put it down! I loved the way it was set in Dubai and even knew the road Finn lived on so I sort of felt part of the whole story!'
Simon, 11, JESS Arabian Ranches

'I was hooked from the first few pages.' Dale, 11, Jumeirah Primary School

'A book that unleashes the dangers of the undiscovered world' Muhammad, 15, English College

'Sea Djinn makes you feel as though you are on a long, exciting journey,' Sophie 9, Jumeirah Primary School

'It is a very exciting book. I think it as good as Harry Potter - very nearly better. We couldn't wait to get to the next chapter because it's so good and Linda stops at really exciting places.' James, 8, Fulham Prep, London

'My son and I both loved Sea Djinn. It became a part of our lives when we read it together. We can't wait for Fire Djinn.' Clare Slater, forty something, London

'Sea Djinn is remarkable. If you start reading, you get trapped inside the book. Also while you're reading the characters come out.' Eunji, 10, Jumeirah Primary School

Sea Djinn

by

Linda Davies

Fear one thing in all that is….
Fear the Djinn.

The Wishmaster. 1993

☙ CHAPTER ONE ☙

IT WAS A RADIANT day with a rip-roaring wind and brilliant sunshine. A day to be on the beach, surfing the waves, NOT sitting indoors doing maths homework. Finn Kennedy waited until his Aunt was distracted, then he eased quietly from the house, hurried across the garden, and climbed over the locked gate to the street. To freedom.

Finn waited for a break in the traffic then jogged across Beach Road. It was hot and he began to sweat, but the shamal carried with it a hint of cool that seemed to have blown in from far away.

Half a mile to the left he could see the outline of the Burj al Arab, towering above the city streets like some monstrous ship run aground. Now he could smell the sea and his heart quickened.

He walked along a street of palms, the fronds clattering like a thousand angry rattlesnakes and as he turned one more corner, there it was, the beach, stretching out like a band of gold, and beyond it the sea, foaming and turbulent with high waves roaring in.

Finn pulled off his sandals and felt the sand hot and soft beneath his toes. The shore was littered with shells, some beautiful white horn shapes, others tiny conches of brilliant orange and red. There were hundreds, as if some profligate sea god had just scattered them there to beautify the beach.

Shell Beach. That's what he called this place, the only place where he had felt happy since he had arrived at Aunt Camelia's house, the 'Pink Prison,' in Dubai four weeks ago.

The sun was beginning to set, and there was practically no-one around on the beach, just a few die-hard surfers making the most of the rare swell, and a couple of dog walkers. Finn stripped off his t shirt and ran until the waves smashed into him, taking his breath away. He forced his way out deeper, diving under the bigger waves that threatened to break over him. With the sun dipping towards the distant horizon, he launched his body on the waves, surfing into the beach with great whoops of delight. This was what he loved best. The sea was where he felt most at home.

He hurled himself on the biggest waves with no apparent sense of fear, but he always came up, laughing and gasping for breath, the spume slaking off his brown body. He was of medium height, lean, with longer hair than most boys got away with, the legacy of spending months aboard a boat where nobody cared about uniforms or hair cuts. It was a sort of dirty honey colour, bleached blond at the tips by the sun and sea, and his eyes were green as the sea itself, sharp, quick to anger when anyone dropped in on his wave, but quick to smile too when someone had a good run. His nose had a bump in the middle. He'd broken it a year earlier when his surfboard crashed into his face during his worst-ever wipe-out.

The sun dipped below the horizon, sending out great fingers of flame across the sky. Boats scudded by, heading for their moorings. The light faded and the glittering sea turned dull, almost threatening, but Finn didn't notice, he was so caught up with riding the waves.

The evening call of the Muezzin drifted out across the water like a melancholy lament to the dying of the day, but still Finn surfed. Only when night had fallen and the other surfers had departed with a friendly 'goodbye' did Finn drag himself reluctantly from the sea. He shivered and pulled on his t shirt. The shamal had eased off, but the wind was still blowing strongly. He supposed he should go home. Aunt C would be having kittens by now, but he couldn't face it. So he stayed a little longer, sitting cross-legged on the sand, staring into the foaming surf as the moon rode up and silvered the breaking waves.

The stars emerged slowly, twinkling in the darkening sky. He could see Venus, shining more brilliantly than all the other stars. He wondered if his parents, who were marine biologists, were looking at it too, from their boat, wherever it was.

As he turned to leave, a shape in the foam caught his eye. He saw a wave rise up, lift something with it, and then in a fountain of spume and moon-silvered water, the thing disappeared. He waited, heart racing, convinced that his imagination was playing tricks on him. Then the water calmed before the next wave broke, and there in the shallows, looking directly at him, was a kind of man. Only it wasn't a man, not like any he had seen. Below the man's shoulders and torso, where the man's legs should have been, there was the sleek, powerful, grey body of a dolphin - a truly enormous dolphin.

Suddenly, a much bigger wave appeared, and the man creature surfed in on it right up onto the sand. The water swirled around him for a moment, and then rushed back into the ocean.

'Hello,' said the man creature.

Finn stared back, disbeliveing his own eyes. Then he smiled. He had never quite believed in the world sold to him by adults. A world where everything had an explanation, where everything was known, by them, the grown ups, where there was no mystery, no kingdom of the unknown. He had always hoped that there was more......

'Hello,' he manged to say. 'Who, I mean, what are you?'

The creature chuckled, a deep, musical sound, like water gurgling over pebbles.

'My name is Triton. I am many things.'

As the creature began to speak, it seemed to Finn as if the ocean itself tried to listen in, for the waves that had recently been so large and stormy became subdued and the roaring became a gentler lapping as the wind suddenly died.

'A long time ago, right back at the beginning of time, when the first oceans swam over this planet's surface, when the first shoots of green grass sprang from the rich earth, when the first air was breathed, when the first fires raged, the Djinns were created from smokeless fire. We are beings, a bit like angels and demons, but we can incorporate into humans, animals, stones, rivers, whatever we choose. The original Djinn were given their own dominions. There are Djinns of the Earth, Air, Fire, and Sea. That is who I am. I am Triton, the Sea Djinn.' A sad look came over the Djinn's face and he paused in his story. 'I am one of two Sea Djinn. At the beginning of time, we ruled over our dominions together, ensuring the well-being of our elements. We lived in the subtle, immaterial world peaceably for millennia.

But then the other Sea Djinn wanted more. He wanted power over my domain and yours. So began the ancient war of the Djinn.'

The Sea Djinn raised one muscled arm. He reached his palm up to the sky, opened it to the stars, then quickly closed his fingers as if around something. Then he placed his clenched fist over the sand, opened his fingers and blew gently on a small flame. Finn watched, mesmerised.

The flames twisted and flickered around some invisible kindling. They swirled and grew there on the beach, until they seemed to take on a recognisable form. Finn peered in and his eyes grew huge.

He saw something that looked a bit like the Sea Djinn next to him, only it appeared more like an eel, long and slithery and it had about it the unmistakeable stench of evil. Finn could smell it in the acrid smoke that curled from the fire. Finn could see it in the creature's eyes, in the way it slithered, and in what it had done. It was slithering, hissing around a large metal cage. Inside the cage, chained to it, sat Finn's mother and father.

Finn gasped. 'No. That's not happening. It's a trick,' he shouted. 'It's not real. It's not real, is it?' he asked desperately.

The Sea Djinn looked grave. 'I'm afraid it is. That is Hydrus, the Sea Djinn of the night, my enemy and y-'

Finn interrupted him. 'What's he doing with my parents? Why does he have them there and what's he going to do with them?'

The Sea Djinn laid a cool hand on Finn's arm. As he did so, Finn felt a surge of electricity shoot through his body.

'He wants their knowledge. He and his legion of followers have been slowly destroying the sea in their own Dark Kingdom for centuries; now many of them are becoming sick and hungry. The Night Djinn is sick, getting sicker every day, so he scoured the earthly kingdom of yours, and found out that your parents were eminent marine biologists, the best around. So he kidnapped them. He's forcing them to come up with a cure for him and his followers, something to make them stronger so that they can vanquish me and mine in the upcoming battle. Beat us once and for all time.'

There was so much more to say, thought the Sea Djinn. There were the two Prophesies, but they would have to wait. He could see the boy was shocked enough as it was.

Finn sunk his head in his hands. Even though his eyes were closed he could still see the image of his parents, chained in the cage, with the evil Sea Djinn slithering around them, flicking its poisonous tongue at them.

Finally, he looked up. As he did so, the Evil Sea Djinn looked up too, and Finn felt as though Hydrus was looking directly at him. The good Sea Djinn extinguished the fire of vision with a sweep of his arm, but it seemed to Finn it was a moment too late.

'You must go now, back to your aunt,' said the good Djinn quickly.

'How do you know about her? How do you know about my parents?' demanded Finn.

'I am a ruler of my dominion. I have my powers.' Triton didn't add that he had been waiting for Finn, for this moment, for a long time.

'Go home,' he said again, more urgently.

'But my parents... I can't leave them there. I have to do something,' shouted Finn to the Djinn who was hauling himself back into the sea.

'Come back here when you can. I will find you. I will tell you.' With a flick of his great tail, the Sea Djinn disappeared into the waves.

❧ Chapter Two ❧

FINN RAN HOME, UNABLE to shake the sensation that he was being watched, pursued by the unseen. So caught up was he by the urge to flee, he didn't notice the expressions of amazement on the faces on the few people he passed. He had no idea that he was running faster than he ever had before, in fact, faster than any normal grown man could run.

Back on Street 21, outside Aunt C's house, he slowed. The gate loomed before him, ten feet of glass with a delicate metal filigree dancing over it. He took the first foothold and pushed himself up onto the gate.

It was easier than it looked to climb, it was the jumping down that was tricky, as steps led down to the gate from the garden, and he had to jump beyond them or risk a painful landing. He launched himself into space and landed with a great thump a good twenty feet from the gate. He gazed round, stupefied. How had he done that? He had almost flown. It just was not possible. His heart beat wildly. His head felt like there were bubbles in it, rising to the surface, making him dizzy. He stayed where he was, crouched on the ground in the middle of the garden, trying to feel normal again.

The sound of a door opening made him jump. Someone was standing, half-concealed behind the door

Oh no, Aunt C, please no. He couldn't face her accusations, recriminations. He focused through the darkness - small, slight body, wildly curling red hair gleaming in the pale light thrown from the street lamps - his cousin, Georgie. Finn said a quick, *thank you*. Georgie beckoned frantically.

'Finn, for goodness's sake. Get in. Where've you been? What have you been up to?' she demanded in a fierce whisper.

Finn ran half-crouched across the garden, like a soldier evading enemy fire. Georgie closed the door behind him and locked it.

'Quick, up to your bedroom,' she whispered. They scurried up the stairs, holding their breath.

'Got you!' said two voices in unison. Finn and Georgie jumped and wheeled round. The twins, Cordelia, whom Finn called Corduroy because of her ropy hair, and Cressida, whom he called Creosote because she was always oiling up to her mother, stood at the entrance to their bedroom, looking smug.

'Just wait till Mummy hears,' taunted Creosote.

Finn took a step towards them. The twins yelped and retreated two steps. Georgie held up a hand to Finn.

'Mummy won't hear. Not so much as whisper,' she announced.

'Oh yeah? How can you stop us?' demanded Corduroy.

'Simple,' said Georgie. 'You say a word, you can forget pizza, pancakes, pasta, pastries. Anything good.'

Since Georgie's father had gone three months previously, her mother had gradually lost the will to cook anything except the most basic meals, so Georgie had taken over more and more of the shopping and cooking. The twins looked sour in defeat. They hung their heads and slunk off.

Georgie grinned at Finn. 'Sorted.' Georgie had a small, angular, determined-looking face and when she smiled she looked positively impish.

Finn made it to his bedroom and closed the door behind him with a huge sigh of relief.

'Spill,' commanded Georgie, hands on her hips.

'Aunt C? Where is she?'

'You're lucky. The twins were being particularly thick with their homework. Half an hour with them and Mum grabbed her head and started moaning. One of her migraines. Went straight to her room and hasn't been out since. She's out for the count, till tomorrow at least.'

'Phew!'

'Yeah, big phew for you. So?'

Finn blew out a great breath. Where did he start?

'All right. But first you must promise not to tell, especially Corduroy and Creosote.'

'As if,' Georgie replied scornfully. Georgie and the twins did not get on at the best of times, but since Finn had arrived and teamed up with Georgie the twins had become even more poisonous than usual.

'You're not going to believe this,' said Finn.

Georgie's eyes grew larger and larger and she actually listened without interrupting, save the odd gasp.

'Flipping heck,' she managed to say when Finn had finished.

'Yeah, or something like that.'

'So what about your parents?'

'I'm going back to the beach tomorrow evening, same time. I'll see that Djinn again. He has to tell me what I can do.'

'Mmm,' replied Georgie thoughtfully. 'Hey, what's that?' she said suddenly, pointing to Finn's arm.

Finn glanced at his skin. It had a luminous tinge to it, which almost seemed to be moving.

'It's shimmering, like the sea at night,' said Georgie.

'He laid his hand on my arm,' said Finn. 'The Sea Djinn. Maybe that's why....' he trailed off. He hadn't told Georgie about his great leap. He thought there was a limit to what he could ask even her to believe.

They talked for a while more, then Finn yawned so hugely that Georgie could see his tonsils. He staggered to bed, collapsed under the duvet and was asleep before his head hit the pillow. Georgie crept up to him, stroked a finger over the shiny patch on his arm. On a whim, she touched the scab on her knee from her latest rollerblading fall. The phosphorescence flickered over her skin. Before her astonished eyes, the scab healed into new skin, and all trace of the wound vanished.

That night, as the children slept, far out at sea, on an island of bones, the evil Sea Djinn writhed and hissed, conjuring visions from flames snatched from the ether. In those visions he saw Finn, saw his house, saw his bed. Awake he stayed, all the long night, deciding what he would do about the human boy, and his parents.

Finn trembled in his sleep, disturbed by nightmares that were rooted in truth.

CHAPTER THREE

THE NEXT DAY WAS a school day. Aunt Camelia, recovered from her migraine, rapped on all the bedroom doors with varying degrees of sharpness, calling out gently to Cordelia and Cressida, who shared a room and were not the sort of children who needed raised voices, calling loudly to Georgie, who was apt to ignore anything less than a shout, and breaking into a full blown yell for Finn.

The yell caught Finn slap bang in the middle of his nightmare, and he woke giving a yell of his own. 'Arghhhhh-'

Georgie ran into his room. 'You all right?'

Finn rubbed his face. His hair was as wild as his eyes.

'Your mother, yelling at me. Thought she was, I don't know... I saw monsters. Had nightmares. Bad ones.'

Georgie gave his shoulder a quick pat. 'Morning for pancakes, I'd say. C'mon. Get dressed quickly and there'll be time.'

Finn needed no more encouragement. He jumped from bed and hauled on his school uniform, feeling a quick glow of affection for his cousin. Without her in this house, he really would have gone mad by now.

Georgie had become an excellent cook. They were a few incinerations to begin with, but Georgie learned quickly when it was something that mattered to her. And food did. Big time. So she became an expert in preparing and cooking burgers with thick, juicy chips, pasta with delicious creamy sauces, pizzas dripping with toppings, fish with crisp golden batter and chips, fried onion rings, chocolate cake, and, best of all, pancakes.

Anything to tempt her mother to eat. Anything to make life look normal, on the surface at least. Food was a comfort they all needed desperately.

Georgie missed her father with an ache that was worse than any physical pain she had ever felt. Like her mother, she refused to believe that he had abandoned them, but she could not believe her mother's wild theories that he had been kidnapped. She thought that he must have suffered a blow to the head, perhaps the boom whacked him when he was out sailing and he developed amnesia. She knew that happened to people. He had probably sailed off to Africa, sold his boat, which was why no-one ever found it, and was working as a teacher in some African school in the bush with elephants roaming the horizon. Every night she thought of him, in Africa, with the elephants.

But she had no time for those thoughts now. She hurried into her short-sleeved white shirt, dragged on her pinafore dress, tugged on her socks and rammed her feet into the grubby black shoes which she had accidentally on purpose forgotten to clean. She clattered down stairs and hit the kitchen like a whirlwind.

So proficient was she at pancakes that she didn't even need to weigh or measure the ingredients anymore. She just shook out the right amount of flour into the food processor, broke two eggs into it, poured in the right amount of milk, screwed the top on as tight as it would go (she'd made a big mistake on that one once, failing to secure the top so that when she hit the MIX button the mixture had swirled round madly, pushed the lid off and exploded out all over her hair and uniform. Her sisters hadn't stopped laughing about it for days.)

She hit the MIX button today with a slight feeling of trepidation, but the lid held firm, and one minute later the mixture was done. Into two saucepans sizzling with butter it went, and pretty soon she had ten pancakes cooked. Two each for everyone.

Georgie grabbed the golden syrup and poured it over her pancakes, passing it to Finn. She was surprised to see him eat only one pancake, then push the plate away with a miserable look. She could see in his eyes he was thinking about his parents and her heart ached for him.

Finn hated his new school. It was called the Jumeirah Academy of Music, known to all as JAM. It wasn't much more musical than other schools, but it sounded artistic and cultured and was apparently very hard to get into so he should be grateful he was there. It had fun things to do but being the new boy was a pain. He missed his old friends and his old teacher back home in Pembrokeshire. He missed his parents and the haphazard tutoring they gave him and his sister when he travelled with them on their boat.

Most of the kids at the new school were okay, he just didn't know them, had no shared history with them, but one or two of them were poisonous. In his first week at JAM, he'd been put in the swim squad and that had earned him the enmity of the boy who had lost his place to Finn.

Just his luck to bump into that very boy at first break. His name was Dagmar Drax. His friends called him Dagger.

'Hey, Fishboy,' called Dagmar. 'Bad smell round here, isn't there, something fishy. Think you can swim, do you, huh? Just try me in the boxing ring, then we'll see who comes out on top.' Dagmar jogged around Finn, eyes narrow with hatred, shadow boxing, just missing Finn's face by inches. Behind him, glowering darkly, was Dagmar's band of buddies, Brian, whom Finn nicknamed Bovine because he looked like a cow and was always chewing, and Colin, whom he called Butthead for reasons that were obvious to anyone who looked at his face. Finn was well and truly outnumbered.

'Missing your parents, new boy?' taunted Dagmar. 'Worried that you might never see them again, I'll bet.'

Finn snapped. He whipped back his fist and punched Dagmar with all his might. Dagmar flew backwards through the air and crumpled to the ground like a giant rag doll. Finn scarcely heard the kerfuffle that followed. Had Dagmar *known*? It was as if he had. But *how*?

Through the confusion of his silent questions boomed the voice of Mr Gusting, the PE master.

'Stand back, stand back, let me get to him.' Mr Gusting pushed his way through the hordes of children who had congregated quickly at the first hint of trouble, and were now watching excitedly.

Gusting took one look at Dagmar's limp body and shouted: 'Nurse! Nurse! Somebody get Nurse Pilchard NOW.'

Then he fell down to his knees and took Dagmar's pulse. At that moment, Dagmar's eyes flickered open and he groaned. He pushed himself up onto one elbow, weakly turning his thick neck from side to side, searching for Finn.

'Easy now, easy Dag,' crooned Mr Gusting. Dagmar was one of his protégées, being captain of boxing for his year, and faster in the ring than the boys a full two years ahead of him. With the interschool boxing championships coming up, Mr Gusting did not want any harm to befall his star.

'What happened Dag?' He asked, his usually harsh voice gentle. 'Did you run into a tree?'

Dagmar managed a miserable shake of his head.

'Hit me,' he moaned.

'Who?' demanded Mr Gusting, looking around, eyes blazing.

'He, he…' spluttered Dagmar, pointing feebly at Finn. 'He did it.'

Mr Gusting looked somewhat doubtfully at Finn, clearly trying to figure out how Finn could have knocked out someone twice his size.

'He did what?' queried Mr Gusting.

'He.... he thumped me,' whispered Dagmar, cheeks flushing red with humiliation.

Nurse Pilchard arrived, squatted down and began to give Dagmar a thorough examination.

'Lie still boy, and lairt me gairt yer fiddlesome tie off,'' she commanded in a Scottish accent so thick and brutal that whatever she said sounded like an insult.

Georgie, who had come up to see what all the fuss was about had to stifle a giggle when Dagmar groaned again under the rough hands of Nurse Pilchard.

She stopped giggling as she watched Mr Gusting march up to Finn.

'Is this true, boy?' he demanded.

Finn nodded. For one brief moment a look of admiration flitted across Mr Gusting's face, then he wiped it off with teacherly disapproval.

'You want to box, get in line to join the boxing team. I don't know what sort of standards prevailed in your old school, but here at JAM we do not tolerate this kind of behaviour. You're lucky you didn't break his nose. One hour's detention.' Mr Gusting turned to follow Nurse Pilchard who was strong-arming Dagmar towards her starched treatment room

'*He's* lucky I didn't break his nose,' muttered Finn, cursing himself. One more hour before he could escape to the beach, try and see the Djinn again and find out how he could rescue his parents.

Mr Gusting, who must have been five yards away, separated from Finn by a wall of chattering children, stopped in his tracks. He turned his head in Finn's direction, and he looked to Finn like a bird of prey intent on plucking out eyes not answers.

Finn looked nervously at the ground.

'He said Dagger was lucky he didn't break his nose,' Butthead gleefully informed Mr Gusting.

'I heard him. Let's make that two hours' detention. Tonight.'

'No, not tonight, please, not tonight,' pleaded Finn.

'Why, get in the way of boxing training?' sneered Mr Gusting. 'My office. Don't be late.' He turned and strode off.

Finn stared miserably after him. Georgie came up to him and patted his arm.

'Bad luck,' she said. 'But well done for thumping that

bully, Dagmar. It's what most kids in this school would love to do but no-one dares.'

'Yeah, well, he deserved it. Did you hear what he said?'

'No,' said Georgie. 'I was playing football. I saw him stop and speak to you, next thing I saw was him flying through the air.'

A few giggles broke out around them. 'Come on,' said Georgie. 'Let's go somewhere quiet.'

They headed away from the centre of the playground towards one of the acacia trees at the perimeter. Brilliant orange flowers lay strewn around them as they sat down in the shade. Finn told Georgie what Dagmar had said.

'But he couldn't know, could he, about your parents? I mean nobody knows, do they, apart from us, and the Djinn of course?' queried Georgie.

'I don't know,' said Finn, rubbing his head. 'Could just have been coincidence, but the look in his eyes, I swear Georgie, he really did seem to know.'

'Coincidence,' Georgie said smartly, keen to find an answer to everything. There was only one thing Georgie liked better than a mystery and that was solving one.

'And that big bully Gusting. Two hours' detention. Can you believe it? How did he even hear me?' complained Finn. 'He must have bionic hearing or something.'

'Maybe he does,' replied Georgie. 'I mean why not? You just did a bionic punch.'

Finally, she succeeded in getting a grin out of Finn. 'I did, didn't I?'

'Now,' said Georgie, eyes gleaming wickedly. 'What shall I do to earn myself two hours' detention?'

❧ Chapter Four ❧

G EORGIE WAS DELIGHTED BY her detention scam. Watching her domestic science teacher spit out the fairy cakes laced with sand was a treat. The only thing that bothered her was her mother's face when she arrived for pickup.

'I'm not in the least surprised by Finn's detention, he always did live by his own rules,' she said, 'but you, Georgie, you know how to behave.'

'Sometimes, Mama, you have to know how not to behave too,' Georgie replied.

Georgie's mother gazed up to Heaven, as if seeking there the answers she was unable to find on earth.

'Oh, Georgie, you are so like your father, and I never could understand him either. I'll see you, and Finn, wherever he is, in two hours,' she concluded sadly, then turned and walked away.

Georgie watched her go with a pain in her heart. Preoccupied, she wandered off in the direction of Gusting's office. He didn't have a classroom, unless you counted the gymnasium, boxing ring, tennis courts, football pitch or swimming pool, but he did have a large office with good views out of two windows. Not that she expected to see much out of them. She'd probably be writing five hundred times : *I must not replace sugar with sand in Petronella Brockness's fairy cakes.*

She knocked.

'Enter,' boomed Gusting. Georgie felt her first flutter of nerves. She'd always suspected that Mr Gusting didn't like her. He wasn't someone you wanted for an enemy.

'Sit,' he commanded, as if she were a dog.

The only other person in detention was a thin boy with unruly dark hair, the white skin of someone who didn't get out enough, and keenly intelligent eyes. He jumped when a few moments later Finn entered and slammed the door behind him.

Georgie winced.

'Still angry are, we, eh, eh? Well, we'll do something about that. Sit down, Finlay,' boomed Mr Gusting.

'It's not Finlay, it's Fi-'

'Do you think I am one bit interested?' asked Mr Gusting. 'Do you think at all?' He smiled, pleased with his attempts at humiliation. 'If you weren't in the swim squad I'd be tempted to get you suspended for assault, but, as it is, you're useful to me so I won't. But, you still need to be punished, so I've got something suitably unpleasant planned for you,' he added, with a malevolent smile. At that moment Gusting's mobile rang. He frowned down at his pocket and snatched out his phone.

'Yes,' he said into it angrily. Suddenly his body language changed. He almost jumped to attention.

'Yes. Right away,' he said in reply. Without a backward glance, he grabbed his jacket off his chair and hurried from the room.

Georgie turned to Finn. 'What d'you think that was all about?'

'Dunno. You think he's coming back?'

'He seemed to forget all about us, didn't he?' said the other boy.

Finn and Georgie nodded.

They sat in silence for a couple of minutes, then Georgie got up.

'What now?' she asked.

'We could just chat for a bit,' suggested the other boy.

'Who are you?' asked Georgie, slightly irritably, as if he had no business being there.

'I'm Fred,' he replied. 'Who are you?'

Georgie and Finn introduced themselves.

'You must really have annoyed him,' Fred said to Finn. 'What did you do?'

Finn told him and Fred let out a whistle. 'Well done! Dagmar Drax deserves a good punching.'

'Exactly,' agreed Georgie. 'What did you do?'

'Forged a note to get out of games.'

'How d'you get caught?' asked Georgie.

'Well, I was pushing it, I suppose. Fourth time in five weeks I did it. He must've got all suspicious, 'cos he rang my mother.' Fred looked miserable. 'No more getting out of games now.'

'What's wrong with games?' asked Georgie. 'Better than maths or urgh, science, surely.'

'Not for me. I'm useless at every kind of sport so far invented, apart from running. I'm quite fast at that. And, actually, I love science. You see I like inventing things.'

'Invent a way out of here, then,' said Finn.

Fred got to his feet, ambled across the office and opened the door. 'What are you waiting for? You've got legs haven't you?' he said to Finn and Georgie who were looking at him in surprise. He seemed on the outside like a good boy, a bit of a swot, but obviously that was not the case.

Fred reckoned he was in enough trouble already, a little extra wouldn't make much of a difference.

'C'mon. He's abandoned us. Taken his jacket. Gone. So should we.'

Georgie and Finn grabbed their backpacks and followed him. They glanced up and down the corridor but there was no-one in sight.

'What are we going to do?' asked Georgie.

'Sneak out, of course,' replied Fred. 'Actually, we just walk out all brazen then no-one will question us. *Act like you own the place and one day you will*, that's what my father's always saying.'

So that's what they tried to do. They got past Miss Naim, the school counsellor, with a smile and a nod, and were just rounding the next corner when they spied Dagmar and his cronies Butthead and Bovine heading towards them.

'There he is, and that poxy cousin of his, let's get them,' yelled Dagmar, breaking into a sprint.

'Urgh,' gulped Fred.

'What now?' gasped Georgie.

'I want to ask him what he knows,' said Finn belligerently.

'When he's alone, Finn. Right now, we're about to get pulverised,' said Georgie urgently. 'C'mon. *Run*,' she exhorted, and set off back the way they'd come. Fred needed no encouragement. He set off after her. Finn gave Dagmar a look of pure loathing, then took off after Georgie and Fred. He soon caught them and all three of them barrelled round the corner together. The long corridor stretched before them, and they could hear the pounding of feet behind them which told them Dagmar and his gang were catching up.

'In here, quickly,' whispered Georgie.

She opened the door to a classroom, and the three of them ducked in.

'Oh no,' she groaned. She'd thought it was empty, but in a far corner stood a tall teacher with a mad thatch of black hair streaked through with a stripe of white, bending over the table where a boy sat watching something bubbling in a test tube above a Bunsen burner.

'*Ah, there you are,*' said the teacher, smiling at the three of them with great enthusiasm. 'I was wondering where you'd got to.'

At that moment, the door burst open and Dagmar and his gang glowered in the doorway.

With surprising agility, the teacher moved to block from view the boy and the experiment with the Bunsen burner.

'Yes boys?' said the teacher in a different voice, a sort of dead, boring voice. 'Are you here for the spelling skills MasterClass? Welcome, come in, sit down.'

'Spelling! MasterClass!' They spat. 'You must be joking,' they all said in unison, then turned and left rapidly.

'Good, that sent them on their way, didn't it?' chortled the rather strange teacher. 'Now, please sit down.'

'Bbbbb-, but, we don't want a spelling MasterClass,' groaned Georgie.

'Who said anything about spelling? That was just to put those ruffians off.'

'Mr Violet?' said the boy.

'Wait one second, Eric. Let me get these three settled.'

'Mr Violet,' came the voice, getting plaintive.

'Now, Georgie, Fred and Finn, I know you must be-'

'*Mr Violet!*' the voice was desperate now. '*Mr V*, it's going to, it's going to EXPLODE!'

He had Mr Violet's attention now. The teacher swung round, gasped as he saw the liquid bubbling and emitting an evil-looking green gas.

'*Take cover,*' he yelled, somehow gathering all the children under his arms and flinging them to the floor under a desk. Above their heads, there was an ominous silence, then the BANG of an explosion and the crashing sounds of exploding glass hitting the walls, the ceiling, anything in range. The children heard the glass raining down on the table above them. They all stayed where they were, breathing rapidly.

'Phew, that was a close one,' said the teacher, still sounding cheerful. He ducked out from under the edge of the desk and unbent his long frame.

'It's all right, you can come out now,' he said.

Cautiously, Fred, Georgie, Finn and the other boy eased out from under the desk.

The teacher stood surveying the room. Papers were littered everywhere as if an entire class had had a temper tantrum and broken glass sparkled in the sun.

'Good!' said the teacher, with satisfaction. 'Eric, now you know how to mix volatile substances and make an explosion.'

Eric nodded, looking pleased.

'That was meant to happen?' asked Finn.

'Absolutely. Of course in an ideal world we would have had more time to take cover, but then the world is not ideal, is it. Far from it in fact. Wonderful, but not ideal.'

'Doesn't it break all the school rules?' asked Fred. 'I mean Health and Safety?'

'Pah!' exclaimed the teacher, bending towards Fred to make his point.

'Pah,' echoed Georgie with a giggle.

'Fat lot of good Health and Safety would do for Eric here when he's locked in at the bl- ah, er, no need to go into detail there, enough to say, you'll be able to blast your way out now, won't you Eric?'

'Yes, Mr Violet,' replied Eric.

'Mr Violet? I've never seen you around here before. Are you really a teacher here?' asked Georgie.

Mr Violet shook his head. 'I'm not on the staff roster, if that's what you mean. No, I'm a sort of supply teacher. I come when needed. Eric summoned me, so I came.'

'Summoned you?' asked Georgie.

'Mm. Thought hard about me. I picked up his thoughts, I responded,' he answered.

'But, but,' spluttered Georgie, still trying to understand, 'why would Eric need to make a mini bomb?'

'I would have thought it was obvious. If you are locked in somewhere, with no key and no other means to escape, then blowing your way out is a rather good solution, no?'

'But why would Eric be locked in anywhere?'

'That, Georgie, is a bigger question than I have time for at the moment.'

'But how do you know he's going to be locked in? Answer me that then?' demanded Georgie refusing to give up. 'And, what's more,' she continued, 'if you know this, then why can't you stop it happening?'

'You mean change the future?' asked Mr Violet, eyebrows arching with interest.

'Yes. After all, you're claiming to know it, so why not change it?'

'Changing the future is beyond me. The best I can do is mould the present so that it can influence the future. That's why Eric is here, that's why you are here.'

'What, me?' asked Fred, looking doubtful.

'All of you,' answered Mr Violet with a smile. 'I need to prepare you, and time is short, so please sit down.' Mr Violet turned to Eric. 'Confident you got all that down pat?'

'Yep. Think so.'

'Good. There's a package on my desk. Take it with you. Keep it with you at all times. Be ready. Remember, you'll be fine. Stay cool and calm.'

Eric nodded gravely, then took a small plastic pouch from the teacher's desk and quietly left the room.

Fred, Georgie and Finn looked questioningly at one another.

'No, Finn, I'm not a lunatic,' said Mr Violet.

'How di-'

Mr Violet just waved a hand. 'Telepathy's a useful skill, especially for you, since you're so prone to rush in to situations.'

'Please,' said Georgie. 'Please tell us what is going on.'

'Clean up time first,' intoned Mr Violet. 'Will you help me?' Without waiting for an answer he crunched his way across broken glass to a small cupboard, which he tapped four times, then pulled out four implausibly long brooms and four large dustpans. Georgie, Finn and Fred blinked, but each took a dustpan and brush, and in a surprisingly short time, the classroom was restored to order. While they were all sweeping up, Mr Violet must have somehow managed to sort out all the papers because they were gone too.

Job done, Georgie, Fred and Finn took their seats at a large desk. Mr Violet pulled up a chair on the other side.

'I cannot explain everything to you, because I don't know it all myself, but I know some of what the future holds and some of what will befall the three of you. If you are to have any chance of survival it will be by working together, using the skills that I am going to teach you and I think you will need. And, yes, Finn, this is related, directly, to what happened to you yesterday, and to what has happened to your parents.'

Finn gasped. 'You know all that?'

'Some of that.'

'Can you help me then, can you help me free my parents?'

'That's why I'm here.'

'But can't you just do something now? You're a grown up, grown ups can do things, sort things, you must be able to help me, now.'

'You've been sold the myth of adult invincibility, Finn,' Mr Violet replied gently. 'There is a limit to what I can do. But everything I can do, I will. This is my fight too. I am on your side. My job is to teach you all as much as I can to arm you, to prepare you for what lies ahead.'

Mr Violet smiled briefly and glanced at his watch. 'We'll need to be quick. We don't have much time. All three of you need to learn Thought Protection and Astral Travel.'

'Astral Travel?' asked Fred, with a bemused look on his face.

'Some people call it Teleporting, but I think that sounds a tad prosaic for what is really rather exciting,' replied Mr Violet. 'Fred, you know a bit about the stars, don't you?'

'A bit. I have a telescope on my balcony. On a clear night I can see - how did you know that?' Fred asked, interrupting himself.

'Another time,' answered Mr Violet. 'Point is, you're the best one to learn Celestial Navigation. And Georgie, you need to learn how to make a sleeping potion, and Finn, you need to learn how to desalinate sea water so you can drink it, and learn how to make glass.'

'Glass!' Shouted Finn. 'You think you're going to help me save my parents by teaching me how to make glass? Are you mad? My parents are lying chained in a cage with that horrible thing slithering around them and all you can do is offer to teach me glass blowing. As if that will rescue them.'

Fred's eyes bulged. *'Slithery thing?* What slith-'

'Actually, if you learn it well enough, it just might,' replied Mr Violet, ignoring Fred. 'You have to trust me, Finn. I can't help you, or your parents, unless you do.'

Finn blew out a great sigh. 'What choice do I have? I'll do anything to help them.'

'Oh, you have a choice, Finn. You can get up and walk out.'

Finn locked eyes with Mr Violet. He considered doing just that. Getting up and walking out. Then he seemed to see, like a video fast forwarding, a series of images, a boat, riding high on a wave, a cliff wall, the awful, slithering thing, someone else, a face he recognised but didn't have time to place, and some kind of island, with living things that he had never seen before. All this passed before his eyes in such a brief flash that he wondered if he were just imagining it. All that remained, were Mr Violet's eyes, the same colour as his name, their previous kindness replaced by a steely determination.

'I'll stay,' Finn said. 'Tell me what I need to know.'

Mr Violet nodded. 'Georgie? Fred?'

'I'm not going to miss this,' replied Georgie.

'Fred?'

'Um, er, I don't suppose you know this, but, er, are the stock markets, specifically London and New York, going to go up or down today?'

Mr Violet seemed momentarily nonplussed. Finn and Georgie looked at Fred like he had suddenly started spouting Martian.

'Give me a moment, Fred.' Mr Violet turned his head sideways as if listening out for something. He stayed like that for a minute or so.

'Bad day, all round, I'm afraid, Fred,' he said, eyes distant. 'Shorting Sun Systems would be a good idea,' he concluded, eyes coming back to Fred.

'And I can really help, can I, with Finn's parents?'

'Not only can you help, Fred, you're essential,' replied Mr Violet.

Fred looked delighted. 'Right, well then, count me in.'

'Excellent! Now, Georgie. Let's start with you. Basic sleeping potion. Here are the ingredients.'

In fifteen minutes, Georgie had learned a new recipe.

'Now Finn,' said Mr Violet. 'What we n-'

The teacher froze suddenly. He glanced at his watch. 'It's wearing off, early. Blast and perdition. Back to Disgusting's office. Quick march.'

The three children giggled. 'That's what we call him.'

'With good reason. Go on. Hurry.'

'You're not coming with us, to explain?' asked Georgie.

'No. And say nothing about this, about me. Just act like you've been in his office all this time, and he won't know any different. Be extremely wary of Dennis Gusting. Stay out of his way in future. I won't always be able to protect you.'

'But how, why sh-'

'Run,' shouted Mr Violet. 'If you go *now*, you'll just make it.' The sudden fear in his eyes made them run. They charged out of the classroom, leaving the door flapping behind them, and hurtled down the corridor. They got to Mr Gusting's office and fell into their chairs, puffing and panting. Seconds later, they heard footsteps rat-tat-tatting like gun-fire round the corner, then the door flew open. Mr Gusting stood there. He screwed up his eyes, scrutinising the three of them.

'Lines?' he demanded.

The children looked in panic at the sheets of paper on their desk. There, before, them, written out neatly in their own individual handwriting, were their lines.

∽ Chapter Five ∾

FRED RODE BACK SILENTLY in the Range Rover with his mother. His mother, however, was not silent.

'Fred, how could you? Detention, with the riff-raff. We are not that kind of family, you know that. This kind of behaviour is simply not acceptable. Do you hear me? Fred? *FRED*!'

'Urgh?' Fred, sitting in the back seat, gazing out of the window and trying to make sense of what he had seen and heard over the past few hours, jumped violently at the lash of his mother's voice.

'What will your father say?' demanded his mother.

'All depends on the markets, doesn't it,' replied Fred.

'Now Fred, don't change the subject. Your father has a very stressful job. He wouldn't be human if it didn't get to him now and then. And, need I remind you, our net worth goes up and down with those markets, so this is serious business. It's not just numbers, Fred.'

Fred thought that's exactly what it was. The rise and fall of the markets never seemed to make any difference to his mother's visits to the shops, beauticians or hairdressers or to the type of holidays they took or to the restaurants in which they dined. It was a kind of obsession, Fred knew that. The value of the portfolio. Like a game of cricket, only the opponents were the friends of his mother and father and there was no such thing as a team. It was every man and woman pair against every other. Silly game, thought Fred, but it amused them. Trouble was, when his father lost, well, Fred wasn't sure he liked being around him very much then. The words 'Bad Loser' jumped into Fred's head before he could stop them. He banished those thoughts with images of Finn's wild eyes and the sense of mystery that clung to him; Georgie, with her impish grin and filthy shoes, and the wonderfully eccentric and raving mad Mr Violet. He'd never met people like them before. They were not the sort of people his parents would like him consorting with and they were all the more attractive for that reason.

His parents were very particular. They wanted a boy who was good at sport, knew when to shake grown-ups by the hand, look them in the eye and address them clearly and intelligently. They wanted a boy who could sail a boat, strike the perfect forehand, score a goal, not an own goal. But he wasn't it. Perhaps there'd been some mix up at the hospital where he was born, maybe he was a changeling, and the real Adam's baby was now scoring goals and shaking hands back in London. But Fred just wanted to invent, to draw things, and then to make them. He could run quite fast if he wanted to, he just never really wanted to.

What he wanted, was friends. Not the sons and daughters of his parent's hand-picked friends, who were all little Miss or Master Perfect on the surface, smiling hand-shakers when the parents were looking on, and thumpers or pinchers when their backs were turned. They didn't like him because he didn't fit in, and, fine, he didn't want to be like them, or like anyone, but friends would have been nice. Now, thanks to detention, he'd found two. In one go! And, somehow, he was mixed up in the same thing they were, although he couldn't quite get his head round references to Finn's parents and some slithery thing.

He'd never had a chance to ask and Finn never had a chance to explain because as soon as he'd walked out of Mr Gusting's office his mother had pounced on him and pulled him away as if the others were plague carriers.

His mother slammed the door and marched into the house. Normally she would quiz him about his day at school, hand him a biscuit if he'd gained enough house points, but today she barrelled straight through to his father's study.

'Caradoc,' she called out. 'You're needed. Family conference.'

Fred groaned.

'What? What's up?' Fred's father came out running a hand through his hair, tie off and shirt buttons open. Always a bad sign. 'Look, Alison, the markets are just a tad busy, it's not going quite so well today,' he said through gritted teeth. Fred's father worked a full day at his office in Emirates Towers, but carried on his daily tussle with the markets long after he had come home.

'That's as maybe, but your son has just spent the past two hours, not in Go-On Maths, but in detention.'

Fred smiled to himself at the thought of the real Masterclass he had been to. Unfortunately, his father noticed.

'You think this is funny, Frederick?' demanded his father. 'We struggled long and hard to get you into JAM. Is this how you repay us?'

'Er, no. Course not,' said Fred quickly. 'Sorry. I was just thinking about something else.'

'Well, I suggest you stop thinking and listen. I do not pay good money to send you to that school only to have you end up in detention, with God knows what undesirables. What, incidentally, did you do?'

'Erm, you know the markets will close down, today,' gushed Fred in a desperate attempt to distract his father. Note forging would not go down well, that much was certain. 'Short Sun Systems, that's what I would do,' Fred added.

Caradoc Adams studied his son with new interest and thinly veiled amusement.

'You would, would you? And since when, pray, have you become a financial expert?'

Fred racked his brain for a convincing explanation.

He took from his pocket the mobile his mother insisted he take everywhere in case of emergency and waved it in the air. 'Crossed line. Heard two guys talking. American accents. One of them said something about the Golden view.'

Fred's father bent down to his son in excitement. 'Goldman view? Could it have been Goldman view?'

'Yes!' shouted Fred. 'That's it. 'The Goldman view.'

Fred's father ruffled his hair, detention forgotten. 'Well done, Fred.' He flicked a quick glance at his wife.

'Sorry, Ally. Got to go. Moolah beckons. Hey, Freddie,' he shouted over his shoulder. 'I make money from this, you get yourself a bonus, O.K?'

'Great,' said Fred.

Fred's mother blew out a deep sigh of frustration. Ignoring Fred, she headed to the telephone to commiserate with her new best friend, Anthea Drax, over what unsupportive brutes men were, of how in so many ways she was actually a *single mother*, but, somehow, still had to spend all day at the hairdressers and gym and mall so that she could remain a *trophy wife*. Fred had heard this conversation a million times before, between his mother and various girlfriends. He knew he could count on a good twenty minutes before he was missed, and probably more, since his parents were giving a dinner party that night, and soon his mother would be busy glamorising herself while the maids slaved in the kitchen preparing a four course meal.

Quickly, he changed out of his uniform, pulled on shorts, t shirt and trainers, grabbed a key and ran from the house.

At the Pink Prison, Georgie was testing out her sleeping potion.

'Cordy, Cressie, I've made a lovely smoothie for you. Full of energy, and good for the skin too. We made it in Food Technology today. I saved it especially for you.'

'Ooh, goody,' said the twins, approaching the glasses hungrily.

Georgie smiled. If she could make the twins sleep, she wouldn't have to give in to their blackmail when they discovered that she and Finn had gone out.

'Oh, Georgie, could I have some, please?' asked her mother, approaching. 'I haven't really had much to eat today.'

Georgie swallowed a groan. She didn't want to give her mother a potion, but her mother looked starving and she never slept well, so perhaps the potion would be good for her.

'Sure, the twins will share, won't you?'

They nodded.

'Here you go,' said Georgie, dividing the potion into three glasses and handing them over. 'Bottoms up.' She watched her mother and the twins drain the glasses.

'Mmm, delicious,' they all said. Georgie wondered if the potion would be strong enough in smaller doses. She glanced at her watch. Mr Violet had said it should take ten minutes to work.

'Now, tea,' said her mother. 'You girls need something a bit more substantial.'

'Can we play in our room first?' asked Cordy.

'Of course. I'll go and see what there is.'

'Shepherd's pie,' said Georgie. She'd made one the night before. Her mother reached down and stroked her hair.

'Thanks, my love. You've saved me again.'

Georgie laid the table, covertly watching her mother washing the salad. After a while, Cecilia began to yawn.

'Mummy, why don't I do that?' suggested Georgie. 'You look a little tired. Perhaps you should have a lie down? I'll cook dinner and call you when it's ready.'

'Oh, Georgie. You are kind,' said her mother, pricking at Georgie's conscience. 'I think I might just do that. I do feel rather tired all of a sudden.'

Ten minutes later, Georgie's mother and sisters were fast asleep in their beds. Georgie headed for Finn's room.

'One hundred per cent success,' she said. 'C'mon. Let's go.'

Fred arrived at the beach puffing hard. He sat down on the sand beside Georgie and Finn and gazed out to sea with a look of fascinated intensity. The sun set in a blaze of gold, and darkness fell quickly. The call of the Muezzin swirled and echoed its way through the streets and out of the city, onto the beach to drift away on the waves. The night air felt soft as velvet on their skin. They waited, scarcely talking, so intent were they on searching the waves. It got darker still, and then the moon rose, casting a silvery glow over the water, helping them see a bit better. Finn gazed out over the waves, but saw nothing. He could feel Georgie and Fred beside him, sense their unasked questions. He knew they couldn't help but wonder if this were all some fantastical story he had made up.

'Perhaps it's because you are here,' he said. 'Maybe he won't show himself if I'm not alone.'

'Shall we go?' asked Georgie.

'I think you'd better,' replied Finn.

He watched them walk away until they were swallowed up by the night. He sat alone, the darkness pressing in on him as he waited. He began to wonder, as the minutes turned to hours, if perhaps it had all been some terrible hallucination, that perhaps he had gone mad. He fought that idea, waiting and waiting until he had no choice but to give up hope, for that night at least. It was long after midnight when he finally dragged himself home.

ᕲ Chapter Six ᕲ

AT BREAKFAST THE NEXT morning, everyone seemed odd. Finn was exhausted. Georgie saw the despair on his face and knew he hadn't seen the Djinn. She had her own worries, while the twins and Aunt C were suffering from the after-effects of the sleeping potion and were puzzled as to why they had not changed out of their day clothes before going to bed. They rubbed their heads and looked queasily at the omelettes Georgie had cooked.

'Oooh, I can't, Mummy. I just *can't*,' wailed Cressida, pushing her plate away.

'I can't either, Mummy,' whinged Cordelia, 'I feel *awful*.'

'I feel a bit weird too,' said their mother. 'Perhaps we're all sickening for something.' Aunt C turned to examine Georgie.

Georgie was wolfing down her omelette looking pre-occupied, but otherwise disgustingly healthy.

'You look pensive,' said Aunt C.

She moved on to Finn. 'You look pasty, Finn.'

'I'm all right,' Finn muttered. The last thing he wanted was to be confined to bed.

'Bed for you two, Cordy and Cress. Georgie and Finn,

you can both go to school.' The twins were delighted by the prospect of a day in bed, while Georgie and Finn were delighted to have narrowly escaped it.

'I wonder if we'll see Mr Violet again today,' said Georgie as she and Finn waited in the playground for the start of school bell. They sat against the wall in the shade of the acacia tree. A dozen impromptu ball games went on around them; basketballs thudded into the ground, making it sound like a mad drummer was at large, and the high pitched giggles of girls playing chase ricocheted around them. Meanwhile, Dagmar and his cronies searched for Finn.

'I don't care about Mr Violet,' said Finn. 'I just want to see the Djinn again, and get to my parents. Somehow.'

'You heard what Mr Violet said. You have to learn what he can teach you first,' replied Georgie.

'Glass-blowing!' spat Finn.

There was a sudden commotion amongst the footballers, mutterings of 'Hey, get off our pitch,' followed by curt instructions to get out of the way, or words to that effect. Finn and Georgie glanced up to see Dagmar, Bovine and Butthead shouldering their way through the footballers.

'Uh oh,' muttered Georgie. 'Here comes trouble.'

'Hey, Finn, you retard, ready for a rematch?' shouted Dagmar,

'With pleasure,' answered Finn getting to his feet. He marched towards Dagmar who had started throwing air punches and was skipping from side to side.

'What did you mean yesterday, about my parents, slime ball?' demanded Finn.

Dagmar's eyes glittered with malice. 'Wouldn't you

like to know what I know, Fish Boy?'

'Just about fill a postage stamp,' replied Finn.

Butthead and Bovine let out a snort of laughter before they could help themselves.

Enraged, Dagmar took a step towards Finn and swung at him. Finn ducked but Dagmar still landed a glancing blow on Finn's head. Finn staggered backwards, stars exploding in his eyes. If Dagmar had caught him full on, Finn knew he would have been knocked out cold. Dagmar was far bigger and probably stronger. Finn knew he would have to be quicker.

Dagmar, encouraged by Finn's stagger, launched himself at Finn. At the last moment, Finn ducked nimbly out of the way and stuck out his foot. Dagmar, unbalanced, tripped over Finn's foot and crashed head first into the concrete. He rolled onto his back, moaning loudly. Finn crouched down beside him.

'What did you mean, slime ball?' he repeated, grabbing hold of Dagmar's hair and yanking back his head. Dagmar said nothing, but Finn looked into his eyes which seemed to change as he did so. He found himself seeing beyond the white, the brown of iris, the black of pupil, the red of broken veins. He saw darkness, edged by flashing lights that seemed to dance and whirl but then slowly coalesced into an image; the same image the Sea Djinn had shown him; his parents in their cage, the evil Sea Djinn writhing and hissing around them.

Finn let go of Dagmar's hair and reeled away from him. Just then the bell rang and a swarm of teachers arrived to lead the pupils off to their classrooms. Dagmar got to his feet and hurried after Finn. 'Got your answer, Fish Boy?' he hissed.

Finn couldn't concentrate on any of his lessons. Finally, Miss Finity, his form teacher, lost patience with him.

She strode up to him, all six foot two of her, and peered down her beak-like nose at him. She had a soft Irish accent that normally made her sound friendly, despite her formidable appearance, but now she spoke sharply.

'Finn Kennedy. Will you please come back to this planet from whichever galaxy you've floated off to. What *is* your problem today?'

Dagmar guffawed from the back row.

'Can you restrain yourself to positive contributions to the class, Dagmar Drax. Such as answering questions, preferably with the correct answer, which would make a pleasant change,' she added with an acid grin. She turned back to Finn, who felt a quick flash of affection for her.

'Well?'

'I'm tired, I s'pose.'

'Tired are we? Well, may I suggest you go to bed an hour earlier tonight?' she said, not unkindly.

Finn felt as if he'd never sleep again. He had seen into Dagmar's mind, and now he knew for sure that Dagmar knew exactly where his parents were. The question was how, and why?

When the bell for the end of school finally rang, Finn felt a surge of relief. He and Georgie grabbed their backpacks and bolted from the classroom. Fred was waiting outside.

'What's the plan?' he whispered. 'You going back to look for the Djinn tonight?'

'Yep.'

'Can we come too?' asked Fred.

'We'll hide, out of sight,' said Georgie, sensing Finn's hesitation.

Finn was torn. He desperately wanted to see the Djinn again, but he was worried the others might put him off. But he really wanted them to see the Djinn for themselves, if only to convince himself that he hadn't gone mad and wasn't imagining everything.

'All right,' replied Finn. 'But you must stay out of sight. I don't want him put off.'

They had lagged behind the other students, all hurrying to get out, and now the corridor was empty apart from them and their footsteps echoing off the marble floors.

'Hang on a sec,' said Georgie, pausing outside a door she had never noticed before.

'What?' asked Fred and Finn together.

Georgie pushed the door open slowly and peered inside. She ducked back out. 'Come on in,' she said.

'Why?' asked Finn.

'Just come,' Georgie repeated.

'Humour her,' said Finn with a shrug, following her inside. Fred followed too and gently closed the door behind him. They were in a white room, utterly empty. Finn and Fred gazed around at the blank whiteness. Georgie stared fixedly into space, face screwed up in concentration.

'And?' queried Finn.

'Wait,' whispered Georgie. 'Listen.'

They all strained to hear something in the silence. Gradually, a noise emerged, so faint at first they wondered if they were just imagining it. It sounded like a distant drumbeat, slightly slurred, as if the drummer had dragged one drumstick lightly over his drum. The beats soon grew louder, and then another door they hadn't noticed in the wall opposite burst open. Mr Violet appeared, slightly flushed and out of breath.

'Phew, got here as fast as I could,' he said to Georgie. 'What's up?'

'You came,' said Georgie, her voice faint with amazement.

'Of course I did. You summoned me. If you do that with enough force, and I can get to you, I will come.'

'You summoned him?' asked Finn. 'How?'

'With her mind,' answered Mr Violet. 'A most powerful tool. As is mine, to receive her message.'

'Cool,' said Fred.

'What is this room anyway?' asked Finn. 'I've never seen it before. It's not a classroom, and that door wasn't there when we came in.'

'Sometimes if you need a space you will find something. Or if you need a way in, you will find it. You need to wish hard, follow your instincts, like Georgie did.'

'Why did you summon him, Georgie,' demanded Finn. 'I can't take any more of this, this talk.' Finn rubbed the heels of his hands into his eyes as if he could dissolve his confusion that way.

'I don't have time for this,' he said, feeling a sudden claustrophobia. 'I have to get to the beach again.'

'It's daylight, Finn. It won't get dark for hours. What's the rush?' asked Mr Violet.

Finn felt he would burn up with impatience. 'You know what the rush is. My parents.' Finn wheeled round, searching for the door. To his horror, he couldn't see one. He ran towards the wall where he had come in and pounded the plasterwork where the door had been.

'Stop, Finn,' shouted Georgie, as she and Fred tried to pull him back. 'It's not there.'

'Get off, both of you,' shouted Finn, flinging them off

with a surge of strength. They both careened backwards, landing heavily.

'Urgh,' said Fred, rubbing his back.

'Ow,' said Georgie quietly, shocked into near silence by Finn's violence. Finn who had continued pounding and scraping against the wall after throwing his friends off, slowly turned. He saw Georgie and Fred lying on the floor. He saw the wary, shocked looks on their faces. He flicked a glance at Mr Violet who was looking at him with an expression that seemed to mingle pity and anger.

'Oh, God,' said Finn rushing towards his friends. 'I'm sorry, Georgie, Fred. I'm so sorry.' He reached out his hands to them to pull them up. Neither Georgie nor Fred took his hands. Slowly they pushed themselves to their feet.

'I am so sorry,' Finn said again. 'Please, please forgive me. I know it's no excuse, but I don't know what came over me. I sort of went mad, and I never meant to throw you off like that. I thought I just gave a shrug, not a fling.'

'It was just a shrug, Finn,' said Mr Violet. 'Time for you to learn some home truths. Number one, you didn't see the door because you lost the ability to see. Yes, you might have seen the obvious, but the door was not obvious. If you hadn't lost control, Finn, you would still have been able to see it, but impatience is your curse. Unless you control it, it will control you.'

Finn shook his head. 'I know. I know. Now look what I've done.' He gestured at Georgie and Fred who were still refusing to look him in the eye. 'How could I have done that?' he asked himself aloud.

'You have come into your fighting strength,' answered Mr Violet. 'The Djinn touched you didn't he?'

'My arm,' answered Finn. 'It felt awesome, like electricity ran from him to me.'

'Some of his power. Hadn't you noticed?'

'Well, I did seem to run quite fast, and do a big jump, then I knocked Dagmar flying. I was a bit surprised by that.'

Mr Violet gave a slight smile. 'Know your strength. Control it. You've made a mess of your fists,' he added.

Finn looked down at his hands. Georgie gasped. Finn's hands were bruised and bleeding from pounding and scraping at the walls.

Finn swore under his breath. Slowly, he sat down and looked up at Mr Violet, as if ready, at last, to listen to him.

'Impatience will get you nowhere, Finn,' said Mr Violet. 'It will cloud your thoughts so you'll make bad decisions. Learn to stay cool, even if you don't feel like it. Search for it. Discipline yourself. Shut up and think, rather than rushing in.'

'Easy to say,' replied Finn.

'Very hard to do,' agreed Mr Violet. 'But unless you learn to do it, you'll stand no chance against Hydrus. You'll never get your parents back.'

'Why can't you help me, since you know so much?' asked Finn, plaintively.

'As in come with you, when you're ready to go?'

Finn nodded.

Mr Violet looked off into the distance for a long time before answering.

'He knows me. He knows everything I can come up with. I've tried to beat him. And failed.'

'What happened?' asked Finn.

Mr Violet sat down, rolled up his right trouser leg. Where there should have been skin, there was plastic.

'He metamorphosed into a shark, took off half my leg. He drank my blood, ate my flesh. He knows my mind and what's in it.'

'How did you get away?'

Mr Violet gave a puzzled shrug. 'That's what's so odd. Having taken off half my leg, he let me go. Swam off. Perhaps he didn't like the taste of me,' joked Mr Violet. Nobody laughed.

Finn lapsed into silence.

'You need to value your friends more, Finn, for their friendship alone,' said Mr Violet. 'And, as it happens, you need them now if you are going to stand any chance of getting your parents back.'

Finn nodded. 'I will, I will.' He turned back to Georgie and Fred. 'Please, guys, come on. I'm really sorry.'

Georgie approached him, gave him a small smile and a tentative hug. Finn grabbed her and hugged her tightly. He released her with a smile. To Fred he offered his hand again. This time Fred took it. Finn had forgotten his injuries and grimaced with pain.

'Oops, sorry,' said Fred.

'No, I'm the one saying sorry,' said Finn. 'Friends, again?' he asked.

Fred nodded. 'Friends,' he replied.

Finn felt a massive relief, but then another thought occurred to him.

'But, Mr Violet, if he knows what's in your mind, how can you teach me to beat him?'

'I'm not trying to replicate my mind in your body. I'm trying to teach you to think in a certain way, with calmness and clarity. I'm arming you with knowledge, a powerful weapon in itself. Take what I teach you, add your own insights to it, use it in the way you think best. Then you will have an alchemy of my knowledge and your brain and spirit, and that, together with help from your friends, might just be enough to beat him.'

Finn digested this. 'Don't get me wrong, Mr Violet, I do want to help destroy him, but even more, much more, I want to rescue my parents. What if I just tried to do that?'

'If only you could, Finn. Neither you, nor your sister, nor your parents will ever be safe until you have destroyed Hydrus. You have this one chance.'

'But why me? That's what I don't understand. I'm just a boy.'

Mr Violet gave a sad smile. 'No ordinary boy, Finn. Have you not heard the Prophesy?'

'What Prophesy?' demanded Finn.

'Triton will tell you more. He is the keeper of the Prophesy, not me.'

'What's it got to do with me?' asked Finn, incredulously.

'Talk to Triton,' replied Mr Violet.

Finn groaned in frustration. He wanted to know now, but he could see that he would get nothing more from Mr Violet.

'Then teach me everything I need to know,' said Finn.

'Right. We need to invent an after school class that Fred's parents and your Aunt C will allow you all to attend. Something that no other pupils will want to attend.'

'A Maths Masterclass,' suggested Georgie, inspired.

'Perfect,' exclaimed Mr Violet. 'I will have a note sent home. You need to get your mother or father to sign, Fred, and you two get Aunt C.'

'Maths Masterclass? I thought you were quite good at maths,' Aunt C said to Georgie and Finn.

'Well, my teacher doesn't seem to think so,' said Georgie.

'And you Finn, of course I have no idea, really, what your maths is like, but if you need the extra lessons, then I'd better sign the form.' She paused for a moment. 'Wouldn't you both rather I didn't though? I mean you're at school quite long enough. Nice to have you home.'

'Oh Mummy, please just sign the forms,' pleaded Georgie. 'We need to start tomorrow.'

Her mother looked at her narrowly, clearly suspicious of Georgie's new-found love of maths. 'You always seemed good enough at maths, but you never seemed keen on it, George.'

'I'll be keeping an eye on Finn,' Georgie hissed to her mother under her breath.

Finn heard well enough and would have spluttered with indignation had he not cottoned on to Georgie's game.

'Ah, I see,' Georgie's mother whispered back to her. 'In that case…..' she hunted down a pen and signed on the dotted line.

◌ CHAPTER SEVEN ◌

'FRED!' YELLED HIS FATHER on hearing the door slam. Fred jumped and wondered what he'd done now.

His father burst out of his study, grinning form ear to ear. 'You ARE a genius.'

Fred looked baffled.

'The Goldman view,' said his father, slapping him on the back. 'Shorting Sun Systems. We made a packet, you and me.'

'That's great, Dad.'

'Certainly is.'

'Er, Dad, could you sign this school form. It's for extra maths lessons.'

'Sure, sure,' said his father, grabbing the form and signing with a flourish whilst scarcely glancing at it. 'Who cares if you're rotten at maths when you're a star at the stock market.'

I'm not rotten at maths, thought Fred indignantly, but he took the signed form and put it in his book bag.

Back at the Pink Prison Finn managed to convince Aunt C he was sickening for something.

'I really need to sleep,' he said as soon as he'd finished an early supper.

'You do look peaky,' she replied. 'Obviously something going around. Go on then, off to bed.

'I feel ropey too, Mummy,' announced Georgie, trying to sound weak and feeble.

Her mother bent down to scrutinise her. 'You look O.K.'

'But I don't feel O.K.,' said Georgie plaintively.

Georgie's mother gave her a suspicious glance. She wondered what was going on. First this new found passion for maths, then this insistence on an early night when she looked fine.

'Oh well, you'll be safe enough in your beds, I suppose. Off you go, both of you.' She gave them each a kiss on the cheek and wandered off distractedly to check on the twins.

'Give it an hour or two?' whispered Finn.

Georgie checked her watch. 'Nine. In the garden, but you better get the ladder from the garage for me. *I* haven't got a handy acacia tree outside my window and I don't really want to jump down twenty feet if I can avoid it.'

'No prob.'

Finn felt he would go crazy waiting to sneak out. He paced back and forth in furious impatience. He just wanted to forget Aunt C and her cautious rules, walk straight out of the front door and rush to Shell Beach. Then he remembered Mr Violet's lesson on impatience. He stopped pacing, forced himself to sit down on his beanbag, leaned back and slowly calmed down.

He started to think of all the questions he wanted to ask the Djinn if he saw him again. When he happened to glance at his watch he saw to his surprise that it was five to nine already. Time seemed to have run much faster than normal. Feeling delighted but puzzled, he cranked open his door. The twin's room was silent. They should be asleep by now. Finn could hear faint strains of music coming from Aunt C's room down the hall - the soothing music she played to try to help her get to sleep. Georgie, he knew, would be ready and waiting at her window, with a stash of emergency provisions in her backpack.

Finn quietly closed his door, turned off his light and padded across his room to the window. He ducked behind his curtains, opened his window and peered out. The moon was half full, hanging in the heavens like a hunchback. He climbed up to crouch on the windowsill and looked down. He could climb down the branches of the acacia tree, or he could just jump. He noticed a clump of Arabian primroses gleaming in the moonlight. They looked a long way away. It was a heck of a long way down. He took a deep breath and before he could think about it any more, launched himself.

For a brief moment, he felt as though he were flying, then he landed with a soft thud exactly on the clump of primroses. He grinned to himself then hurried off to the garage to fetch the ladder so that he could release Georgie.

Fred was already waiting for them on Shell Beach. He leapt into the air when they arrived behind him and softly said his name.

'Argh. Don't do that,' he said, heart pounding.

Finn gave an apologetic grin. 'Sorry. Hard not to creep up on someone on sand with the waves breaking in the background.' Finn glanced around. Apart from the three of them, the beach was deserted.

'Right, you two stay here. I'm going on down the beach to see what I can see.'

They nodded and watched him go.

'Think he'll really see something?' Fred asked Georgie when Finn was out of earshot.

'You don't believe him?' Georgie asked.

'Well, I want to, and something kind of tells me I should, but it's hard to, isn't it?'

Georgie nodded. 'It is hard. I want to believe him too, and I do, really. And there's all this strange stuff with Mr Violet and him appearing when I wanted him to. That sort of makes the rest of it seem more real, doesn't it?'

The two of them got stuck into a discussion of Mr Violet and who exactly he was, as Finn sat down a few hundred yards away, right at the water's edge.

At first, Finn, could hear their voices carrying softly across the sand to him, but then the sound faded and it was just him and the ocean.

He waited, alone, the dark of the night hanging around him like a soft cloak. The moonlight dappled the waves with silver and high above the stars glittered. The warm water of the ocean lapped at his feet. Finn gazed out into the depths, trying to will the Djinn to appear, as Georgie had willed Mr Violet.

He still wondered about that. He found it hard to believe, but she seemed convinced she had conjured him, and Mr Violet said that she had. Well, if she could do it, then he was sure he could too.

'Triton? Are you there? Are you there? Come back. Please. I need you. I'm here, waiting for you on Shell Beach. I want to know what to do next. Please come.'

He focused all his heart and mind on wanting. He put all of his fears for his parents and all his yearning for them into trying to call the Djinn to him from his watery kingdom. His eyes were closed and he was trying to see the Djinn with his mind's eye. When a voice spoke, he jumped in alarm.

'You can open your eyes now.'

It was the Djinn! Triton was in the shallows, smiling at him.

'You came,' Finn almost yelled, he was so excited.

'You called me, but I was always going to come back to you. There is much to do, much to discuss.' The Djinn looked away over Finn's shoulder. 'Why don't you invite your friends over?' he suggested.

'You can see them?' asked Finn. All he could see was folds of darkness where he thought they were.

'Not with my eyes but I know they are there. Call them o-' the Djinn stopped suddenly. He turned his head and seemed to scent the air with his nostrils. Immediately his kindly manner changed. 'Quick, come with me,' he urged. 'Climb on my back, hold tight, and take a deep breath. I'm going to take you under the water.'

'But, b- how will I breathe?'

Triton saw the fear in Finn's eyes. 'Trust me. Now climb on. Quickly.'

Finn just had time to hear the roar of a boat's engine before he waded into the water and climbed onto the Djinn's back.

It was the strangest feeling. The part of Triton that was man met the smooth grey skin of a dolphin half way down his back, where Finn clung on. The man's skin was warm and tough. The dolphin's was cool and slippery. Finn wrapped his arms round the Djinn's chest, took a huge breath and clung on tight. With a flick of his huge tail, Triton swam out into deeper water then dived down under the waves.

Finn felt the salt water sting his eyes, so he closed them tight. He felt the sea skim past him, sluicing off him, almost as if he too were a sea creature. He went fast, so much faster than he had ever swum, and if he hadn't been so terrified wondering when he was going to get his next breath, he would have loved it.

Just as he felt as if his lungs were about to burst, he felt the Djinn slow down. He opened his eyes which immediately began to water furiously, but he could see nothing. He had never experienced a darkness like this. It was total. He might as well have been blindfolded.

The Djinn slipped away from underneath Finn, took hold of his arm and pressed into his hand something which felt like a shell. He guided the shell thing to Finn's lips, and Finn felt bubbles come from it. The Djinn seemed to want Finn to bite the thing. He was talking but Finn's ears were ringing so much he couldn't hear the words. Finn was so desperate for air he began to panic. Then, suddenly, he understood. The shell was like a mouthpiece on a snorkel. He bit round it, held his nose with his fingers and with a quick bolt of fear breathed in the sweetest air he had ever tasted. He gulped some more and as his lungs returned to normal, his panic ebbed away.

He felt the Djinn move slightly. He opened his eyes again. This time, instead of pure darkness, a dull glow suffused the ocean around him. Finn could just make out the Djinn in the water by his side, holding one of his arms to anchor him. In the Djinn's other hand was a kind of squid that was the source of the eerie greenish light. Finn's eyes were streaming painfully. The Djinn reached out and very gently he swept his fingers back and forth across Finn's eyes, so close that he touched his eyelashes. In a few moments, Finn's eyes stopped watering, the painful stinging ceased and he could see much better. Finn smiled and looked around in wonder.

The Djinn followed Finn's eyes and moved the jelly-fish around so that it illuminated their surroundings. Finn found he was standing in an underwater cave. He couldn't see how deep it went, the light didn't extend that far, but he could see the ceiling.

It was about twenty feet above them, opalescent, like mother of pearl, gnarled in places with rocky spurs that descended downwards like daggers. Fronds of green sea grass drifted languidly in the current like a mermaid's hair. The floor of the cave was rocky and uneven. Finn's body wanted to float upwards, and it was only the Djinn's hold on him that stopped him from drifting up and impaling himself on the rocky spurs.

The Djinn seemed to read his mind. He reached behind him and took hold of something which he passed to Finn. It was a small rock. Finn reached out to take it and staggered under the weight. It felt as heavy as a rock ten times its size. The Djinn smiled at the amazed look in Finn's eyes.

'It's meteoric rock, much denser and heavier than anything from this earth,' said the Djinn. The ringing in Finn's ears had stopped now and he could hear that the Djinn's voice was higher underwater. It was almost bell-like, perfectly clear. It made Finn think of the cries of whales. He wished he could say something back, but he daren't take the shell from his lips.

'Think your words to me,' said the Djinn.

'You can understand my thoughts?' Finn asked in his mind.

'I can. Of course most humans do not think very clearly, and that can make it difficult. You'll find they are meant to be thinking about one thing, say maths homework, but that only occupies about one tenth of their thoughts. The rest of their mind is taken up with wondering what's for dinner, feeling resentful that they have to sit inside doing homework when they'd rather be outside in the sunshine, and trying to kick their brother or sister under the table without their mother seeing. And adults are even worse. They spend so much time trying to disguise their true thoughts from other people they end up not sure what they're even feeling or thinking themselves.'

Finn burst out laughing. Bubbles of laughter shot from his mouth and drifted up to the roof of the cave. He quickly put the shell back to his mouth and took a few deep breaths.

'What is that thing?' thought Finn, nodding to the sparkling squid.

'That thing, as you so rudely call him, is a photo-phore. I'd try not to insult him again if I were you as he's a powerful creature. If he feels upset, or under threat, he can release a cloud of light so brilliant it can dazzle you.'

'Er, right. Sorry,' thought Finn.

'No matter,' replied the Djinn. 'You might need that knowledge one day. Keep one on you. They're meant to live in the deep, but certain species like this one can come up higher for short periods.'

Finn nodded and wondered immediately how or why he would *keep one on him*.

'Where are we?' thought Finn.

'We are in the Cave of Light,' answered Triton.

Finn was about to say that it wasn't light, it was gloomy, but then he noticed that since they had arrived the cave had grown lighter. A glorious golden light reflected back at them from the mother of pearl ceiling. Then Finn saw that the light seemed to be flowing from Triton himself.

'The Cave reflects back what you have inside you,' explained the Djinn, gesturing towards Finn. Finn noticed, amazed, that light was flowing from him too.

'Wow!' he mouthed, sending another trail of bubbles up to the ceiling.

'Why did we have to leave the beach?' Finn thought.

'I don't know if they're all right, but I'll try to find out,' answered the Djinn.

'What?' thought Finn confused.

'You were thinking about your friends on the beach, wondering if they are all right.'

'Oh, yes I was. I wondered who was in that boat, and then I worried that it must have been someone bad. That's why we had to flee.'

'I think it was someone bad. I cannot be sure of that because I didn't allow them to get close enough to tell, but instinct is normally correct, even at a distance. I couldn't risk them getting close,' said Triton.

Finn nodded. 'You said you'd find out if they were all right. How can you do that?'

'Watch.'

The Djinn reached down to the seabed, picked up a conch and blew on it. Out pealed a single note, high and haunting.

Back on the beach, Georgie and Fred searched desperately for Finn.

'Maybe he swam out to that boat or something,' suggested Fred.

'Why would he do that?' cried Georgie, but she and Fred studied the boat which was approaching rapidly. They could just make out several figures standing at the front. They seemed to be scanning the waves.

'Oh God,' said Georgie in disbelief. 'It's Mr Gusting, and, and, Dagmar, and the boat's coming ashore. It's a hovercraft!'

With a roar of its engines the hovercraft came out of the sea and hovered over the sand towards Georgie and Fred. They backed away rapidly, but the hovercraft stopped suddenly just twenty feet from them. Someone switched off the engines and the hovercraft settled onto the sand with a groan. The sudden silence rang loudly in their ears. Georgie glanced about. There was no-one else on the beach. No-one to help them, no one to witness….Georgie felt her stomach clench with fear.

There was another man on the hovercraft. It was difficult to make out his features in the darkness, but they could see something of him. He was thick set, built like a wrestler. His hair was dark and thick, slicked back, shining in the moon-light. He was standing quite still, but a feeling of violence emanated from him. Georgie shuddered as his eyes found hers. He studied her for a few moments and Georgie had the distinct sensation he was looking into her mind. He then turned his scrutiny upon Fred who twitched under his gaze.

As if satisfied, the stranger stepped from the craft, and, followed by Mr Gusting and Dagmar, he strode up to Georgie and Fred. All Georgie's instincts screamed at her to turn and flee, but she thought perhaps these people knew where Finn was.

'You two!' bellowed Mr Gusting. 'What are you doing here?'

'Er, we ,er, er-' gulped Georgie.

'What are you doing here on this beach?' he demanded, even more angrily.

'It's a public beach,' said Fred, recovering first. 'We're allowed to be here.'

He could see Mr Gusting struggling with that.

'You impertinent weasel,' hissed Mr Gusting, a vein throbbing in his temple.

'We're not at school now. You can't tell us what to do,' said Georgie with a confidence she didn't feel.

Mr Gusting and the other man laughed. 'Oh can't I?' demanded Mr Gusting, taking a step closer, his eyes gleaming menacingly in the darkness.

'Take one step closer and I'll scream,' said Georgie.

Again the two men laughed, this time joined by Dagmar.

'Awww, is the baby scared?' he taunted, 'will the baby start blubbing? Bet I can make you blub.'

'You are such a pathetic bully, Dagmar. You'll never make me blub. Vomit perhaps,' said Georgie.

Dagmar lunged towards her but the other man caught him by the sleeve. Dagmar snarled like a chained dog.

'They don't matter,' said the unknown man. 'Leave them to it, they're just a waste of time.'

For a long time, Mr Gusting stared at Georgie and Fred. He seemed to be trying to make up his mind. He looked from one to the other, his dark eyes cruel and merciless. Georgie and Fred were terrified.

Reluctantly, Mr Gusting looked up at the other man and made a murmur of agreement. 'You're right. They're unimportant. Worthless in fact.'

Georgie felt the flush of humiliation redden her cheeks. She would pay him back for this, she vowed silently.

'Where's your friend, the boxer?' Gusting demanded suddenly.

They both feigned ignorance.

'That Finlay boy,' shouted Mr Gusting.

Georgie shrugged. 'How would I know? And his name is Finn, not Finlay.'

'I don't care what his name is,' snapped Mr Gusting. 'I thought you were cousins,' he continued.

'We are, but we're not joined at the hip.'

'Detention for you. Answering back.'

'I'm not at school,' yelled Georgie, anger triumphing over her fear.

'Ah no, you're not. But what would your mother say, out on the beach at night with this boy, eh, eh, what would she say?'

'Leave us alone or I really will scream,' said Georgie.

'Yeah, clear off,' said Fred.

The other man spoke in a commanding voice to Gusting.

'Come on, let's get to the village. We're wasting time. He's not here.'

He strode back to the hovercraft. Shooting a look of loathing over his shoulder, Dagmar followed.

'I'll deal with you two another time,' said Mr Gusting. His lips twisted malevolently before he climbed back into the craft, switched it on, reversed back into the sea and sped off with a roar, shooting a plume of churned water high into the air.

CHAPTER EIGHT

IN THE CAVE OF Light, Finn felt a slight vibration then suddenly a barracuda sliced through the water. With its jutting lower jaw and vicious-looking teeth only inches from him, the barracuda regarded him intently through its limpid eyes. A sharp blue light emanated from its head. Finn floundered backwards.

'It's all right,' said the Djinn reassuringly. 'He's a friend.'

Triton stroked the barracuda's back and made a series of strange high pitched sounds.

With a quick flick of its tale the barracuda turned and disappeared into the darkness.

'Er, who was that?' asked Finn.

'Barbary. One of the fastest fish in the sea, and totally loyal. Wouldn't want to cross him though.'

Finn shook his head in amazement. 'How can all this exist? You and the evil Djinn and Barbary? I still can't get my head round it, even when I'm looking at it all with my own eyes.'

The Djinn smiled. 'Life on this planet began in the sea, billions of years before there was life on land. Is it really so surprising that we have evolved so much in that time, or, for that matter, that we have wars of our own, just like humans?'

'No,' thought Finn. 'Not if you put it like that. So, er, does the Loch Ness Monster really exist?'

'Of course she does. Bit of a show off, allowing herself to be seen all over the place.'

'She, er, has a choice?'

'Without giving away her secret hiding places, yes, she does.'

Finn was just getting started, but suddenly, Barbary was back. The fish made a long stream of sounds, to which the Djinn listened intently. He then bowed to the fish, who bowed back and swam languidly away.

The Djinn didn't speak at first. He stared into the salty radiance, his green eyes thoughtful.

'It was good we hid. They were his agents. They bothered your friends, but no,' he raised his hand quickly to reassure Finn, 'they didn't hurt them. They left them alone and went on to the home of my friends. We don't know what they wanted there, but we know it will be nothing good.'

'The home of your friends?' thought Finn.

'The fishermen's village at the far end of Shell Beach. The fishermen there are my friends. They are actively on our side. Their fight is ours.'

'Are there bad fishermen, on the other side?' thought Finn.

'Unfortunately, yes. Most of the huge trawlers that ravage the ocean's riches for a start. For thousands of years, humans have caught fish to eat. They used to fish with simple nets and sailing boats, but now they use motor boats and huge nylon nets. The fish do not stand a chance, nor do dolphins, turtles or sharks. Millions are caught every year in those death-trap nets meant to catch something else,' the Djinn answered, anger flashing in his eyes.

'What did they do at the fishermen's village?' asked Finn.

'Just appeared to be scouting around. They sailed back and forth, waking everyone with the roar of their engines. Then they left.'

'You said they were his agents?'

'My enemies, and yours. Hydrus's agents.'

Finn sucked hard on his conch shell, but only a thing stream of air came out.

'I need more air,' he thought to Triton.

'Come on. Get on my back. We can go back to the beach now.'

Finn clambered onto Triton's back. He just had a moment to look around the fabulous underwater cave again, trying to commit it all to memory so he could describe it exactly to Georgie and Fred. He took the last breath of air from the shell, then Triton gave a huge flick of his tail and they sped out of the cave into the enveloping darkness.

They soon broke the surface and Finn took a deep breath. He looked for the sea shore, but saw nothing but empty sea all around him.

'We're going to dive again,' warned Triton. Above the ocean, Finn noticed the Djinn's voice had become deeper again.

Finn took another huge breath, then closed his mouth and his eyes as the Djinn plunged below the surface.

Less than a minute later they broke the surface again. Finn opened his eyes and gulped in air. They bobbed gently in the waves a hundred yards from the beach. The Djinn swam a small circle, checking all around. There was no sign of the enemy boat.

'You can get off now,' said the Djinn.

Finn slipped from Triton's back and looked up at him expectantly.

'You need to feel at home in the sea,' said the Djinn. 'Tread water here and we'll talk. It's safer than on the beach.'

'O.K,' replied Finn. 'Tell me what I can do to reach my parents.'

'Listen to Ulysses for a start. Stop being so stubborn, not to mention impatient.'

'Ulysses?' asked Finn, confused.

'Mr Violet.'

'Ah. Yeah, er, I was a bit difficult.'

'I heard.'

'Who is he?'

'An extremely skilled operative. My best. You're lucky to have him for a teacher.'

Finn nodded, chastened. 'But he's not a teacher at my school, is he?'

The Djinn laughed. 'No. I don't think most school governors would approve of the things he teaches, although I have no doubt the pupils would.'

'So, he's one of your agents. But are there teachers who are enemy agents?'

'There are. Pupils too. Just as you are a Light Fighter, so there are Dark.'

'What's a Light Fighter?'

'The Light Fighters are on the side of the four Djinns of the Day. They, we, use the weapons of light to fight. The Dark Fighters support the Night Djinns, and they use the weapons of darkness.'

'What are the weapons?'

'The weapons of light are clarity and brilliance.'

When Finn didn't look impressed, the Djinn smiled and continued.

'Guns and knives are so obvious, Finn. Think of a diamond.'

'It's beautiful,' shrugged Finn.

'Yes it is. But it's also the hardest substance on the planet, tempered by heat of thousands of degrees. It's harder and more lethal than any knife.'

'A big one maybe.'

'Oh, there are big ones in the sea, like you've never seen. And there are thousands of smaller ones, just lying in the sand of South Africa's Forbidden Coast. Perhaps I'll show you one some time. You can fight with small diamonds too. You can use their brilliance to dazzle someone, or for morse code. You can see with light, you can also blind with it. You can use the sun's rays to start a fire to cook food, or to burn something to a cinder. You can use a mirror to see behind you, or to make someone think he is seeing an exit when in fact he is walking into a wall of glass. You can build a prison of glass so perfect that it is invisible. The only way you know you're in it is if you touch the walls. Like most weapons, the weapons of light can be used two ways. You'll learn all of this from Ulysses Violet.'

'Why can't you teach me?'

'I will, when I can, but you have so much to learn, and I have a kingdom to run.'

Finn gave a sheepish smile. 'What else do I need to do?'

'Learn the art of patience. Find the Pearl of Wisdom. Find the Dark Djinn.'

'The Pearl of Wisdom? What's that?' asked Finn.

'There are two Pearls,' answered the Djinn. 'The Black Pearl, which teaches the beholder the black arts of evil, and the White Pearl, which brings wisdom and clarity to whoever possesses it. Many years ago, Hydrus stole the White Pearl of Wisdom from me. I tried to get it back. I summoned a storm of such fury,' the Djinn smiled at the memory, 'all I could do was cause Hydrus to lose the Pearl. I never did find it again, and neither did he. It's been lost for over a thousand years. Perhaps it shattered in the storm. Even then it was ancient, very fragile, but Hydrus believes it still exists and in all that time he has hunted it. He wants it because he thinks it will help him vanquish me and the Light World, and also because of the Prophesy. Did Ulysses tell you anything of that?'

'Not much. I asked him to, but he said you were Keeper of the Prophesy and I had to ask you.'

'And so I will tell you,' answered the Djinn with a grave nod. 'The Prophesy says that there will come a boy, a Prince of Atlantis, who will find the Pearl, who will learn from it the secret of how to vanquish the Dark Djinn. So Hydrus will do anything to get to the Pearl first. Before the boy prince does. Before you do, Finn.'

Finn floundered in the sea and took a gulp of water. 'I'm not a *prince*,' he spluttered.

'Your parents, Finn. Both your mother and father come from an unbroken line that goes all the way back to Atlantis. When such a woman and man come together and have a child, then the child shall be a prince or princess of Atlantis. You must have noticed, Finn, that you are different in some ways.'

Finn nodded glumly. The differences had not always made him happy.

'You love the sea. You love to swim. You swim better than anyone you know, although you hold back, don't you? You are afraid to show anyone what you can do,' said Triton.

'I don't want to be a freak,' muttered Finn.

'Having a gift doesn't not make you a freak. Being different does not make you a freak, Finn. Who wants to be normal?' Triton asked with a smile, gesturing at his own body.

Finn laughed. 'I see your point.'

'Be who you are. Use your powers and they will grow. They will need to if you are to have any chance of beating Hydrus.'

The Djinn suddenly focused on something over Finn's shoulder. Finn followed his gaze.

He could see two small figures moving jerkily up and down the beach.

'Your friends,' said the Djinn. 'Searching for you. Come on. Let's go and reassure them.' He hadn't told Finn of the second Prophesy. That would have to wait, and perhaps it was just as well, he thought.

Finn climbed onto the Triton's back and together they surfed in on a breaking wave.

On the beach, Georgie froze. 'Fred,' she yelled. 'Fred, there's something here, coming in on a wave, it's, it's, Finn, and, oh my goodness, I think it's him. It's the Djinn!'

Fred wheeled round and ran back to where Georgie was standing, staring open-mouthed at the shapes in the waves.

Finn's grin was enormous as he slipped easily off the Djinn's powerful back.

'Fred, Georgie, meet Triton, the Sea Djinn.'

The Sea Djinn lay in the shallows, propped up by his arms. He nodded to Fred and Georgie. His eyes looked on them with benevolence and he gave them a smile of surprising sweetness. Georgie had expected to feel at least a bit scared of him, but she just felt awe and an incredible sense of happiness and safety, as if nothing bad could ever happen as long as he were near.

When Georgie and Fred had got over their amazement at meeting the Sea Djinn, they started peppering Finn with questions.

'Where did you go?' asked Fred.

'Yeah, we were worried as anything,' added Georgie. 'How could you just disappear?'

Just managing to get the odd word in, Finn told them. Each new thing he revealed unleashed another volley of questions, but Finn could feel a sense of urgency emanating from the Sea Djinn.

'What happened to you two?' Triton asked Georgie and Fred.

Quickly, they told Finn and the Djinn about Dagmar and the stranger and Mr Gusting. The Sea Djinn's eyes narrowed and his look of benevolence vanished.

'They know you're a Light Fighter. Perhaps they even know more. You'll have to be extremely careful,' the Djinn said to Finn.

'Dagmar knows about my parents,' said Finn. 'He was teasing me about never seeing them again, and then this morning, when I looked into his eyes I could see the same image of them, in their prison with Hydrus slithering around them.'

The Djinn nodded gravely. 'You can See. Good, you must use that more, but all three of you must learn to block Seers otherwise your every intention and conversation and secret will be known to them. This stranger, whoever he was, was obviously looking into your minds,' he said to Georgie and Fred.

'I could feel something, a sort of shock almost,' said Fred. 'It made me twitch.'

The Djinn hissed in a breath.

'What's wrong?' asked Finn, worried.

'This was no ordinary Seer. He was the Thought Thief.'

'Did he steal our thoughts?' asked Georgie, horrified.

'Some of Fred's, yes. Did you feel anything? It can feel as if someone is pulling threads from your brain, or, if he's in a real hurry, you just feel an electric shock as he downloads a chunk of your memory.'

Georgie shook her head. 'I just felt a sort of burning sensation, very slight, like you do when someone is really scrutinising you.'

'Or reading your mind,' corrected the Djinn,

'But what did he steal from me?' asked Fred. 'I can't remember losing anything.'

'That's just it,' replied the Djinn. 'You won't even know that you've been robbed because you'll no longer be aware of those memories that have been taken.'

'How horrible,' said Georgie.

'It is. Thankfully, not many people can do this,' said the Djinn. 'A good, or should I say, evil and skilled Seer can, but few of them reach that level. Most of them can just copy your mind data, not remove it. This man must be very high up in the organisation. They are escalating,' said the Djinn, almost to himself.

'But how can we protect ourselves?' asked Georgie.

'You have to project your mind out of your body, then they can't find it.'

'What, like Buddhists do?' asked Fred.

'Exactly,' replied the Djinn.

'But that takes years to learn, I thought,' said Fred.

'It does, but there are a few tricks you can try. Ulysses will teach you.' The Djinn paused to survey the sea. 'I must go now, and you must all go home.'

He reached out a hand and one by one touched all three of them on the head. Phosphorescence from his fingers gleamed on their hair and they all felt a glow that began to permeate their entire bodies, like liquid warmth.

'Go safely,' said the Djinn with a bow, and then he turned and with one flick of his huge tail, disappeared into the breaking waves.

Finn and Georgie walked with Fred to his house which was about a quarter of a mile away down Beach Road.

'I don't know what to say,' said Fred, still reeling with amazement at meeting the Djinn.

'Neither do I,' added Georgie.

'That's a first,' said Finn, and they all laughed.

'He makes you feel…..' began Fred.

'As if anything is possible,' suggested Finn.

'Yes, exactly,' said Georgie as Fred nodded.

'And, as if everything is much better, just knowing that he exists,' added Georgie.

'Here's my house,' said Fred, pointing at a large white edifice that rose up behind a high white-painted wall. 'I really hope my parents are flat out. I'm not sure I'll be able to fib my way out of this one.'

'Good luck,' said Georgie, as Finn gave Fred a leg up onto his wall. Fred waved from the top.

'See you in the morning.'

'Yeah, see you,' Finn and Georgie called softly, as Fred dropped with a thud into his garden and hurried across the grass.

Finn and Georgie headed back to the Pink Prison.

Fred managed to sneak in to his bedroom undetected. He undressed quickly and fell asleep dreaming of the Djinn and his friends.

CHAPTER NINE ∞

FINN, GEORGIE AND FRED spent most of the next school day concentrating hard not on their lessons, but on avoiding Mr Gusting. During morning assembly, they all felt his eyes boring into them, but, following the Djinn's advice, they had made sure they were sitting well back from the front, and when they felt his eyes upon them, they shuffled left or right until the person sitting in the row in front blocked them from him. They weren't sure if he, like the unknown man, was a Seer, or a ThoughtThief, but they weren't taking any chances.

As assembly finished, they watched the teachers file out, then they crept stealthily through the corridors, losing themselves in the milling bodies of crowds of other pupils.

'Good luck,' Finn and Georgie said to Fred as they separated to go to their different classes.

Georgie and Finn arrived at their class without incident, but once there they had to endure the taunts of Dagmar.

'Aww, it's de blubby baby and her fwend. Nice twip to the beach? Shame you missed it Fishboy. Back home sobbing about your parents, I'll bet.'

That finally drove Finn over the edge. His self control snapped. He leapt up, his chair crashing to the floor behind him, and he launched himself at Dagmar, sliding across his desk and crashing to the floor on top of him. Miss Finity whirled round from the blackboard and was upon both of them in what seemed like less than a second.

'What has got into you?' she yelled, yanking them apart with surprising strength. Neither answered. They just glared at each other with deep loathing.

'Detention for both of you, for the next week.'

'You can't do that,' yelled Dagmar. 'My father won't allow it. He-'

'Yourrrrr fartherrrr won't allow it?' enunciated Miss Finity in a quiet growl no-one had ever heard her use before. 'He's welcome to come and discuss with me the upbringing of his son if he cares. I shall make myself available any time for such a fascinating and lengthy discussion.' Her eyes twinkled venomously.

She manoeuvred Dagmar back into his chair and dropped him like a fly. She let go of Finn and gave him a meaningful look.

'I'm aware of your Maths MasterClasses, Finn. I'm sure that Mr Violet can find something to teach you for a second hour. That can serve as your detention.'

Finn bit back a smile and tried to look upset. So Miss Finity was on his side. She was a LightFighter. She looked at him again and gave him a slight nod, and he knew she'd read his mind. He sent her a heartfelt *thank you*, and resumed his seat.

The rest of the school day passed without incident. Finn, Georgie and Fred managed to avoid Mr Gusting and Dagmar, who brooded darkly but kept his distance.

They met up outside Fred's classroom at the end of the day.

'Where d'you think he'll be this time?' asked Fred.

'Let's just go to the same place as last time,' said Finn

They found Mr Violet waiting for them

'Right,' said Mr Violet. 'Let's get started, ASAP. We have just one hour for Georgie and Fred. Finn, thanks to your antics this morning and the good works of Miss Finity, you will have two hours, every second of which you will need from what I hear, so, w-.' a violent knocking at the door silenced him.

'Drat it,' muttered Mr Violet under his breath. He got to his feet and limped over to the door.

Four mothers and their extremely unhappy offspring were loitering outside.

'Yes? Can I help you?' asked Mr Violet in a tone of voice that said the opposite.

'Yes,' said one of the mothers. 'We want our children to do the maths class too. They all need it, don't they, if they're to do as well as they should.'

'Give me strength,' muttered Mr Violet under his breath. 'I'm sorry, but that won't be possible.'

'Why not?' demanded the mother, her second chin quivering indignantly.

'Because your children can all do their maths extremely well. Take them home and let them play for once. Now if you'll excuse me.' Forcibly, Mr Violet pulled the door shut in their astounded faces.

'Saints preserve us from Alpha mothers,' he said. 'Now, the first thing we'll start with is astral travel, the science of projecting your mind and taking your body with it, if you wish to. Very useful. First, you can throw your mind while keeping your body stationary to evade a Thought-Thief. Got to make sure you re-unite mind and body after though. We've all seen the odd body wandering round that has clearly lost its mind. Not a pretty sight I'm sure you'd agree. I much prefer moving body and mind together. Let's say you are standing in front of a chasm which you need to jump. If you visualise yourself flying through the air and landing safely on the far side, then, if you concentrate hard enough and the leap isn't too enormous, you should be able to manage it. With a lot of practice first of course.'

'Er, how can we learn that in a classroom?' asked Fred doubtfully.

'You can't,' replied Mr Violet as if it were the silliest question he'd ever heard. 'Come here, all of you.' He stretched out his long, fine hands to them, taking Georgie's hand in one, and Fred's in the other. 'Finn, grab hold of Georgie's hand. Hold it tight. Do not, under any circumstances let go.'

They all did as they were asked and stood expectantly.

'Are you ready?' asked Mr Violet.

'For what?' asked Georgie, her heart beginning to race.

'Astral travel, as practised by a master, even if I say it myself. Hold on tiiiiiiiiiigggggggggggghhhtttttt.'

The next thing they knew was a great, rushing sensation; a blur before their eyes, a whoosh past their ears, then came a thud, and a feeling of heat.

'Wonderful. We made it!' exclaimed Mr Violet.

Finn found himself lying on the sand in the desert, atop a large dune, gazing up at Mr Violet, who was gleefully brushing sand from his trousers. Georgie and Fred lay on the sand beside Finn. There was a heat haze shimmering all around them. Far away in the distance they could see the attenuated skyline of Dubai. Save for the weird ringing in everyone's ears, there was no sound. They might as well have been in another world.

'I'm not here, am I?' Fred asked in a tiny voice. 'This hasn't happened has it?'

Georgie suddenly jumped to her feet and let out an enormous whoop.

'That was amaaaaaazing,' she yelled, spinning around, arms outstretched like an aeroplane.

Fred and Finn watched her and began to laugh. They laughed so much that tears rolled down their cheeks. Mr Violet watched them with an indulgent smile for some time before finally saying:

'When you've quite got yourselves back under control.'

Slowly, all three straightened up and looked at Mr Violet with a new respect.

'What was that? How did you do it?' asked Georgie.

'I visualised where I wanted to be, then I visualised being there. And, voilà, here we are.'

'Where, exactly are we?' asked Finn.

'Fifteen miles from school. Now, time to try it alone.'

'Whaaaat?' exclaimed Georgie.

'See that little chasm over there?' asked Mr Violet, pointing to a wadi bed in the desert that must have been fifty feet deep and forty feet wide. 'That's what we need to build up to.'

'Impossible,' declared Georgie, shaking her head so decisively her long tendrils of hair lashed back and forth across her face.

'No. Nothing is impossible. You have to believe. We'll start off small,' said Mr Violet, marking out two parallel lines with his good leg. 'Ten feet across,' he announced. 'Perfect for beginners. Fred, you start. Come on, come here and stand where I am.'

Fred glanced quickly at the other two then slowly made his way over to Mr Violet.

'Get your balance, still your mind, and see your landing. See it with all your being, focus all your energy on landing there.'

He waited while Fred stood beside him, breathing loudly.

'When you're ready,' said Mr Violet quietly.

Fred took a few moments and launched himself. He landed heavily in the sand, well short of the second line. He got up rubbing his bottom.

'You didn't believe you could do it, did you?' asked Mr Violet

'No,' replied Fred. 'Not really. I'm not much good at sport. Never have been.'

'Says who?' demanded Mr Violet.

'Well, my mother and father actually.'

'What? They actually say that to you?'

'No, not to me. About me. When they have their friends around, and they're all talking about their children, you know how it goes.'

'No, actually, I don't Fred,' said Mr Violet gently.

'Well, they say, um, *Petronella's doing advanced Gymnastics this term, is Fred in her class?'* and my mother goes, *'no, no. That's not Frederick's thing, you know. His piano occupies much of his time, and science of course, and maths. He does Go-on.'*

'GO-ON?' demanded Mr Violet, incredulously.

'It's advanced maths,' explained Fred.

'I see,' said Mr Violet. 'That just means they're pushing you in those directions, doesn't it, Fred? It doesn't mean you're no good at sport, does it?'

Fred thought about this for a while. 'No. I s'pose it doesn't.'

'Right then, let's have another go.'

Fred lined up, a look of angry determination in his eyes. He prepared himself, launched, and landed a good two feet further away than on his first jump.

'Well done,' said Mr Violet. 'Big improvement. Now keep practising. SBL. See, Believe and Launch!' he enthused, waving his arm through the air as if conducting an orchestra.

It took five more attempts, but on the sixth, Fred landed clear of the second line.

'I did it!' shouted Fred, jumping up and looking at the line in amazement. 'I did it!'

'Excellent!' exclaimed Mr Violet.

Georgie and Finn ran over to Fred.

'That was brilliant, Fred,' yelled Finn, patting him on the back so hard that Fred staggered forwards into Georgie.

'It was amazing,' agreed Georgie, steadying Fred.

Fred's grin just kept getting bigger. 'It felt amazing. Like I was flying almost.'

'It didn't look like a jump,' agreed Finn. 'One second you were here, the next over there. I can't say I actually saw you move.'

'You wouldn't be able to,' said Mr Violet. 'Astral travel moves you at the speed of light. Now, a few more goes for you, Fred, to consolidate, then Georgie's turn.'

Fred had got his leaps down pat, executing four more perfect ones, each getting bigger than the last. Sweat streaming down his face, he collapsed in the shade of a palm tree while Georgie lined up. She paced back and forth as if planning a run up. Her brow furrowed in fierce concentration. Finally, she jumped and landed about three feet away.

Mr Violet walked up to her as she sat scowling at the sand.

'You're not meant to be jumping Georgie. Forget trying to move your body. It's your mind we're dealing with here. You need to see yourself landing beyond the line. You need to *see* your body landing there and you need to *believe* it.'

Georgie got to her feet, muttering, *see it bonehead, just see it.*

Finn went over to sit with Fred. He didn't want to put Georgie off by watching. He knew how fiercely competitive she was.

After six tries, Georgie was still not getting it. She was pouring with sweat, trembling with effort, and Finn guessed, not far from tears of anger, although, proud and stubborn as she was, she would never let them fall.

Mr Violet was trying to talk to her, but she just shook her head at him and he backed away.

Finn could bear it no longer.

'Hey, Georgie, what's up?' He could see she was almost vibrating with frustration.

'I. Just. Cannot. Do. It. I. Am. So. Stupid.'

'Georgie, stop being a drama queen. Calm down and get on with it,' said Finn casually, as if none of it really mattered.

He turned to walk away but wheeled round as he heard a shriek. Georgie had landed beyond the line.

'I did it, I did it, I did it!' She yelled triumphantly.

'I kept telling you to relax,' said Mr Violet. 'You need to be in a state of relaxed concentration. *CCR.* Confidence, Concentration and Relaxation. With those you can go far,' he declared. 'Now, Finn, your turn. No pressure or anything, but we are running short of time.'

'All right,' said Finn, trying to visualise where exactly he wanted to land. He turned and walked back behind the line. Georgie, Fred and Mr Violet watched him intently. Finn stood there for a few seconds, looking straight ahead. Then he disappeared.

'What the devil!' exclaimed Mr Violet, shielding his eyes and scanning the horizon. 'I should have known. I should have warned him,' he said, more to himself than to the others.

'Where's he gone?' asked Georgie, panicking.

'I have no idea,' replied Mr Violet. His forehead was creased with worry. 'He could have gone anywhere.'

'Aaaaah!' came a yell from the other side of the void. Finn was standing there, eyes wild with excitement. 'That was awesome!,' he hollered. Suddenly, his face sobered. Mr Violet was eyeing him furiously.

'This is not a game, Finn,' yelled Mr Violet. 'You could have gone round the bend and we'd never have got you back. You are toying with power. You're like a toddler driving a Ferrari. NEVER do that again. You follow my instructions and do not show off, or-'

'I wasn't,' protested Finn. 'I just wanted to see how far I could go.'

'And where, pray, did you go?'

'To the ice cream shop at Park and Shop.'

'Oh no. Can this get any worse?' demanded Mr Violet. 'Please don't tell me anyone saw you arrive?'

Finn looked awkward. 'Well, there were these twins. Their mother was mopping ice cream off the floor so I don't think she saw me.'

'And the twins?'

'They did see me. Their little eyes opened wide.'

'How old were they?'

'Oh, about two.'

Mr Violet exhaled heavily. 'Hopefully their mother will put down whatever they said to her as a sugar high, or else just pure imagination. Children are rarely believed when they talk about the fantastic, fortunately for us. Right, Finn, since you're so adept, perhaps-' he stopped suddenly, turning his head like a dog sniffing the air, and lifting his ears to different positions. 'We have to go back. Our classroom's been discovered. If our exit's closed we cannot return without great complication. You're not ready for that. Georgie, Fred, hold my hands. Finn, visualise the classroom. There's no time for two jumps. Can you do it?'

'Yes,' said Finn, summoning every ounce of will.

'See you theeeeeeere,' yelled Mr Violet, disappearing with Fred and Georgie.

Finn waited a moment. He looked around the desert. The silence rang in his ears. He was utterly alone. If he failed to get back.......Stop it, he admonished himself. Go. Now. Do it.

⟋ Chapter Ten ⟍

BACK AT THE SCHOOL, Mr Gusting was on the warpath.

'Here's the classroom, deputy headmaster,' said the alpha mothers. 'The teacher was so rude to us. Unacceptable. There he was, with three pupils and he refused to take our children here. Told us to go away, in no uncertain terms.'

'Right, well ladies, I am most upset to hear that. Please, allow me to sort this out here and now,' he said, looking forward enormously to a good verbal scrap.

Mr Gusting took a deep breath, shot his cuffs and threw open the door. He stepped across the threshold like a gunfighter ready for a show down, and stared at.... An empty classroom. He looked round in puzzlement.

'Well?' came the demands from behind him when all they heard was silence and the sounds of Mr Gusting's angry breaths.

'Well ladies, it seems you have the wrong classroom.'

The mothers barrelled in behind.

'No. We do not have the wrong classroom. This is the right one, isn't it Jennifer?'

'It is. Without a shadow of doubt,' came back the

supremely confident answer.

Mr Gusting wandered round. He could smell it, salt water, just a trace, but enough to know. His face turned red with anger. He blew out a heavy breath in an attempt to control it. He turned back to the mothers.

'Well ladies, look for yourselves, there is no teacher here. No pupils. No Master Class.'

The ladies looked and saw nothing. Regretfully they trooped out.

Miss Finity arrived suddenly outside the classroom.

'Mr Gusting,' she said importantly. 'Phone call for you. I think it's the Minister for Sport,' she whispered confidentially. Mr Gusting left the mothers and practically sprinted towards his office.

'Right, ladies,' said Miss Finity, sliding her long arm round the shoulders of two of the mothers with surprising force. 'Perhaps you'd like to see the mathematics modules I am developing. Makes Go-on look like kindergarten stuff.'

With exclamations of delight, the mothers tripped away down the corridor.

Seconds later, Mr Violet, Fred and Georgie landed with a bang in the corner of the classroom.

Mr Violet sprang to his feet. 'Come on, Finn. COME ON. You can do it,' he urged, his voice desperate.

Suddenly there was a whooshing sound and Finn landed in the other corner.

'Thank God,' said Mr Violet. 'Well done, Finn. Now, Disgusting's been here. He'll be back any minute when he realises the phone call was a hoax. Clear off now, all of you. *Run*,' he urged. They took one look at his face and they ran.

CHAPTER ELEVEN

MR GUSTING WAS ON the phone, not to the Minister for Sport, who mysteriously had not been on the line when he had got there, but instead to Ivan Drax whom he had just rung urgently.

'There's something going on,' declared Mr Gusting portentously. 'I'm sure Finlay's the one, and I think that charlatan Violet is helping him.'

'Is he now? Very interesting,' mused Drax. 'I would not underestimate Ulysses Violet if I were you, Dennis. He is a powerful fighter.'

'So what do we do?' asked Mr Gusting.

'First of all, we find out if Finn Kennedy really is the one,' instructed Drax.

'The Djinn's salvation?'

'Or his end. Remember, there are two Prophesies, involving the same boy, the same Prince of Atlantis that Hydrus has been waiting for. In the one, Hydrus drinks his blood and takes his youth, his power, his life. In the other Prophesy, the boy vanquishes Hydrus.'

'Do we inform The Dark One we think we have found him?' asked Mr Gusting.

'We have to,' answered Drax. 'But first we *must* be

sure. The spies have been whispering for some time about a boy who can swim like a fish. The Dark One has had his suspicions for a long time, remember. That's one of the reasons he kidnapped the boy's parents, because he thought Finn might be the One, but time is running out and now we need to know for sure.'

'How?' asked Mr Gusting.

'Organise a swimming competition for tomorrow,' instructed Drax. 'I'll get Dagmar to goad the boy. We'll see what he can really do. Oh, and check between his toes.'

'Check between his toes?' asked Gusting incredulously.

'For webbing.'

'There is no webbing. I would've noticed something freaky like that, and so would Dagmar.'

Drax smiled. 'Check for surgical scars.'

'And, if he is the One, why not just kill him?'

'Because,' replied Drax, an edge of impatience sharpening his voice, 'he could be the Djinn's salvation, could he not? Hydrus would kill us if we made a mistake. Look, it's all going according to plan. We kidnapped his parents, we've got him here. Now we confirm he is the One, and then, if he is, we spring the next stage of the trap.'

'Which is?' asked Mr Gusting.

'Let's just say bringing Finn Kennedy a little closer to his destiny,' answered Drax, his voice cold with evil.

Mr Gusting put down the phone with a shudder of anticipation.

CHAPTER TWELVE

$\mathbf{M}$R AND MRS CARADOC Adams were giving yet another dinner party and it was going with a swing. They had three other influential couples there, all chatting animatedly whilst quaffing ice cold drinks and munching delicious canapés that the maids had laboured over all day. Mrs Adams discreetly checked her watch. Twenty minutes until dinner was served, just time for Fred to do one of his piano recitals.

She excused herself and set off for Fred's bedroom, her high heels beating out a tattoo on the marble stairs. She stopped outside Fred's closed door and knocked.

'Fred? Fredieeeeee,' she trilled. When there was no reply, she knocked rather hard. 'Fred,' she hissed. When there was still no reply, she pushed open the door impatiently. No Fred. And he wasn't in his bathroom either because she checked that. When had she seen him last? She was wracking her brains just as she heard footsteps on the stairs behind her.

'Fred!' Where have you been?'

'In the garden, Mummy,' he replied. 'Just admiring your plants.'

That brought a swift smile. 'Mm. They are lovely aren't

they? But, darling, you have to change. Navy trousers and white shirt. Quick, quick! Then come down and play.'

Fred groaned inside. Not again. When would she realise he was a boy, not a performing seal?

'Now Fred,' said his mother, brushing an infinitesimal speck of fluff from his navy trousers. 'We have a particularly important guest here this evening. Your father is very probably going to do some extremely lucrative business with him, so it's important we impress him. Understood?'

Normally Fred would have said a dutiful; 'Yes, Mum,' but after the day's excitement, after something that he enjoyed and that felt real, he didn't think he could go on acting.

'Look, Mum, I really don't enjoy this. Do I have to do it?'

His mother's ruthlessly plucked eyebrows shot up her Botoxed forehead.

'What has got into you Fred? Of course you have to do it.'

'Why?' asked Fred for the first time.

His mother's mouth formed a perfect O of surprise. 'Why? I'll tell you why. Because creating the right social and business life is important. It's a job, just like Daddy's. He picks shares on the stock market. I pick friends. In both cases you have to pick the winners, back your judgement, invest heavily, time, money, effort. Then you get the payoff down the line.'

'I thought you gave all these dinners because they're supposed to be fun.'

'Fun?' his mother asked as if it were a dirty word. 'Fun is very much secondary. What counts is knowing the right people, being on the right guest lists, having access to the right level of society. It's called *belonging*, Fred,' she concluded, as if that explained everything. Fred just wanted to belong to a family.

'Now, Fred, enough chat. Let's go downstairs.'

His mother always insisted on introducing him to everyone before he played, and now he prepared himself for the ritual. He dutifully shook hands with all but one of the guests. His mother seemed to be saving this guest for last. The man was standing with his back to Fred, talking to Fred's father. He was medium height, thick set and dark. Something about him hovered in Fred's memory. Then the man turned round, and Fred gasped.

Fred saw the look of recognition flicker briefly across the man's face before he replaced it with a look of strangerly solicitude.

Fred forced himself to mouth a greeting and extend his hand to the man he had seen on the boat the night before with Mr Gusting and Dagmar. The man gripped his hand with one of those handshakes that certain men seemed to feel the need to inflict, even on small boys. Hand throbbing, Fred wondered if he'd ever manage to play the piano again. He felt as if all his bones had been crushed. Then he registered the name and what his mother was saying.

'And Mr and Mrs Drax have a boy at JAM too,' she said. 'Dagmar. I'm right, Ivan, am I not? His name is Dagmar?'

The bone crusher nodded.

'I must arrange to have you all over for a weekend barbecue, as soon as we all find a slot in our diaries,' his mother continued, beaming. 'What do you say to that, Frederick? Wouldn't it be nice if Dagmar came round with his parents?'

Yeah, about as nice as inviting round a family of hungry anacondas, thought Fred. He managed a weak

smile, and then gratefully followed the lifeline thrown him
unwittingly by his mother as she took him by the hand and
led him to the grand piano.

Distractedly, he took his seat. His mind was elsewhere,
and he knew he hit a few wrong notes from the frowns on
his parents' faces, but their guests clapped enthusiastically.
Fred bowed and quickly made his escape.

As he climbed the stairs, he felt eyes following him.
He knew without looking it was Dagmar's father who was
watching him. He felt a tingle down his spine. A Thought-
Thief, he realised with horror. He tried to throw his mind
far from his body. He imagined his mind landing on his
boat, moored a whole mile away.

At the top of the stairs, he turned and looked straight
back into those sinister eyes. Fred knew a bully when he
saw one. Ivan Drax was as repugnant as his son. Why on
earth had his parents invited the horrible man to dinner?
Then it hit him. He was obviously the man who was going
to do business with his father. Fred just knew that was a bad
idea. He tried to do what Finn had described; he tried to
see into the man's mind. He got a brief pulsing image; red,
like spilled paint, swirling on a dark, rippled background.

The adults ate, drank, chattered and laughed in the large,
candle-lit dining room. They were having far too much
fun to notice the large fern tree in the corner. Even if, out
of the corner of their eyes, they saw some of the fronds
move occasionally, they put that down to the breeze which
wafted in through the open windows.

After more than an hour of crouching, Fred's legs were
beginning to turn numb, and the fronds tickled his nose so
much that he finally couldn't help himself and let out an

almighty sneeze. Luckily for him, at that exact moment, his father gave an enormous guffaw of laughter at something Mr Drax had said.

'Ah, that was a good one, Ivan, my friend,' said his father, getting to his feet. 'Now, Alison, Darling. Could you lead everyone out into the garden? I think we'll take our coffee and petit fours outside.'

'Certainly, Darling,' replied Fred's mother. The guests got slowly to their feet and began ambling out.

'Caradoc, just a second,' Mr Drax said, laying a hand on Fred's father's arm. 'Let's you and I take a few private moments to go over our scheme. What do you say?'

'Oh, of course, certainly,' replied Fred's father.

Mr Drax smiled, as a shark might when sighting prey. 'Let's get started.'

Behind the fern, Fred listened, eyes widening in shock, and then narrowing in anger.

Fred arrived at school the next day exhausted and simmering with rage.

'Hey, Finn, Georgie,' he shouted, arriving at a run and sliding down in the shade of the acacia tree beside them. 'You'll never guess what I heard last night.'

Finn looked at Fred in surprise. Fred hadn't struck him as an angry person, but he looked positively seething.

'C'mon. Spill,' urged Georgie.

'O.K. Right. Well, last night my parents gave another one of their ghastly dinner parties. I have to play the piano to entertain the guests, so I came down to play, got introduced to all the guests, and you'll never guess who was there.'

'Mr Violet?' tried Georgie.

'No. Dagmar's parents. Mr and Mrs Ivan Drax. My mother went on about how we must get Dagmar round for a barbecue. I think I'd deliberately choke on a drumstick just to get out of it, but anyway, that's not the point. At the end of dinner, my mother takes everyone out into the garden, but my father and Dagmar's Dad, Ivan, stay back, and they start talking.'

'Where were you?' asked Finn.

'Hiding behind an ornamental fern,' answered Fred proudly. 'My mother grows them especially big. It was a great place to hide. So they start talking about this project. My father's bank is going to be lending Dagmar's father a ton of money to knock down the fisherman's village to build some fancy marina. It's almost finalised. But my father can't know. He can't know that's where loads of Triton's supporters live. He would never do it if he knew. But Ivan Drax knows, I'm sure he does. I bet he supports Hydrus. When my father asked him how he was going to look after all the fishermen whose homes and moorings were going to be destroyed, he just gave a horrible chuckle and said: 'Don't worry, Caradoc. I'll take care of them.'

'Meaning?' asked Finn.

'I think he-' Fred faltered at this point, 'you see, I tried to see into his mind, and I saw this image. I kept seeing it all last night. Finally I figured out what it was. It was blood, lots of blood, swirling around on the sea. I think he's going to kill them.'

THERE WAS A COMMOTION in the classrooms that morning as the teachers announced there was going to be an impromptu swimming gala for Finn's year. Finn and most of the class were delighted because it meant they would miss a couple of lessons. Dagmar paraded round the classroom as if preparing for battle. Fred and some of the other sports haters complained bitterly.

'Odd,' observed Georgie. 'What's going on?' she asked Miss Finity.

'I have absolutely no idea, Georgina,' Miss Finity replied, looking vexed. 'Dagmar, sit down, will you,' she yelled. 'The sooner it's over the better, in my opinion. Go on out, all of you. Go and get changed, then line up by the pool. Mr Gusting will explain all, I'm sure,' she added acidly.

Finn got into his swimming trunks. He felt his heart beginning to pump harder, the way it always did before a race. Finn watched Mr Gusting marching round, organising pupils of similar standard to swim against each other. After half an hour he was growing impatient. Fred had swum. He'd come third out of four.

'Result!' he'd exclaimed, grabbing his towel and coming round to join Finn. 'At least I wasn't last this time.'

Georgie had swum too, determinedly coming in second in a fast race. Then, finally, Finn was summoned. He gave a wry smile. There was Dagmar, placed in the lane next to him. On his other side was Mahmoud, an excellent swimmer, who was faster even than boys two years older than him, and in the far lane was Hugh, a friendly boy wearing a shark's tooth necklace, who'd just been promoted into the swim squad.

'Right,' boomed Mr Gusting. 'Are you ready?'

The boys nodded. As Finn adjusted his goggles, he noticed Dagmar give a salute. He followed his gaze and saw a thick-set, swarthy stranger nod to Dagmar. Then the stranger turned and fixed his eyes on Finn. Even from a distance Finn could feel the sense of the violence emanating from the man.

'Ready to be thrashed, Fishboy,' hissed Dagmar. 'I'm gonna show you what competitive swimming's really about.'

'Go ahead,' replied Finn.

'Oh I will, Fishboy. I will.'

Finn heard the whistle blow and dived into the water. As he hit the surface, a body plummeted into his. A fist slammed into his head. Dagmar had dived straight at him. Finn felt stars explode in his head. He kicked out for the surface, but Dagmar had grabbed hold of his ankle. Finn needed air, desperately, but he could see Dagmar wasn't in a hurry to let go and he knew Mr Gusting wouldn't be in a hurry to dive in and rescue him. Be calm, he told himself. The blood pumping round his body slowed and suddenly his need for air wasn't so great. Alright Dagger, you thug, if you want to play games, thought Finn, whipping his body round and grabbing Dagmar by the ankle. He used his other hand to ward off the blows Dagmar was trying to rain down on him, and to push at the water to keep them both under. He wasn't sure how long they had been under, but he suddenly saw panic enter Dagmar's eyes. Finn smiled and held on. Next thing he knew, there was an explosion in the water beside him and a hand was grabbing him and dragging him off Dagmar. Finn surfaced and watched a soaking Mr Gusting haul Dagmar from the water. The boy's pugnacious face was white with fear.

Mr Gusting, veins bulging with fury, pushed Georgie and Fred, who had both come running up to Finn, out of the way and turned to Finn.

'*What* did you-' Mr Gusting's yell was drowned out by a horde of pupils in uproar.

'Finn didn't start it,' yelled Tom, a boy with a wild mop of hair and a keen sense of justice. 'It was-'

'It's all right,' cut in a smooth voice from behind. Finn wheeled round. The stranger was standing there. Unlike Mr Gusting, he was utterly calm. The pupils fell silent.

'Dagmar can look after himself,' continued the stranger. 'Let them race.'

Mr Gusting stepped back. 'Right. Well. You can race, Dagger?' he asked, concern flashing across his face.

'Of course he can,' said the man icily. 'Can't you, Dagmar?'

'Yes Father,' Dagmar replied stiffly.

Ah, thought Finn, with a flash of anger. Dagmar's father - the man who was plotting to destroy the fishermen's village. Finn almost, but not quite managed to feel sorry for Dagmar, to have a father like that.

The men stepped back. The boys lined up.

'Good luck, Finn,' called out Lara, a pretty girl from Fred's class.

Mr Gusting blew his whistle and the boys dived in.

Finn wasn't taking any more chances. Suddenly this whole thing felt like a set-up.

He dived as far as he could, and then undulated his body underwater, trying to put as much distance between himself and Dagmar as possible. He did a whole length underwater, surfaced, took a quick gulp of air, tumble-turned and swam back. It was many seconds before Hugh, Mahmoud and then, finally Dagmar finished the race. For a few moments, there was a stunned silence and then applause broke out. Georgie came running up to Finn.

'You beat them by nearly one length, Finn. That was amazing!'

'I know. I'm a bit shocked myself,' said Finn. He thought of the Djinn. Use your powers, he had said. Use them and they will grow.

Suddenly, Finn was conscious of Mr Gusting behind him.

'Sit down, Finn,' commanded the man. 'I thought I saw blood on your feet. I need to examine your toes.'

'I didn't cut myself,' said Finn, shrinking back.

'I'll be the judge of that,' replied Gusting. He grabbed Finn's foot, spread the toes and scrutinised them. Wordlessly, Finn let him. Gusting examined the other foot, then, seemingly satisfied, he got up and walked away.

Finn dipped his feet into the pool, to wash off Gusting's touch.

'What on earth was that all about?' asked Georgie.

'I have no idea,' said Finn, 'but whatever it was, I didn't like it.'

Nor did Mr Violet. Watching from a first floor class-room window, he saw Gusting and Drax observing Finn and whispering. He saw the fight, with Finn holding his breath for minutes, then he saw Finn swim fast and lithe as a dolphin from one end of the pool to the other and back again, thrashing the other swimmers. When Gusting then got down and examined Finn's toes, Mr Violet let out a roar of rage and sorrow. He knew what Gusting would have found - the scars from a surgeon's removal of the skin that had webbed Finn's toes. Now the Dark Fighters knew beyond any doubt that Finn was the Prince of Atlantis of the Prophesy, and that changed everything.

CHAPTER FOURTEEN

A S SOON AS THE school bell sounded at the end of the day Fred, Finn and Georgie rushed out into the corridor and headed towards their special classroom. Finn worried that Dagger would be stalking him, but there was no sign of him.

Mr Violet, looking unusually serious, was waiting for them. 'Come in, co- what's happened?' he asked, quickly pulling them into his classroom and closing the door behind them.

Fred told him what he had overheard at the dinner party and about his dream. Mr Violet listened in silence, his eyes faraway. For a long time afterwards he said nothing. Fred, Finn and Georgie all tried to see into his mind, but all they could discern was a floating blueness that meant nothing to them.

'What are you going to do?' asked Finn.

'I've been trying to transmit a message to Triton, but he's not picking up. I can tell he's preoccupied. I'll try later, but now, look, we have to get on. Things are accelerating.'

'Why?' asked Finn, thinking of his parents. 'And how?'

'The elements are raging. All the Dark Djinns are seething. You'll hear it soon enough on the news.'

'What? What's happened?' demanded Georgie, glancing uneasily at Finn.

'I'm going to give you a crash course today,' Mr Violet continued as if he hadn't heard the question. 'Finn, first we'll do glass blowing, then water desalination if there's time.' Mr Violet approached a long table covered with a cloth that was bulging mysteriously. He removed the cloth with a dramatic swish, then left Finn gazing at what was underneath in bemusement as he turned to Fred and Georgie.

'Right, you two can practise astral travel, or, astral jumping in your case since I think ten feet is your record to date. I won't supervise you closely. I think you can safely move around this classroom, from end to end, avoiding the windows of course.'

To a chorus of grunts of failure, whoops of success and yelps of pain as Fred and Georgie landed awkwardly, Finn learned about glass making and blowing.

'Right, your basic ingredients,' said Mr Violet, gesturing to three piles of what looked like sand on the table. 'First, sand. Plenty of it around fortunately. Next limestone, then sodium carbonate. The limestone is essential as it reduces the melting point of sand from 1700 degrees centigrade to 850 degrees. But you have to get the proportions right - 75 per cent sand, 10 per cent limestone and 15 per cent sodium carbonate. Next you need your heat source.' At this he produced a magnifying glass so dazzling that Finn had to look away, and Fred who had just landed with a bang behind them blundered blindly into them. When the three of them had disentangled again, Mr Violet continued. 'When you have your glass mixed, you then take this blow pipe and you literally blow the glass into the shape you want. Try to envisage the shape. Makes it easier.'

'Er what shape will I want, and why?' asked Finn, still struggling for the life of him to see any use for glass blowing.

'That, I'm afraid I don't know,' replied Mr Violet.

'But, but, how can you know just part of the story, part of what I have to do, but not all?' Finn stammered with confusion.

'Because the future is not fixed. Your fate could take you along many different paths. It is not my job to determine your fate, to tell you what to do. I need to arm you for whatever you may face. I have certain intuitions as to what that might be, but that is all.'

Finn felt a fury of frustration. 'Why can't I just take a gun, blow his brains out?'

'If only it were that simple. He can read your mind, first of all, unless you are very skilled at blocking. He would see a gun in his mind's eye and his spies would see it visually. Even if you did manage to fire off a shot, he would just change into a whiff of smoke and the bullet would pass harmlessly through him. But a pile of sand, some silicone and carbonate, what would he think of that? Nothing. You have to out think him, plan an indirect attack.'

'But how?' asked Finn despairingly. 'I don't even know where to start.'

Mr Violet said nothing. His eyes got that faraway look in them again. Then he started to hum. To Finn's amazement, Mr Violet's voice came at him, not from his body, which was still humming, but from across the classroom.

'There is one way to capture a Djinn,' said Mr Violet's voice. 'It won't kill him, but it would contain him, and effectively paralyse his supporters who would be leaderless.'

'How?' queried Finn.

Fred ceased his jumping and came to listen in.

'It's as the legends say. You capture him in a bottle.'

Finn laughed. 'Great. How on earth would I get a bottle big enough in the first place, and then how on earth would I persuade him to go into it? It's impossible.'

'You'd better get used to thinking the impossible, Finn. Then acting on it.'

'Just like that,' replied Finn, doubtfully.

'It's as simple or as complicated as you choose to make it. You're just young enough to do it.'

'What does that mean?' asked Finn.

'Well, the older you get, the more your imagination shrinks. Most adults are boring old things, no imagination whatsoever. Age and school knocked it out of them, but you, you have no excuse. Adults see shrinks, that's slang for psychiatrists, when actually they should be seeing unshrinks, or expanders, aargh-' yelled Mr Violet, tumbling to the ground as Georgie crashed into him.

'Precision, Georgie, please,' he said plaintively. Finn noticed that Mr Violet had stopped humming and his voice now seemed to come directly from his body.

'We're meant to be on the same side,' Mr Violet muttered to Georgie.

'Crashing into you just gave me an idea,' said Georgie. Can we can use astral travel as a weapon? Land on someone?'

Mr Violet looked pained. 'A tad inelegant, but if you can't think of anything better.'

Finn chuckled and felt the tension inside him ease just a notch.

'Now, a quick stint of water desalination,' announced Mr Violet. 'You can all listen in then have a go.'

After ten minutes of Bunsen burners and water evaporation and capture and recondensation, Finn, Fred and Georgie had all managed to desalinate a small quantity of water.

'Excellent!' declared Mr Violet. 'Now, I have some homework for you,' he added to a chorus of groans. 'Relax. It's not maths or food technology. Morse code.' Mr Violet took out three booklets from his surprisingly capacious jacket pocket and spun them through the air to his students. 'Not exactly rocket science. You can consult these in your own time and practise sending and receiving coded messages with each other. You can also practise seeing into each other's minds, and other people's if you like, although you won't be sure how accurate you're being that way,' he chuckled, 'but it can be fun.'

The warmth faded from his face. 'Be careful, please. All of you.' He looked directly at Finn. It seemed to Finn that he wanted to say something else but the moment passed.

'Goodbye,' said Mr Violet, almost sadly it seemed to Finn. He laid his hand lightly on Finn's shoulder. 'I hope I have helped,' he said.

'Of course you have,' replied Finn, who had grown to like Mr Violet very much. 'And you will again, won't you? I mean, we will see you again, won't we? You will come?' asked Finn.

'Yes,' replied Mr Violet. 'I will. Now, go.'

'Mummy, please can you turn on the news?' asked Georgie politely.

'Why?'

'Please, I want to hear it.'

Georgie's mother gave a heavy sigh. She thought

perhaps her daughter was hoping to hear news of her father and so she took pity and switched on the car radio and tuned it to a news station.

Georgie and Finn sat listening in silence, the city speeding past them unseen. In one part of the world a volcano had erupted and had killed hundreds of people. In another a hurricane had killed hundreds more who were trapped in flattened buildings and more still who drowned in the storm surge the winds had created. In another part of the world mud slides killed thousands, and so it went on, the litany of bad news, of death and disaster, floods and fires.

'Enough,' said Georgie's mother, switching off the radio. 'It's almost biblical, like a series of plagues,' she added.

'No,' said Georgie. 'It's like the war of the worlds.'

∽ CHAPTER FIFTEEN ∾

'M UMMY, DO YOU HAVE our class list?' asked
Georgie innocently.
'Why?' asked her mother, instantly on the alert.

'I just want to ring Melanie and I can't find my
address book.'

'It's stuck up over there, on the fridge,' said her mother
with a shrug. 'You see it a hundred times a day.'

'Oh, no, I meant I really want to write Mel a letter. I
think that would be better.'

'Why?'

'Her dog died. She's very fond of it.'

'You want to write her a letter of condolence for a
dog?' asked her mother incredulously.

The twins caught her tone and giggled.

'Shut up you two,' said Georgie piously. 'Don't you
have any compassion?'

Her mother raised her eyebrows, but let it pass. She
disappeared upstairs and came back a few minutes later
with a sheet of paper.

'Here.'

'Thanks, Mummy,' said Georgie, rapidly scribbling
down an address. 'Here you are,' she said, handing back the

sheet of paper and disappearing quickly upstairs.

Finn followed her in a leisurely way. Upstairs he shot a look over his shoulder to check the twins weren't spying. No sign of them, so he tapped quickly on Georgie's door and went in.

'Got it,' she said. 'Dagmar's address. It's on Beach Road.'

'It would be,' said Finn, referring to the mini palaces that dominated plots that were far too small for them. 'Well done George. Now, all I need to do is find my binoculars.' He turned to leave.

'Can't I come?' asked Georgie. 'Fred too? We could be lookouts. After all, you might need someone to watch your back,' she argued.

'Thanks, George, but I want to go alone.'

Dagmar Drax's house was a huge edifice of glass and concrete. It overlooked the sea and seemed to be glowering at it. Helpfully, there was a large eucalyptus tree right outside the boundary wall. Unhelpfully, there was also a bright street lamp shining on it like a spotlight. Finn searched around in the gutters and finally found a small rock. He took aim and with a loud smash the bulb shattered and crashed to the ground. Finn hoped there was enough muffling noise going on inside the house to mask the sound. He waited anxiously for five minutes, hiding behind a parked car, but no-one came out to investigate.

With his binoculars swinging around his neck, Finn climbed the eucalyptus tree which was shrouded in darkness now. He found a spot quite high up that afforded him the perfect view of a series of brightly-lit rooms; family room, a couple of boring office-type rooms, a very formal room framed in heavy curtains that Finn hoped would not be drawn. He settled down to wait, hoping that it would not be in vain.

For over half an hour, nothing happened. Finn began to feel stiff and cramped crouched in the tree, but he wasn't about to give up. Cars passed, their headlights sweeping beneath him. He watched a stray black cat slink along the pavement towards his tree. The cat stopped close to the tree and gazed knowingly up to where Finn was hiding. Finn gazed back down at it, willing it to go away. He felt it was almost pointing at him with its inquisitive nose. Then the cat decided to climb the tree, and with a series of energetic leaps, it made its way to Finn's hiding place.

Finn felt a mixture of pleasure and annoyance. He felt the cat might somehow draw attention to him, but he liked cats and had a particular admiration for feral ones who lived by their wits. This one was sweet and friendly. It nuzzled up to him, allowed itself to be scratched, gave a brief purr, then extracted itself from Finn's grasp, climbed up to the next highest branch and sat there, seemingly keeping lookout too on Dagmar's house.

Finn watched it, puzzling over it for a while, then he turned back to continue his scrutiny of the house. Suddenly, movement caught his eye. The door to the officey room had been thrown open, and Bonecrusher Drax had walked in with Mr Gusting and two other men Finn had never seen before. One was short, with close-cropped dark hair and a pointed beard, the other was tall with straggly greying hair pulled back into a ponytail. Finn knew with a flutter of excitement that they were up to something.

He watched them sit down around a table. Drax sat at the head of the table, facing Finn. Perfect! Finn got out his binoculars and trained them on the man's swarthy face. He wished he could lip read. He wondered if that would be any easier than mind reading. He watched Drax get up and pour out four drinks, pass them round, then resume his seat. Then they seemed to settle down to business. Finn kept his binoculars trained on Drax's head. He didn't really need them, but thought they might help. *Right, now, here goes*, he told himself, focusing his mind on Drax's. He watched him steadily for five minutes, fighting the urge to fidget. He got nothing. Dispirited, he let the binoculars drop. He rubbed his eyes, thought of his parents, and of the evil Djinn, and of Triton and Mr Violet. He seemed to hear Mr Violet's voice in his head. *Have faith*, he said.

Cloudy, swirling at first, then progressively clearer, images began to form in Finn's mind. He saw a boat bobbing in a mooring at the marina at night time. It was not a sailing boat, but a power boat with two large engines at the back. It was wooden and surprisingly decrepit looking. He would have thought that only new, gleaming yachts belonged in Drax's mind. The next image was of the two new men, carrying two holdalls that looked very heavy, into the boat. Then the boat started up. Suddenly Drax jumped up, rubbing his head. He marched towards the open window, threw it open and glared out, straight at the tree. Straight at Finn's hiding place. The other men had jumped up too and were staring out. Finn held his breath in fear. It was as if Drax knew he was there. Could he see him? Were the eucalyptus leaves too thin to cover him? If they could spot him, he was trapped. Should he stay still, or shimmy down the tree immediately, and run for...... his life is what it felt like, for there was something murderous in Drax's gaze.

Then it occurred to Finn. Drax must have felt his mind being read. Before Finn could decide what to do, the cat started up a slow, agonising wail in the way cats do when they want to attract a mate. On and on it went. Finn saw the men raise their glances to it and then break out into hard, male laughter. Drax swore at the cat, yelled at it to shut up, then slammed the window and went back to his seat at the head of the table.

Finn looked up at the cat in wonder.

'Thank you,' he whispered under his breath. The cat looked back at him, its amber eyes holding his and Finn recognised an ally. 'You're a Light Fighter,' he whispered. The cat blinked in seeming acknowledgement, then took up again its silent scrutiny of the house.

Finn took a minute or so to get back into the right mind set. Drax was talking again, seeming to ask questions of the two men, then with an almost audible click, the images started unfurling again from Drax's head. The boat sped through darkness towards light. Finn recognised the fishermen's village. As the boat approached, it slowed and Finn saw a dinghy being lowered. Then both men climbed down into the dingy, leaving the boat without anyone aboard. Finn watched. The dinghy sped off towards open sea, but the wooden boat continued its course towards the fishermen's village. On and on it went. Finn began to feel sick. He knew what was coming. He saw the crash, saw the blinding flash of light, heard the dull, obscene thud of the explosion once in his own mind, then in Drax's. The cat let out a yelp, or maybe it had been Finn himself who had cried out. He knew he had no time to waste. He shimmied down the tree and ran towards Fred's house as fast as he could.

Fred's house was only a few hundred yards down Beach Road. Like the Drax's but to a lesser extent, it was lit by a profusion of up-lighting and protected by a wall that ran round the entirety of the garden, making entry difficult for burglars, and for Finn. Chest heaving from his sprint, Finn glanced left and right then he clambered up onto the wall and dropped down onto the grass on the other side. He waited for a few moments, crouching in the shadows, and then when he was sure no-one was around, he ran quickly to the house where he ducked down below the windows.

He had no way of knowing which was Fred's bedroom, or even if he'd be in it now. Unlike at the Drax's, all the curtains were drawn. He moved cautiously round the house, then risked backing away into the garden to get a better look at the rooms. On the upper level, he saw what he guessed was the bedroom of Fred's parents. It had a huge window fronted by a large balcony covered with the plants of which his mother was apparently so fond.

Finn moved on round the house. He eyed up a room with a balcony and a telescope. Finn remembered Fred saying that he had a telescope on his balcony. A light shone through, encouragingly. Fred was there, but how to attract his attention? Or perhaps there was a better, if riskier way……..

Chapter Sixteen

F**RED WAS IN HIS** bedroom finishing up his maths homework under the close supervision of his father. The markets had suffered a bad day. Fred's father was in a bad mood and so Fred suffered. Just three more questions left to do; dastardly hard ones. He frowned at the paper swimming before his eyes.

'Dad, I think I've had enough for now,' he said quietly.

His father gave him a withering look. 'Enough, really, have you? Do you think if I turned to Apex Bank and said half way through my day that I'd had enough they would be impressed? No,' he said, answering his own question. 'They wouldn't, would they, Fred, and so tell me, why is it different for you?'

Because I'm a boy, Fred wanted to say. Because I've already done all my school homework, and this is extra GO-ON maths work and yet more pressure on me. He opened his mouth, but just then his mother's voice cut through his thoughts.

'Caradoc! Caradooooooooooooooc! New York calling,' she trilled importantly.

Relief flooded through Fred. Now his father would be on the phone for ages and would hopefully have forgotten all about his son's maths by the time he got off it.

'Yup, coming,' he called out. 'Sorry, Fred,' he said expansively.

'That's okay' replied Fred, just managing to hide his relief. His father closed the door and then seconds later there was an almighty crash. Fred wheeled round in shock to see Finn landing on top of his desk. A pile of books tumbled to the floor with a crash of their own.

Fred stared at Finn open mouthed. Finn grinned back in triumph.

'What the heck-'

'Freddie? Are you all right?' called his mother. The sound of her footsteps climbing the stairs sent both boys into a panic.

'Oh, fine, just tripped over my chair,' improvised Fred quickly. The footsteps paused.

'Dangerous things, chairs,' muttered his mother. The footsteps faded away going downstairs.

Fred and Finn breathed again.

'What are you *doing* here?' whispered Fred.

'Crisis,' replied Finn. 'We've got to go and get Georgie now.

'Give me ten minutes,' said Fred. He changed rapidly into his pyjamas, ruffled his hair, then turned to Finn.

'Get into my bathroom and hide behind the shower curtain. Stay there until I come and get you.'

'All right, but hurry.'

Fred opened his door and headed downstairs. 'Muuum,' he called plaintively.

'Yes, darling,' replied his mother appearing from the kitchen carrying a tray of drinks.

'Mum, I feel really tired. I'm going to go to sleep now.'

His mother put down the tray, took his face in her hands and searched it for any signs of illness.

'Feeling all right?' she asked. 'You do look a bit flushed.'

'Oh, I'm fine. Just played a hard game of football in the sun today and I didn't sleep very well last night.'

'Mmm. And you've been having those extra lessons, the maths Masterclass. Not surprised you're tired. Alright then, off to bed. I'll check on you later.'

'Don't worry about me,' said Fred, stretching up to kiss his mother on her cheek. 'You just have a nice drink with Dad. He needs cheering up.'

His mother looked momentarily gloomy. 'He does, doesn't he? Wretched markets. All right, darling. Sleep well. See you in the morning.'

'See you in the morning,' echoed Fred, as if to confirm it.

'Good,' said Fred to Finn, pulling back the shower curtain. 'I don't think Mum'll check on me at all tonight, so let's get going.'

Finn stepped out of the bath. 'Right, hold my hand.'

'*What?*' demanded Fred.

'We're going to do some astral travelling, you and I, and since you don't know where we're going, you'd better hold my hand.'

'Er, all right then,' replied Fred. He took hold of Finn's hand. Nothing happened. Moments passed and still nothing. Finn's face was contorted in concentration.

'I'm really trying,' said Fred, apologetically.

'So'm I,' replied Finn. 'One more time,' he said. The boys waited another minute or so, concentrating so hard their heads hurt.

'Nope,' said Finn, exhaling loudly. 'Not working.

C'mon. It's not far. Ten minutes at a jog.'

Stealthily Fred opened his bedroom window and peered out.

'Jump?' he asked Finn, looking unhappy about it.

'Yep. I'll go first. If you sort of dangle off the balcony I'll try to catch you.'

'Don't just try. Catch me, please,' said Fred with a nervous grin.

Finn sprang from the balcony and landed deftly. Fred climbed over the edge of the balcony, took a deep breath and jumped towards Finn. Finn steadied his landing but both boys fell over with a thud. They froze, hearts racing, but there were no sounds of Fred's parents coming to investigate.

Ten minutes later the boys were at Finn's house, in his bedroom, having climbed up the acacia tree to get there. Fred was puffing from the run and the climb.

'I need to get fit,' he said. Finn grinned. 'All this'll do the trick. Right, you'd better hide in my bathroom while I go and get Georgie.'

Finn checked her bedroom. Empty. He hurried down the stairs. Georgie was in the kitchen, peering at something in the oven. Finn could hear the television in the next room, and guessed that Aunt C was in there. By this time of night, the twins would be in bed.

'Georgie,' he whispered. 'We have to go.'

Georgie looked up from the oven with a start. 'Don't do that, creeping up,' she said, then, noting the urgency on his face, she asked quickly. 'What's up? What happened at the Drax's?'

'Come on upstairs, I'll tell you there.'

'Wait, I have to get these rock cakes out of the oven or they'll burn. Give me a minute.'

Georgie pulled on a pair of bright orange oven gloves and extracted a baking tray from the oven. She quickly prised the rock cakes free and set them on a rack to cool and turned off the oven.

'We might need those,' said Finn, taking a plastic bag and tipping them into it. Georgie pursed her lips.

'Just let them bang into each other, why don't you,' she said with exasperation.

'Go and tell your Mum you're going to bed,' he whispered. 'Act all tired. Make it look like you're asleep in your bed, pad it out with something, then come to my room, and, Georgie, hurry. Please. It's an emergency.'

'All right,' said Georgie. 'Give me a few minutes.'

Five minutes later, Georgie was in his room. 'Fred!' she exclaimed. 'What are you doing here?'

'Dunno. Finn just materialised on my desk, then dragged me off here. He wouldn't tell me anything until you got here.'

'Right,' said Finn. 'Here's what's going on.' Quickly he told then what he'd seen in the Bonecrusher's head.

Georgie and Fred listened, eyes widening with horror.

'I was right,' exclaimed Fred. 'I saw blood swirling on the water.'

'You were,' agreed Finn.

'So what are we going to do?' asked Fred.

'Let's summon Mr Violet,' said Georgie.

'No time,' said Finn. 'We've got to stop it ourselves.' He grabbed his rucksack, chucked in a bottle of water and zipped his Swiss army knife into a side pocket.

'What!' exclaimed Fred and Georgie together.

'We've got to get aboard that boat and somehow stop the bomb going off, or throw it overboard or something.'

'How?' asked Fred.

'I'm working on it,' replied Finn.

CHAPTER SEVENTEEN

THE BOATYARD WAS QUIET, save the metallic chinking of the halyards slapping against the masts. The night swathed the boats in darkness, but still the gleam of white hulls glowed discreetly in the light of the stars. Lines of boats bobbed innocently at their moorings. The fresh tang of the salt water drifted on the breeze.

The sound of an engine followed by car doors slamming broke the quiet. Sudden half-suppressed footfalls disturbed the calm. The tall man and the short one carried their heavy holdalls aboard the ill-kempt wooden boat, moving cautiously, careful not to jolt their murderously volatile cargo.

They stowed the bombs carefully in the cabin, in the storage space under the bed, before making their way back up on deck to check the dinghy had no holes and that the engine was working. They had to make sure their getaway was guaranteed, that they would be long gone when the bombs exploded and the inferno raged.

They grinned at each other. The bombs were huge. The destruction of the fishermen's village would be total. So what if some of the neighbouring houses were taken out too. There was a word for that, legitimised by politicians:

collateral damage. Not their problem. The job would be done. They cared not a jot for the war being fought. They were mercenaries, available to the highest, most ruthless bidder. The man with the big house on the beach would be well pleased and they would be well rewarded.

They thought of the money that would soon be theirs as they lowered the dinghy from its stanchions and began to check it over. It was sound. No visible leaks. They hauled it back onto the stanchions, reverse way so that they could check the engine. One of them held the dinghy steady while the other pulled the starter cord. Nothing. He tried again. Still the engine refused to kick into life. The man tried again but still the engine lay silent. The man swore loudly.

'What's the problem?' asked the other one.

'How do I know? There's no time to strip it down, we'll have to find another engine somewhere, switch it. Come on, I think I know where we might get one.'

'What about the bombs?'

'Leave them where they are. No-one's going to steal a bomb are they, you idiot?'

'What if they did?'

'Arghh,' groaned the tall man in exasperation. 'There's a padlock on one of them. Lock them together and round the vertical stanchion under the bed.'

Two miles away, in the fishermen's village, the boats bobbed gently at their moorings too. In their small huts, the fishermen's wives and children slept in their beds, lulled by the faint breeze, comforted by the soft lapping of the waves on the seashore.

Normally on a night such as this, clear with calm seas, the boats would be out, the fishermen balancing on deck, scanning the water for signs of fish, or slowly letting out their nets, or painstakingly hauling them in, glitteringly alive with fish. But not tonight.

A quiet murmur of voices could be heard coming from the biggest of the boatsheds. The huge door had been pulled closed, but a chink of light escaped through the thin gap. Inside, the cavernous space was bisected by a channel of sea water like a small canal. This was normally used as an easy entryway for boats that needed repair work, but this night it was empty of boats. Instead, half in half out of the water, his great face gnarled with worry, Triton talked with his supporters.

There, in the water alongside him and surrounding him was an array of sea creatures large and small. There were seahorses, bobbing delicately. There were stingrays and barracuda. The limited space was packed. Lined up on the rafters were scores of seagulls. In the ocean beyond, shoals of fish swarmed. On the beach, crabs ceased their scuttling to listen, their acute receptors picking up every word in the universal language of the sea which all its creatures understood. Beyond the shoals of fish, a praetorian guard of dolphins and sharks patrolled and listened. Later they would relay the message to their brethren in the wider ocean.

On the raised concrete platforms at the waterside, sat rows and rows of humans; the fishermen and other Light Fighters. Mr Violet sat next to Miss Finity. Mr Violet kept rubbing at his ear with a sense of unease. He had a vague feeling he was being summoned, but he couldn't pin it down, either to a person, or to a place.

He tried to shake it off and concentrate on Triton's words.

'Thank you all for being here,' said the Sea Djinn. 'It is many a year since so many of us have gathered in one place like this, and I am honoured. I've brought you here to warn you, and to ask you all to give your help to three human children who have joined our fight.' He went on to describe Finn, Georgie and Fred.

'I'm fairly certain which boatyard it is,' said Finn. 'My father took me there to see a tall ship being built when we came to visit you a few years ago, Georgie. It's the one down by the port.'

'So how do we get there?' she asked.

'We can try astral travel,' replied Finn, 'but I don't think it'll work.'

'Well if you think that I'm sure it won't,' replied Georgie.

They linked hands and tried anyway. After a few minutes, groaning with frustration and effort, they gave up.

'Oh, no,' said Fred. 'I think I can guess. Another jog.'

'It's about a mile,' said Finn. 'You've done that already.'

'I know, that's why I'm exhausted. All right, come on,' replied Fred.

The tall man and the short one were struggling with an engine they had stolen from a life raft attached to a boat at the far end of the boatyard. They had also got hold of a wheel barrow and were loading the motor into it with some difficulty. The short one banged the propellers against his fingers and cursed loudly.

'Shut up,' shouted the tall one. 'This is supposed to be a covert operation. Covert,' he roared. 'That means secret and QUIET.'

'So stop shouting, you fool,' shouted the short one.

'Who are you calling a fool?' yelled the tall one.

So intent were they on their argument that they didn't hear the footsteps of the three children, creeping up on them.

Finn, Fred and Georgie hid behind a generator shed and listened to the voices. Finn took a peek at the men.

'It's them,' he whispered.

'What now?' whispered Fred, goose bumps rising on his arms.

Finn glanced around. 'I can't see the boat.'

'Let's hide behind that row of boats over there,' whispered Georgie, pointing to a row of huge motor yachts gleaming in the darkness. 'Then we can have a better look.'

Finn nodded. Quickly the three of them scampered across the open expanse of concrete and took cover behind the boats. They froze, scarcely breathing, wondering if they'd been seen. They heard one more furious, 'SHUT UP,' and then an ominous silence from the men.

The silence stretched, but then came sounds of grunts and scrapings suggesting that the men were still fiddling with the engine.

'I think the boat might be moored at the outer edge of the marina,' said Finn, eyes searching. 'But it could be right or left from here.' He thought for a moment. 'Come on. Let's try left,' he decided.

They padded along in the moonlight, past the silent boats. Finn felt a growing panic as there was no sign of the wooden boat. He could almost feel a clock ticking in his heart. He knew that time was running out. They approached one particularly enormous boat at the end of the line. Finn walked up to it in despair. As he reached it, he saw, hidden by the sheer bulk of it, the wooden boat, sitting in its lee, bobbing blithely in the water.

'This is it,' he said excitedly to Fred and Georgie. 'Come on, hurry.' They all glanced around. There was no sign of the men, but they saw the dinghy on the stanchions, the engine lying on the deck and they guessed the men would be back any minute.

They stepped quickly across the narrow expanse of water between the dock and the side of the boat.

'What now?' asked Fred.

'We make sure the bombs are on board, then we motor away before the men get back, then when we're far enough off the coast, we dump the bombs over the side, then motor up the coast, beach the boat and get home.'

'Okay,' said Fred, wondering how on earth they would manage all that. 'Let's find them.'

They all raced around the boat, as quietly as they could. It was Georgie who found the handballs. She called out softly to the others. 'I think I've got them.'

Fred and Finn ran down into the cabin. 'Yep, those are the ones,' said Finn.

'Right, let's go, we-' suddenly he stopped and they all froze. They could hear voices and a strange squeaking sound; the wheelbarrow carrying the stolen engine.

'Oh, God, what do we do?' gasped Georgie.

Fred and Finn glanced round wildly. They were trapped. 'Hide, in here,' urged Finn, holding open the door of a cramped loo. 'Let's just pray they don't need a pee.'

All three of them jammed into the loo and closed the door behind them. Moments later they heard footsteps and grunts as the men heaved the motor up on deck. Then they heard fiddling and curses and the roar of an engine firing and the sudden silence as it was switched off again.

'Better check the cargo,' said a rough voice. Next, they heard footsteps tripping down the stairs and approaching. They froze, hardly daring to breathe.

They heard raspy nasal breathing coming from the other side of the door.

'Cargo here,' said a mocking voice.

'Right, let's go set off some fireworks,' came the reply from the deck, followed by raucous laughter that turned the children's stomachs.

The footsteps retreated back upstairs and Fred, Georgie and Finn breathed again.

A little later, they heard the deeper roar of the wooden boat's engines kick into life. Slowly, the boat reversed from the dock. Once out in the open water, the engines roared into a higher gear and the boat shot forward into the night.

In their cramped hiding place, Georgie, Fred and Finn braced themselves against the walls. Each time the boat rose up over a wave, it slammed down on the other side, shaking them to their bones. After ten minutes, cramped and shaken, they were all facing their own battles with sea sickness.

Please let me not throw up all over the others, Fred repeated silently to himself. Georgie tried to imagine that she was in a cool, quiet room, lying on her bed, curtains wafting in a gentle breeze.

Finn forced himself to stay calm as he figured out a new plan. He knew that if they got caught, they and the entire fishing village would be killed.

Suddenly, the engines eased and the boat slowed right down. They could hear the voices of the men now.

'Right, I'll get the dinghy down. You go and set the bombs. We'll set the boat to full speed. Two minutes should do it.'

There was a grunt of response and footsteps on the stairs. It was the nasal breather again. They heard his joints pop as he crouched down by the holdalls. They heard the sound of him unzipping them, then they heard the electronic peeps as he set the timer on first one bomb, then the other.

'Two minutes,' the man yelled. 'Let's go.'

They heard him run up the stairs, then the engine roared into a high gear again and the boat shot forward.

'Now,' roared Finn. 'Let's throw the bombs over board.' They burst from their hiding place and bent down to haul the bombs out. Only then did they notice in the glare of the bright overhead light that the holdalls were locked in place. With a yell, Finn ran up the stairs. 'Follow me, quick,' he roared.

They all ran up on deck. Finn ran to the wheel. It was braced in place with two sticks. He grabbed the sticks and pulled them away. Then he hauled at the wheel. Thirty seconds must have passed and the boat was hurtling towards the fishermen's village. The boat veered perilously to one side and began to turn. Fred and Georgie were flung into the side rail. They grabbed onto it and held hard. Finn grappled with the wheel pulling the boat around, away from the fishermen's village. He could see the lights from it, twinkling in the darkness, then the boat came round and faced the open sea. It was still too close, just a few seconds more, he said to himself. He counted; one, two, three, four, five... when he came to fifteen, he could see, some way ahead, the dinghy with the men in it, staring in disbelief as the boat bore down on them.

He called to Georgie and Fred. 'We're going to have to jump.' He eased back the throttle and the boat began to slow. He knew it would be bad at this speed, but the seconds were running out. The boat was still bucking and jumping over the waves. Finn grabbed the sticks, jammed the steering wheel in place again, then hurried across to Georgie and Fred.

'We have to jump, now,' he said. 'Get onto the rails and jump as far away from the boat as you can.' He saw in his mind the propellers churning. They had no lifejackets and no-one, save the bombers, knew they were there. But they had no choice. Finn calculated it was thirty seconds or less before the boat would be blown to smithereens.

They climbed onto the rails and jumped.

The impact hit them like concrete. Water, hit at speed, was not the gentle yielding substance of the swimming pool or bath. It was a hard, unforgiving element and the breath was slammed out of them. Finn recovered first. He wheeled round in the water. He saw Georgie, floundering, but above water. He checked for Fred. There was no sign of him. Finn felt a wail of panic rising in him.

'Fred!' He yelled. 'Fred, where are you?'

Nothing. Then he saw a disturbance beneath the waves. He swam at it as fast as his gasping lungs would allow, took a huge breath and dived down. His hands struck a flailing limb. He grabbed it and kicked for the surface, pulling at handholds of an elbow, a shoulder, until Fred's head emerged, eyes wild.

'Breathe,' urged Finn. 'You're all right, you're all right. I've got you. Breathe.' He knew all about drowning swimmers, how they could take you under in their panic, kill the two of you. His father had taught him all about them. Knock them out was one solution, but he didn't want to hit Fred. He just grabbed hold of his arms and stared hard at him. Fred seemed to see reassurance in his eyes for he ceased thrashing and went limp. Finn trod water and held him up.

'There, you're okay now.'

Fred nodded.

Careful to keep hold of him, Finn turned to check on Georgie. She was swimming slowly towards him and Fred, panic in her own eyes.

'You okay?' asked Finn.

She nodded and opened her mouth to speak. Finn never heard her words. Behind him the water exploded in a plume like a huge reverse waterfall. The sky lit up with orange and red. The sound of the explosion rocked them. Burning debris from the boat sailed lethally through the air. They heard it splash and sizzle into the sea around them. Their chests felt thumped again. They turned and saw the sea on fire.

In the fishermen's village, they all heard the explosion. The fish swam like an exodus out into the open water. Triton exchanged a look with Mr Violet and swam out into the sea after the fish. The humans ran out and stood on the sea shore. They all looked with horror at the flames leaping into the sky.

Half of the dolphin and shark brigade swam to check on Triton, the other half headed towards the explosion. There, in the water, they found Finn, Fred and Georgie.

The children first glimpsed the dorsal fins gliding through the water about ten metres away. There was one particularly huge shark with a jagged fin that looked like a battle wound. Georgie could not help herself. She began to scream. Finn saw the sharks, felt his own terror, knew there was only one chance. He thought of Triton, thought of the Barracuda and he tried to think at the sharks.

'Help us', he thought. 'We are friends of Triton.' If the sharks were on the side of the Night Djinn, they'd be dead, but they might be dead anyway, so what did he have to lose?

'We are Triton's friends,' he repeated. 'We are Light Fighters. Help us, *please*.' He knew that both Georgie and Fred were too weak to swim to shore. Without help, they would drown.

CHAPTER EIGHTEEN

'WHAT HAPPENED?' DEMANDED MR Drax, in a voice tight with rage. The short man sat before him in the immaculate study. His clothes dripped water onto the marble floor and his face oozed blood from a vicious gash cut by flying debris from the exploded boat. The tall man had not been so lucky. His body now floated in the open sea. He had been hit by metal from one of the propellers and had died instantly.

'There were three of them, on the boat. They must have stowed away. They turned it round, faced it towards us. I saw them jump into the water, then the boat exploded, right by us.....' he thought of his dead friend and he couldn't go on.

Mr Drax gave him a look of contempt. 'Who were they?' he asked, getting up to pace around. 'We must have a leak somewhere. Someone has talked and the Light Fighters got onto us. We'll have to find out who they were.'

'They were children,' said the short man.

Drax's eyes opened wide. 'Were they now? Hmm, I think I know exactly who they are.' He smiled for the first time. 'Now where's that class list?' he mused to himself.

'What are you going to do?' asked the short man.

'Deal with them,' replied Mr Drax.

CHAPTER NINETEEN

THE LEAD DOLPHIN, DAUPHIN, and the lead shark, Jagged, studied the boys and the girl.

'They're the ones Triton spoke of,' said Dauphin.

'Are they?' mused Jagged, almost reluctantly.

'Look at them. I'm sure you fancy a quick snack and I don't want to get in your way, but just open your eyes. And listen,' he continued excitedly. 'That one,' he jutted his bottle nose at Finn. 'He's communicating.'

Help us, the dolphin and the shark heard. *We are Light Fighters, please, help us.*

'All right, all right,' conceded Jagged. 'We'll help them.'

'I'll handle them,' said Dauphin. 'You get any closer and they'll die of fright.'

The shark gave a leering grin and with a lazy swish of his tail, swam off.

Dauphin called to his friends. Two of them came up close.

'Help them,' he said. He turned back towards Finn. 'Come nearer,' he communicated. 'Swim over here and hold onto my fin.'

Finn understood him and let out a yelp of delight. 'They're going to help us,' he yelled to Georgie and Fred.

He guided Fred towards one dolphin that seemed to be smiling in a kindly way at them. He didn't let go until he was sure Fred had a tight grip on the fin. He turned to see Georgie holding onto her own dolphin with a grin of relief. He turned back to the dolphin who had spoken to him.

'What is your name?' he communicated.

'I am Dauphin,' answered the creature. 'The one with the white strip on her nose is Delphine, my mate, and the huge one is Azhad.'

'Am I pleased to meet all of you,' thought Finn, taking hold of the fin.

The dolphins whipped around and sped through the sea, making sure their passengers remained above water as much as possible. They occasionally dived beneath the surface, then with a great lash of their bodies, they leapt free into the air. Finn wasn't sure if they did this to go faster, or just for the joy of it. He felt exhilarated after the terror of the evening, and tried to gauge when Dauphin was going to dive so that he could hold his breath.

'Where are we going?' communicated Finn, for the dolphins were heading not to shore, but out to open sea.

'To a safe place,' replied Dauphin, speeding up.

Ten minutes later, they arrived at a small island. The dolphins showed no sign of their exertions, but Finn, Georgie and Fred were all puffing hard from the efforts of periodically having to hold their breath, and from having to cling on for dear life to the speeding dolphins.

The dolphins slowed right down as they approached a deserted cove. They took their passengers in, and Finn saw the shady contours of a cave. The dolphins swam into it. It should have been dark, but Finn noticed a globe of light emitting a golden radiance. The globe moved slightly and

Finn realised that it was a squid.

Another movement caught his eye and he saw, rising from the water, the huge, muscled torso and head of Triton. Finn felt a surge of relief when he saw him. He started to speak, but Triton cut him off.

'Rest, get your breath,' he said gently, nodding to a broad shelf at the side of the cave, just above water level. Finn, Georgie and Fred let go of the dolphins and clambered up onto the shelf. Finn looked at Dauphin and communicated a huge 'thank you' to him. Dauphin inclined his head to receive the thanks.

Then Triton himself spoke to the dolphins in a series of high pitched pips that sounded like radio transmission and Finn thought that he too was thanking them. He realised then that he, Georgie and Fred were under Triton's official protection and it felt good. He shuddered at the thought of what would have happened if the dolphins hadn't rescued them.

Triton waited until their breathing had returned to normal. 'What happened?' he asked, speaking now as a man.

Between them, Finn, Georgie and Fred told their story, beginning with Fred overhearing Mr Drax's plans for the fishermen's village, then his dream about blood on the water, then Finn told Triton about discovering Drax's plan to blow up the boat and with it the fishermen's village. Georgie took over and told Triton how they got onto the boat and had to hide. Finn finished up the final bit with turning the boat around, jumping into the sea and seeing the night explode as the bombs ripped the boat apart just a hundred metres from them. Triton's eyes switched between them, and they felt the dolphins watching them too.

When they had finished speaking, a silence fell upon the cave, broken only by the soft lapping of the water and the slight movements of Triton and the dolphins in the current.

'You saved many lives tonight,' Triton said gravely. 'You all risked your own lives to do it. I thank you on behalf of my Kingdom of the Sea.'

Neither Finn, Georgie nor Fred knew what to say. They nodded awkwardly, but Georgie beamed.

'For the rest of your lives you may call on us at any time,' continued Triton.

They didn't know exactly what this might mean, but all of them were electrified by the promise.

'The men who planted the bomb, did they see you?' continued Triton.

Finn thought back to the moment when the three of them had stood by the rail, preparing to jump from the speeding boat. He had glanced at the bomber's escape dinghy and for a few, brief moments he had locked eyes with the men.

'Yes,' replied Finn. 'They saw us.'

The Sea Djinn thought for a while.

'You cannot go home now. They will hunt you down and they will kill you.'

Fred and Georgie felt gripped by fear, but Finn was focusing furiously on a plan.

'What if we escaped to sea?' he asked. 'What if we went to find my parents, went to rescue them?'

'You mean try to locate Hydrus's lair? Sail right up and do battle with him and his forces?' asked Triton

Finn nodded. 'That was always meant to happen, wasn't it, sooner or later? It just seems like now is the right time.'

Triton nodded. He turned to Fred and Georgie. 'What about you two?'

'I know those men would kill us,' said Georgie. 'I saw it in their eyes; I heard what they said about killing all the people in the fishermen's village. They didn't care at all. I can hardly go to the police, they'd just think I was mad. I can't go home, much as I want to. I can't begin to think how my mother will take it when she discovers I have disappeared, or my sisters, but I have to do it. For Finn, for his parents and for my father too.'

'You father?' asked Fred.

Thoughts and memories swirled round Georgie's head.

'Perhaps my mother was right all along. Perhaps my father has been kidnapped. I'm sure there's a connection to what's happened to Finn's parents. I can feel it.'

Georgie turned back to Triton. 'Do you know anything about my father?' she asked.

The Sea Djinn shook his head. 'I don't. I have made enquiries already, because I happen to agree with you. I think he was kidnapped. But I haven't heard anything back yet,' he added.

'I've made up my mind anyway,' said Georgie. 'I want to go with Finn. I want to fight with him. And I want to try to find my father.'

Triton nodded. 'You realise what you will be risking?'

She knew. She knew all right, and she gave herself no more time to think about it.

'I know. And I'm going.'

'And what about you, Fred?' asked Triton. Fred thought of his home, his perfect, empty, lonely home, and then he looked at his two friends. He had never felt so good, so alive, and yes, half the time, so terrified since the three of them had hooked up together.

'I want to go with Finn and Georgie,' he said simply. Then he smiled. 'And, it just so happens that I have the perfect boat.'

Finn grinned back at him. 'I was hoping you'd say that.'

'Can you sail?' asked Fred.

'Is Miss Finity Irish? Of course I can sail. I was born on a boat. I grew up on one. Most kids learned how to ride a bike. I learned how to sail. What kind of boat is it?'

'A big one. Goes like the wind. A thirty eight foot catamaran.'

'But that's enormous,' said Georgie. 'We can't sail that on our own.'

'Of course we can,' they both answered.

'When do we go?' asked Fred.

'Before first light,' replied Triton.

Georgie gasped. 'But what about provisions?' she asked. 'And how long d'you think we'll be away? We'll need to go home and get our stuff.'

'You cannot go back to your houses,' said Triton. 'They will be waiting for you, even now. We will obtain everything needed then you must go. Any requests?' he asked.

'Food, loads of it. And water. Flour, yeast, seasonings. Clothes, warm ones, and swimmers. Oh, and towels,' said Georgie. 'And sun cream.'

The Djinn nodded. 'Fred?'

Fred thought for a while. 'A mirror.'

'A what!' exclaimed Georgie.

'For Morse code,' replied Fred tersely.

'White paint and black. A paintbrush, and turps,' said Finn. 'Oh, and some chocolate, please. Lots.'

Triton raised his eyebrows. 'I'll do what I can, but time is short and Hydrus's people are ruthless. They'll be hunting you as we speak. I want you to be long gone before dawn.' He turned back to Fred with a look of urgency.

'Now, where is this boat?' he asked.

☙ Chapter Twenty ☙

The dolphins towed Finn, Fred and Georgie back into the open sea, then on towards Fred's parents' yacht club.

The gleaming, streamlined catamaran was moored on the outer pontoon. The dolphins gently towed them right up to it.

'There she is,' said Fred pointing proudly.

'*ALISON*' was written in large blue letters on the white hull.

'It's an awesome boat,' said Finn.

Trying not to splash, the children let go, thanked the dolphins again, climbed up the ladder and boarded the boat. They jumped as a quiet voice addressed them. For one horrible moment, Fred thought it might be the bombers come to get them, but it was Mr Violet. His hair looked wild and his eyes were darting anxiously this way and that. His nervousness put Finn even more on edge.

'Er, right, um, I've put together some kit,' said Mr Violet. 'Food's in the fridge. I've got you all spare clothes. Finn, I've got this for you.' He handed over two zip lock bags of grainy powder.

'What?' Finn started to ask. Mr Violet was giving him meaningful looks he didn't quite understand so he fell silent, took the bags and shoved them down into the side pocket of his backpack and promptly forgot about them.

'Now, as for charts,' continued Mr Violet more briskly, 'there aren't any for where you are going.'

'So how do we get there?' asked Finn, heart sinking. How do you plot a course to somewhere that doesn't exist on any chart, he wondered. East of the sun, west of the moon? Beyond the horizon, left towards the sunrise? Perhaps celestial navigation was the way? He would need help from above to find this place. For the first time, the sheer enormity of what they were undertaking dawned on him. The madness of it made him smile.

'Use your eyes. Use your mind's eye. You saw the place, didn't you?' said Mr Violet. 'I know the legends. I was taught them long ago,' he continued, suddenly dreamy. 'And I have Seen a certain amount of your journey in my mind. You must sail beyond the Known Sea, across the Sea of Tranquillity, past the Bay of Honour, over the Ocean of Storms, past the Marsh of Dreams, through the Sea of Crises and on until you get to the Serpent Sea. Then you will find Bone Island, and that, my friend, is as far I can See.'

'Yes, wonderfully picturesque,' answered Finn exasperatedly, 'but where is all that?'

'That I do not know,' answered Mr Violet.

Finn gave a roar of frustration. 'It could be anywhere.'

'No,' replied Mr Violet. 'It is somewhere and you will find it. You will see it.'

'You have to use sea sense,' came Triton's voice from the water. 'A shark can detect one millionth of a volt of electricity in the water. This is their sixth sense. You all have it, you pure humans, now you must develop it.'

Finn left the others and went down the steps to the water's edge where Triton rested.

'Trust your instincts, Finn. Use what Mr Violet and I have taught you. Follow your guides. They will find you. You must recognise them. There will be allies and tools for you to use. The sea will provide. Be ready to use everything at your disposal. This will be a fight to the finish. It is either you or Hydrus. Only one of you can survive. If you don't finish it now, you will have to some other time, sooner or later. At least this way it is at a time of your choosing.'

Finn nodded. 'I'm ready. I want to save my parents, to try to find Georgie's Dad if he's there, and to destroy Hydrus, but sometimes, I still can't help wondering, why me?'

'You know the Prophecy, Finn. You are a Prince of Atlantis. This is your fate.'

'So, if this is my fate is it known too who wins this war?'

A look of infinite sadness crossed the Djinn's face.

'No, Finn. I'm sorry. The outcome is not decided. It is all in your hands, and those of your friends.'

'So, I, we, could lose?'

Triton nodded. 'You could. Make sure you don't.' Triton gave Finn one last long look, then he reached out his finger and touched Finn lightly on the centre of his chest. Finn immediately felt the warmth flood his body. Before he could say anything, Triton withdrew his hand and vanished under the water. Finn went back up on deck. Fred and Georgie had finished all the checks. Mr Violet had disappeared.

'Ready?' asked Georgie.

'As I'll ever be,' answered Finn, wondering if he would ever see Triton or Mr Violet or this shore again.

∞ CHAPTER TWENTY ONE ∞

I THINK YOU SHOULD BE Captain,' said Fred.

'It's your boat,' replied Finn.

'You can sail better,' countered Fred.

'You know the boat better,' parried Finn.

'Stop being so flipping democratic,' snapped Georgie in a frustrated whisper. 'Whoever's at the wheel is Captain, and since you're sitting there now, that means you, Finn,' continued Georgie. 'We'll all take turns.'

'Fine,' replied Finn and Fred, relieved to have had that settled.

Finn started the engine which rumbled into life. In the water the propellers churned.

Georgie hopped back onto the pontoon, untied the ropes, threw them on deck and jumped back on board. Then she pulled in the fenders while Fred acted as lookout and Finn manoeuvred the boat back from the pontoon and out towards open sea.

They all expected to hear voices at any moment, calling them back. They felt horribly exposed. The floodlights of the marina illuminated them like candles on a birthday cake. They imagined hungry eyes on them. Finn pulled up the throttle, making the boat go as fast as he could without risking it crashing into the other boats in the marina. He couldn't wait till he cleared the end of the pontoon and found open water. *Ten, nine, eight....* He started a count-down in his head. By *one*, he had rounded the pontoon and he felt the very real possibility of escape. He opened the throttle fully and they accelerated away into the open sea. His voice drowned out by the roar of the twin engines, Finn gave a whoop of joy.

Two minutes later, they had escaped the brilliant light thrown over the surrounding sea by the marina and they were shrouded in darkness. Finn turned the boat into the wind, switched on the autopilot and killed the engines.

'Let's hoist the sails,' he called softly.

They worked well as a team. Once they'd got the main-sail and the spinnaker up, Finn went back to the pilot's seat. Georgie and Fred joined him.

'Where now?' asked Georgie.

Finn gazed towards the horizon, off to the east. 'Look, dawn's coming.'

The first rays of dawn lay like a sliver of gold at the edge of the sea.

'I think that's where Triton's kingdom is based,' Finn said. 'He would be where the light comes first. I think Hydrus will be west, where sun sets, where darkness falls.'

'I'll second that,' said Fred. He took the wheel and set a course south into the open sea and west towards the sunset.

'Let's go and check out the supplies,' Georgie said to Finn. They both went down into the cabin, leaving Fred alone on deck.

Fred sat in the pilot's seat, watching the light creep across the horizon.

Can you steal your own boat, he wondered. It was a wonderful thought. He'd always been so good, always been the dutiful son, born the weight of parental hopes and expectations that would have taken several children's shoulders to carry without being stooped and bowed. In the pilot's seat, he straightened up as the weight fell from him. For the first time in his whole life it seemed to him, he was doing exactly what he wanted. He wouldn't pretend that part of him wasn't terrified, but a larger part was just plain exhilarated.

He glanced up at the sails, hauled them in tighter and smiled in pleasure as the boat quickened to his touch. Below the hulls, the water sang as they passed. The sun burst above the east horizon with a blaze of fire. Light flooded the ocean, which in a matter of minutes turned from dark sapphire blue to a shimmering, glinting azure blue. It occurred to Fred that now that the cloak of darkness which had shielded them was gone, they were totally exposed.

Finn reappeared ten minutes later, looking pleased.

'I've been thinking,' said Fred. 'What if they send out the coastguard or something, helicopters, start hunting for us?'

'You mean your parents?' asked Finn.

Fred nodded.

'You think that when they discover you've disappeared and the boat's gone too, they'll really think it's you who's taken the boat?'

'I don't think they'd exactly leap to that conclusion, but,' Fred added a little guiltily, 'I know my mother will be frantic and she will make the police search everywhere and that includes the ocean.'

'Hmm. It's not your mother or the coastguard that really worries me,' said Finn.

'The Dark Djinn?' asked Fred.

Finn nodded. 'I get the feeling he can look across the ocean and see me, wherever I am. When Triton conjured an image of him out of fire, I could have sworn he was looking right back at me. It took a few minutes, but then he seemed to focus right in on me. Triton felt it too, because he threw the fire into the water and extinguished the image right at the moment I felt Hydrus looking at me.'

'If he can look at you, perhaps you can sort of lock onto him, figure out where he is,' suggested Fred.

'Fred, you're brilliant,' said Finn excitedly. 'The only problem is that I may give away our own whereabouts in the process.'

'I conjured Mr Violet, remember,' said Georgie, who had come up and been listening intently to the conversation.

'I'm not sure I want to conjure the Dark Djinn,' replied Finn, shuddering at the thought.

'If we could just conjure his image, in fire, like Triton did,' suggested Fred.

'It's something to try,' agreed Georgie.

'Maybe,' mused Finn. 'Let's just sail on a bit this way first. I want to get the hang of this boat before we try anything. And I think Fred's right; the coastguard might be looking for *ALISON*. We need to try to disguise her.'

'Call down the fog,' came Fred's distant voice, as if he were day dreaming.

Finn gave a bark of laughter. 'Simple, guys. We just call down the fog, but, just in case that doesn't work, look what I've got - paint and brushes.'

'While we're at it, let's give her a fun name,' said Fred gleefully.

'All right,' agreed Georgie. 'You choose.'

'Sinbad!' decided Fred, with a smile.

CHAPTER TWENTY TWO

THEY CRACKED OPEN A bottle of lemonade to celebrate the re-naming of their boat.

'To Sinbad,' they all said with a cheer, clinking their plastic glasses. The boat gave a sudden lurch as it crested a large wave and lemonade bubbled over the sides of their glasses and ran stickily down their hands. They laughed.

'I think that was a buck of approval,' said Fred.

'Boat's gone from sounding like a respectable woman to sounding like a pirate,' said Finn. 'I know which I'd rather be.'

'Maybe we need to be a bit piratical too,' mused Georgie.

'More than a bit,' replied Finn.

'Of course, it is supposed to be bad luck to change a boat's name,' said Fred, worrying again.

'It'd be worse luck to get hauled back by the coastguard,' replied Finn.

'Amen to that,' agreed Fred. They all drained the last of their lemonade when suddenly they heard a distant whop, whop, whop. They looked at each other in alarm.

'Helicopter,' mouthed Georgie.

'It's a long way off. Sound travels far over water. Maybe it won't see us,' suggested Finn.

Fred had a sickening sense that it would. They scanned the skies.

'There it is,' shouted Georgie, pointing at a black speck. For a few moments, it seemed as if the helicopter was moving away from them. The speck became infinitesimally smaller, but then it seemed to shift course, the distant throbbing of the rotors grew louder and the black speck grew into a large dot on the horizon.

'Oh no,' moaned Fred. 'They can't catch us now. We haven't even got going.'

'Get below,' shouted Georgie. 'Both of you.'

'What?' asked Finn and Fred in unison.

'They won't be looking for a woman sailing the boat.'

'You're not a woman,' said Finn.

'Get below. Now,' said Georgie, pulling on her baseball cap, rolling a small towel and shoving it down her t shirt.

The boys disappeared quickly into one of the sleeping cabins. Georgie puffed out her chest and waved gaily as the helicopter drew nearer.

It flew overhead with a tremendous roar and she waved as if she were quite delighted to see it. She looked hard to see the insignia of the coastguard on the 'copter, but couldn't see it. The helicopter flew on and turned slowly in a great arc. This time it flew about a couple of hundred feet above the sea, but off to the side of the boat.

They're reading the name, thought Georgie. The machine seemed to hover in place for a while, and then, finally, reluctantly, it seemed to Georgie, it flew off. Georgie gave a great whoop of delight and, when the 'copter had totally disappeared from sight, she called down to the boys.

'We fooled him,' she said joyfully. 'Let's have something to eat to celebrate. I've got some sarnies in the saloon.'

They all went below and quickly wolfed down the thick, club sandwiches dripping with mayonnaise that Georgie had made earlier.

They ate quickly, washed the sarnies down with water and went back on deck. As they did so, Sinbad gave a sudden shudder and lurch. The wind hit their faces and filled the sails. It was if they had entered another room. The old one had a nice, gentle, civilised wind; this one almost reeled with a wind that felt feral. Sinbad accelerated suddenly

'Let out the sails,' called Finn. He let out the mainsail, while Fred let out the spinnaker. Sails re-trimmed, Finn looked round. There was no sign of any other boat, or helicopter, or land. It felt as if the sea was theirs. Sinbad streaked sinuously through the waves.

Finn steered her, content with the speed for a good fifteen minutes, then he turned to the others who had come to sit by him on the pilot's bench. 'Let's see what she can really do, shall we?' he asked them.

'Okay.' replied Fred. He hauled in the spinnaker while Finn did the mainsail. The boat quickened beneath them and they felt as if they were flying. Conditions were perfect; a keen wind but moderate waves. They sailed on easily for another few hours. Georgie and Fred had both gone below for a nap. The exhaustion of the past few days had finally taken its toll.

Finn felt it gnaw away at him, but he was still running on adrenalin. He was never happier than when at sea. Piloting this huge, fast boat on his own was a joy. He imagined that every minute brought him closer to his parents. It brought him closer to Hydrus too, but for the moment he pushed the sea serpent from his mind. The waves glittering in the sun were almost mesmeric. Finn let his eyes drift almost lazily on them, enjoying their abstract rhythms and beauty.

Suddenly, he checked his watch. It seemed to be getting dark, but sunset was still hours away. He stood and turned to look at the sky behind them.

'Oh no,' he said quietly.

He switched on the autopilot and ran down into the cockpit, yelling to Georgie and Fred, asleep in their respective cabins.

'Wake up, Georgie, Fred, wake up, now. Hurry!'

'Wha-' they emerged slowly, sleepy and bleary eyed, but they snapped fully awake when they saw Finn's face.

'What's happened?' asked Georgie.

'It's what's about to happen. Where're the lifejackets?' Finn asked Fred.

'In here,' replied Fred, indicating a space under his bunk, pulling out three.

'Get them on,' said Finn, shouldering his own and snapping it secure before running back up on deck.

Glancing nervously at each other, Georgie and Fred hauled on their lifejackets. Out on deck, they followed Finn's gaze. In the distance, from the sea to high in the sky, there towered storm clouds, black, bulbous and terrifying. They could already feel the wind quickening.

'The Sea of Storms?' mused Georgie.

'Definitely. Whether or not it's the right Sea of Storms, who knows,' replied Finn. 'Let's trim the sails as tight as we can,' he continued.

'Are you mad?' asked Fred.

'We're going to try to outrun it,' said Finn.

They tightened the sails and Sinbad angled up in the water, one hull slicing through the air as they accelerated.

The wind speed increased and the hull rose higher out of the water. Georgie gasped with fear as the boat sped faster through the growing waves. Moments later, the first drops of rain spattered their faces as the outriders of the storm hit them.

Finn gazed at the clouds in disbelief. They had come out of a blue sky, out of nowhere, and they were bearing right down on them, as if targeting them.

Suddenly a horrible thought occurred to Finn. It's him. It's Hydrus and he's coming after us. He looked at Fred and Georgie, who had hooked themselves onto the safety line. Finn followed suit, wondering how they were going to get out of this. Catamarans were fast, this one was super fast, but the storm was gaining on them and they were sailing in open sea. There was no safe harbour to run to. They were just fleeing for want of any better idea, in the hope that the storm might burn out before it got to them, but Finn didn't think it was going to.

The splattering of rain increased to a torrent and soon they were all soaked and shivering. The sky was darkening all around them now, in front as well as behind, and visibility was falling in the blinding rain.

The boat began to buck and toss as the waves grew higher. Fred inched his way up to Finn.

'We have to let the sails right out,' he said. 'The winds are getting stronger. If we stay close hauled we're going to capsize.'

'I know.'

'Well let's do it then,' screamed Fred.

'Just give me a few minutes more.'

'For what? So we can capsize,' screamed Georgie, who had gripped her way along to join them.

'I can see something,' said Finn scanning the sheets of rain ahead of them.

'There's nothing there, just rain,' said Fred.

'There is, just-'

Georgie had started to scream. She was standing up, grabbing hold of the pilot's chair and pointing behind them. There, in the clouds, a thousand feet high, was the face of Hydrus, mouth open, tongue spitting, eyes demented with hatred. Georgie fell silent as the others looked on.

'We run,' yelled Finn. Georgie and Fred just nodded.

Finn kept his eyes ahead, on the sheets of water falling through the sky and on the waves, rearing up. One big one and they would be flipped over like a matchstick. Around them the wind screamed. It was freezing and as bleak as death, as though it had raged in from some far away frozen waste. The boat whined agonisingly as the fibreglass hull tore through the water. The halyards whipped frenziedly at the mast. The boat was leaping and falling up and down the cresting waves as if crazed. They were all white with cold and terror, struggling to stay upright, to grip on as wave after wave crashed and broke over the boat, sucking at them with a demented fury, trying to pull them over and down into the frothing mayhem. They all knew this couldn't go on much longer.

'There!' yelled Finn, pointing. Ahead, through the maelstrom of water, a darker shape appeared. An island, cliffs and they were about to slam right into them. Behind them, gaining second by second, the elements screaming his coming, was Hydrus. Ahead was a thousand foot wall of sheer rock. Below them was the boiling sea. Out of this, there was no way.

'Life raft,' yelled Finn, but the wind stole his words, and a wave, toweringly massive, hit the cliffs, rebounded and flipped the boat as if it were idly tossing a coin. The lines holding the safety harnesses snapped like string and Finn, Georgie and Fred were catapulted through the air and into the frenzied sea.

This was hell, a moving, swirling, black, wet hell. Georgie fought with her arms and legs flailing, kicking, and struggling against this dragging death. She hit the cliff with a thud that smacked the breath out of her. The receding wave sucked her away again, and when she got her breath back she saw the next wave coming at her and she knew it was all over. The wave picked her up, carried her still higher and higher. She waited, almost losing consciousness, not fighting now because there was no point. She braced herself, waiting for the impact. She felt a thud below her. She heard the ricochet as water smashed into rock, and suddenly something hit her and the darkness was absolute.

CHAPTER TWENTY THREE

FINN WAS IN THE water fighting for his life. Something came within reach and he grabbed it automatically. It was his backpack. He clung onto it. He saw the cliff in front of him before the next wave swallowed him in its trough. All he could see were walls of water, then he was rising up and up on the water wall, climbing on the biggest wave he had ever seen. He took a huge breath, waited for the impact. Thud. His body hit the cliff and the water held it there. He felt the pressure would squash all the breath from him, crush his ribs. His fingers scrabbled, but where there should have been cliff there was space.

He strained to see. There seemed to be some kind of cave, high on the cliff wall, but then the waves receded and down he fell, lower and lower in the body of the wave. It churned and he gasped and took in water. He spat it out but there was no air to breathe. Just more water. He fell to the trough then another wave picked him up. He began to see flashes of light as his oxygen-deprived body began to give out. One chance, he said to himself. Get to the cave, the cave. He kicked and fought with all that was left of his strength. He thought of his parents and his sister, he thought of Fred and Georgie and he kicked again. He rose up, and saw the shelf approaching. Please keep rising, please. He kicked violently, his fingers scrabbling through the water, and suddenly they found purchase. He touched the cliff. He felt empty space, and then there was a hand grabbing at him and a voice screaming.

'Cling on, kick, come on Finn, *hold on.*'

It was Fred, and he had him. Finn kicked once more and Fred dragged him in.

The floor of the cave was cold and rough hewn.

'Georgie?' gasped Finn 'Where's Georgie?'

Fred shook his head.

Finn tried to look out, to scan the mayhem of water outside, but he could see nothing save spray and spume and darkness. No tumble of red hair, no bright yellow lifejacket. He crawled deeper into the cave and collapsed on the floor.

'She's gone,' he said dully. Fred couldn't manage to say a word. Like Finn, he buried his face in his hands. They stayed like that, both of them, for a long while.

'How did you get up here?' asked Finn, finally. Knowing that Fred was a weak swimmer, it amazed him that he hadn't drowned.

'I saw it, the cave. The waves were smashing me against the cliff face and I just couldn't get high enough to climb in, so I just willed myself up, saw the cave, saw myself jumping from the water, and I got here.'

'Astral jump,' observed Finn.

'Yes, I s'pose.'

'Well done,' said Finn. 'I just wish Georgie had managed to do it too. Why couldn't she?' wailed Finn, plaintively.

'It was so hard,' said Fred. 'I could hardly think straight. I just knew I would drown if I didn't do something and then I just remembered Mr Violet's lessons.'

'I didn't even think of it,' replied Finn. 'In the heat of the moment everything goes out of your head.'

'It's stopped,' whispered Fred suddenly. 'The storm.' Where there had been the screaming wind and the roar of the waves, there was now an awful quiet.

'D'you think that means he's gone?' continued Fred. 'Or is he outside now, searching?'

Tentatively, they crawled forward to the edge of the cave. The storm clouds were gone, save one patch of black in the middle distance. Elsewhere, the sky was blue.

'Maybe it was a hurricane and we're in the eye,' said Fred.

'I don't think so,' replied Finn.

'Should we try to summon Mr Violet,' suggested Fred. 'Perhaps he can help us search for Georgie.'

'Let's give it a go,' said Finn.

Both boys fell silent and concentrated as hard as they could on Mr Violet. Finn tried to imagine him materialising in the cave beside them. Their brows furrowed with the effort. Nothing happened.

After about ten minutes, Finn turned to Fred.

'I th-' suddenly he froze. The sound of a motor carried across the now calm water. The roar grew louder. Both boys threw themselves down onto the floor of the cave and craned their necks to see. A huge power boat rounded the side of the island. Three figures were visible. As the boat got closer, they recognised the faces; Drax - father and son - and Mr Gusting. Fred and Finn lowered their heads and listened.

'They're here somewhere,' shouted Drax. His hard, cruel voice carried up to the cave with awful clarity. 'Hydrus saw them, he chased them here, he saw the boat go down.'

'So all we'll find is their bodies. Why bother?' asked Dagmar.

'Because Hydrus wants them alive,' answered his father. 'He needs Finn, remember, for the Prophesy.'

'So why'd he make such a big storm and sink 'em?' persisted Dagmar.

'Because he overdid things, as usual,' replied his father acidly. 'He was meant to scare them, to drive them through the Ocean of Storms and on towards Bone Island. He was meant to dismast them then, and we would come along just in time to *rescue* them, but he overdid it and I don't think he foresaw that they would try to outrun him. They wouldn't have capsized if they'd let out the sails. They have guts, those kids,' he added.

'And what if they are dead? If Hydrus killed them?' asked Dagmar.

'Then Hydrus will be in a rage to end all rages and that makes life dangerous for us all, so we'd better hope to Darkness we find them holed up somewhere, alive,' replied his father, handing him a pair of binoculars. 'Scan the cliff-side. I can see a cave up there.'

'Send up Raptor,' came Mr Gusting's voice.

Fred and Finn cranked their heads up a fraction and saw Dagmar go below decks. He returned with a falcon fluttering on his outstretched arm. He leaned in to the bird and spoke softly to it.

Fred and Finn eased back deeper into the cave.

'Lie still,' whispered Fred. 'Pretend you are grey, that there is nothing in you to interest anyone. Pretend that you do not really exist.'

'And?' asked Finn desperately.

'I do it in the playground. I was bullied. I learned to make myself invisible.'

Finn tried, he tried desperately hard.

'You're trying too hard,' whispered Fred. 'I can practically feel you struggling. Just let go of everything. Pretend you are nothing but cold rock.'

Finn tried to imagine he was dead. He thought of Georgie and wished he were dead. This was his entire fault, all his doing. He heard the beating of wings. He heard clawed feet land and scrabble on the stone floor of the cave just feet from him.

Dead, you are dead, he told himself. He felt the bird's eyes sweep over him, had the sensation that it was lingering on him. He did not breathe, did not move. Neither did the bird. He began to feel his heart pound in his body. How long could he keep this up? How long could Fred, he wondered. He heard the bird take a few steps closer. He imagined it poking out its beak to peck him, but then suddenly, there were shouts from below and the bird gave a squawk of alarm. He heard its feet scrabble, then the soft whop of its wings as it took off and flew away from the cave. He waited a few moments more before letting his breath out in a great puff and sucking in the dank, dark air in greedy lungfuls. Beside him he heard Fred do the same.

'That was close,' Fred whispered. Finn grunted. He was listening to the shouts below. Carefully he inched forward until he could see.

First thing he saw was a streak of yellow in the water - a yellow lifejacket. Then he saw a body, limp, seemingly lifeless, but moving at speed. Georgie, it was Georgie, face-up in the water but she looked quite dead. Then Finn saw the pale grey nose of a dolphin pushing her towards the edge of the island, as if to round it and disappear.

But then there was a commotion in the boat. Finn and Fred saw Dagmar stand and aim a harpoon gun straight at

Georgie. Before Finn could scream out a warning, Dagmar let the harpoon fly. There was a sickening thud, a high pitched squeal of agony and a spurt of blood gushed into the air. It was the dolphin, hit in the head, murdered.

Mr Gusting gave a cheer, then jumped into the water and swam towards Georgie.

'I've got her,' he yelled.

Finn felt a sick dread in his stomach. He watched, feeling more fear than hope. He watched Gusting pull at the limp, lifeless body. Finn could see the red curls, dank and soaked. Her white face, bleached of all colour. His heart wept. Then suddenly, the lifeless form heaved and vomited up a cascade of seawater onto Mr Gusting. Gusting recoiled in disgust.

'Er, stop that now,' he yelled. 'Or I'll get Dagmar to harpoon you too.' He pointed at the floating corpse of the dolphin, the harpoon sticking hideously from its head.

Georgie heaved again in response and then began to pound Gusting with flailing fists. Finn stifled a shout as Gusting slapped Georgie across the face.

'You pigs,' came Georgie's weak voice, but she didn't fight back. Finn could see she was desperately weak, but she was alive and he felt a surge of elation. Anything was possible again.

He and Fred watched as Gusting dragged Georgie up to the boat. Drax pulled her onto the deck. None of them saw the shadow of the other dolphin in the water. It was Delphine, grieving. She aimed herself like an arrow at the boat, stared at the face of her mate's killer until she had memorised every feature and then with the ocean and the body of Dauphin as witness, she swore vengeance. She would wait, she had the patience of the deep, but she would have her revenge.

'Where are the others?' boomed the voice of Mr Drax, yanking at Georgie.

Finn could see Georgie's look of misery even from a distance. 'I don't know,' she answered desolately.

'We'll hunt for the bodies for another hour,' said Drax. 'If we don't find them, then perhaps, somehow, they managed to escape, although I doubt it. They're probably at the bottom of the sea, along with the boat, and Darkness help us if they are.'

'We should let her join her friends, don't you think?' came Mr Gusting's voice.

Finn clenched his fists. For a while there was silence. Finn contemplated jumping from the cave, swimming to the boat and then what? He could not overpower the three of them, but he could try something. He had to. He was preparing to move when Drax spoke again.

'No. Let's take her with us. If they are alive, they will come for her. We can try to placate Hydrus with that as a plan.'

'How can they follow us?' asked Dagmar. 'Their boat is sunk.'

'Maybe they'll swim,' replied his father derisively. 'After all, she'll make good bait, won't she, for those little fish boys?' The three of them laughed.

'We'd better leave,' said Drax, serious now. 'The Dark Lord sent out a summons, and we'll have to hurry if we're going to make it in time to pass through tonight. He's going to be angry enough as it is.'

Finn and Fred heard the roar of the boat as it turned and continued to search. After a while, it veered away from the island and accelerated into the open sea. The boys continued to watch it until the noise of its engines was just a distant echo in their heads. Then they were utterly alone.

Finn turned to Fred.

'I don't think Mr Violet's coming, d'you?'

Fred shook his head. 'Mr Violet said we were meant to sail beyond the Known Sea, and that's how it feels, like we've travelled beyond everything I've ever known, and we're completely cut off.'

Finn felt that too, but he fought against it.

'We'll get out of here,' he said fiercely. 'Somehow. I promise you. And we'll get Georgie.'

NIGHT FELL AND THE temperature dropped. Georgie shivered on the boat. She felt sick with terror. She wrapped her arms more tightly around herself in an attempt to keep warm. Mr Gusting had attached a chain to the side of the boat and padlocked the end of it round her ankle. With every lurch of the boat it cut into her skin.

'Just in case you try to escape,' he'd said with a sneer.

Georgie watched the blood running down her ankle. She was in shock. She could not get her mind around how quickly everything had gone wrong. She was living a nightmare. She wanted to cry, but she knew it would be no use. Who would heed her tears? Her captors would only laugh and she would not give them that satisfaction.

Where were Finn and Fred? Had they plummeted down to the depths with the boat, or were they by some miracle alive? She decided to believe that they were alive. No bodies had been found, despite the search. And they *had* been wearing life jackets. They would have floated. They *had* to be alive. Georgie refused to believe that the fight was over so quickly. What was her part in it now? Just bait? How could she fight? There was something she could do; she felt the idea of it fluttering around her consciousness like a moth outside a lit window.

Perhaps she could leave some sort of trail, something to let someone know that she had been kidnapped and that she had passed this way. She groped around her feet in the darkness but there was nothing. She felt in the pocket of her shorts; her fingers closed around a pen, sparking an idea. She glanced to the front of the boat. Gusting and the Draxes were all facing forwards, ignoring her. Slowly and silently, she began to take off her life jacket. Once she had removed it, she turned it inside out and began to write, in the darkness.

This is Georgie Sherwood. I have been kidnapped by Mr Gusting, a teacher at JAM, and by Ivan and Dagmar Drax. My friends Finn Kennedy and Fred Adams have been shipwrecked off an island. Please help us. Please find us.

She was about to toss it overboard when Mr Gusting turned around suddenly.

'You, girl, what do you think you are doing? Put that back on right now. We need you alive.' He grinned horribly. 'Someone very important wants to meet you.'

'Who?' asked Georgie.

'The one true Ruler of the underwater world. The Dark Djinn.'

The underwater world. Georgie shuddered in fear. Would her father be there, she wondered. She would focus on that and nothing else. After a while, exhausted and lulled by the motion of the boat speeding across the waves, Georgie fell asleep.

She woke with a start some time later. Drax was shouting and glowering at Gusting.

'We're going to miss it. Can't you make this thing go any faster?' he yelled.

'Well, we could throw her overboard,' Gusting responded, nodding at Georgie.

'There it is!' yelled Dagmar, pointing into the darkness.

Georgie edged up and tried to see what he was pointing at.

'Faster, give it everything. We have half a minute,' yelled Drax.

The boat screamed across the water, engines roaring, the hull thudding down with great, sickening bumps that bruised Georgie's body. Suddenly, through the darkness, she saw the outline of an island, bone-white in the moonlight. The boat was racing toward the beach at full speed.

They were going to crash. Surely they couldn't stop in time. Georgie braced herself. At the last moment, Gusting cut the engines and the boat rode right up onto the beach, the sand rasping under the hull. The men leapt out, pulled the boat up further.

'You stay and guard it,' yelled Drax to his son, who immediately started to moan.

Drax and Gusting unlocked the padlock and pulled Georgie from the boat. She screamed and pummelled Gusting with her fists. He slapped her face so hard she saw stars, then he dragged her into the sea. They are going to take me out and drown me, she thought. Then she saw ripples of water, spinning round in front of her - a whirlpool. Her gut clenched in terror. They were swimming right for it. Gusting dragged her right into the centre and stopped. All she could hear was the sound of the whirlpool and the men's rasping breaths. Her own breath seemed trapped in her lungs. There they waited, until Drax swore.

'We missed it. Probably by seconds. Damn the Light World,' he yelled, slamming his fist down into the water.

It was quiet now, Georgie noticed. The whirlpool had gone.

'Back to shore,' grunted Drax. He and Gusting struck out for the beach, leaving Georgie to make her own way. She paused, looked around, wondered if now was her chance to escape. Yeah right. What would she do, swim off to sea? Swim back to Dubai? Feeling a wave of water break over her head like desolation, she swam to the shore and followed her captors.

Dagmar, his father and Gusting dragged the boat further up the beach and round behind a rocky outcrop. Drax and Gusting headed off towards a cave, leaving Dagmar covering as much of the boat as he could with seaweed. He was doing a good job. You could hardly see the boat. It just looked like a big scrubby bush.

Georgie walked up to Dagmar. 'Where are we?' she asked.

'Bone Island,' he replied.

Georgie gave a start. Bone Island. Mr Violet had spoken of it. He'd said it was as far as he could See of their journey. Did that mean it would end here? she wondered with a shudder.

She walked on up the beach. The wind chilled her soaking clothes and she needed the shelter of the cave, even if Drax and Gusting were in it.

Once inside, she saw the men had made a camp fire and had begun to cook rations they'd pulled from a cool box. The scent of frying fish wafted into the air. Despite her misery, Georgie realised she was starving.

'Can I have some?' she asked.

'Well that would be less for us, wouldn't it?' answered Gusting.

Drax and Gusting laughed out loud.

Georgie bit back tears and vowed to herself that somehow or other she would get her revenge on these men.

∽ Chapter Twenty Five ∾

EARLIER THE SAME NIGHT, Fred and Finn had drunk the last of the water in the bottle Finn had in his backpack, eaten a square of chocolate each, and then fallen into an exhausted sleep on the rough floor of the cave.

They awoke the next morning to the sound of seagulls screaming. They sat up sharply, disoriented and afraid. It seemed to Fred as if the seagull screams were human. It took them both a few seconds to remember where they were and what had happened and then the bleak reality flooded back.

They looked at each other and each saw the grimness in the other's eyes, but both boys smiled bravely.

Finn wanted to speak, but first he had to check the sea. He lay on his tummy and inched to the edge of the cave. The sea stretched out for limitless miles before him, limpid and pale in the weak dawn light. He scanned the water for any sign of Georgie, the Draxes and Gusting, but as he'd expected they were nowhere to be seen.

His head throbbed and his mouth felt cracked with dryness. He knew if they didn't drink soon they would be in trouble.

'All clear?' whispered Fred.

Finn nodded. 'Sleep well?' he asked with a sarcastic grin.

'Yeah, so comfy this bed,' said Fred gesturing at the rocky floor of the cave. Finn stretched and suddenly froze mid-stretch. Fred followed his gaze to the ceiling of the cave, around six feet above them.

'Drops of water,' said Finn. 'See them?'

Fred nodded. 'Evaporated and re-condensed sea water. We can drink it!'

'Exactly. Thank you Mr Violet!' exclaimed Finn. 'C'mon, lift me up.'

Finn grabbed his empty water bottle and Fred hoisted him up. Finn stretched up and nudged the drops of water into his bottle. It was agonising, painstaking work, but after what seemed like an age they got a couple of inches of water.

Finn passed the bottle to Fred, who was red-faced with the effort of hoisting Finn.

Never had water tasted so good. His lips and throat were parched. The water slipped down in an instant and he fantasised about more. He quickly passed the bottle to Finn before temptation became too much and he swigged all of it.

Finn sucked down the water. The cool liquid, even if it carried the dankness of the cave, tasted like nectar.

Finn carefully replaced the lid and stashed the bottle in his backpack.

He moved back to the edge of the cave and sat, cross-legged, gazing out.

'Hey, Fred, come and look at this.'

Fred hurried over to his side and squinted at the sea.

'What?'

Finn pointed. 'See, over there, just breaking through the troughs of the swell. See it?'

Fred squinted harder.

'Something pointy.'

'It's the mast. It's Sinbad's mast!' declared Finn.

'Er, that's great Finn, but, er, what do we do about it?'

Finn turned to him, his eyes alight with excitement. 'The sea can't be more than forty feet deep there. We can dive down, get hold of some rations, some bottles of water. And, if my memory hasn't gone bananas, there should be a dinghy there somewhere, with an engine and a petrol tank.'

Fred looked from the vantage point of the cave to the spot in the waves, about sixty feet away.

'Er, so we jump out of the cave, swim for the boat, then bob around in the open ocean and take turns diving down into it.'

'You got a better idea?'

Fred heartily wished he had. He shook his head glumly.

Finn threw on his backpack, secured it tightly and inched forward to the edge of the cave. He grinned at Fred. The prospect of action, of doing something, made him feel much cheerier.

He studied the water and the wave pattern for a while.

'It's deep enough here,' he concluded. 'Safe to jump. Bombs away,' he yelled, hurling himself away from the cliff face, out into space. He accelerated through the air. Ten, twenty, thirty, forty feet, then his feet smacked into the water. Down he went, still surprisingly fast. Wow, he was going deep. He began to feel a panic coming on, but then he slowed down and after what seemed an agonisingly long time to him, weighed down by his wet clothes and ruck-sack, he began to head for the surface. He kicked as hard as he could, pumping his arms, then emerged from the water and took a great gulp of air.

Fred watched from the cave, mightily relieved, for a moment. Then it was his turn. Finn watched him, standing silhouetted against the dark background of the cave.

Oh, God, thought Fred. Why do I have to do this? He thought for a moment of his bedroom at home, safe and welcoming, then he pushed down all thought and leapt.

The shark watched the second boy hurl himself into the water. He smiled to himself. He watched the legs thrashing in the water, just a few yards from his mouth. It was murky at this depth, so he knew the boy wouldn't see him. The boy flailed some more, then kicked his way to the surface. The shark watched him move away. He gave him a decent head start, then with one lazy switch of his powerful tail, he caught up and circled slowly, nearly forty feet down, watching the four legs thrashing above him.

Fred swam hard till he got alongside Finn. The current was pushing both boys back towards the cliff wall so they couldn't risk hanging around.

'C'mon,' said Finn. 'Let's kick for the boat.'

It was about fifty feet away, a long fifty feet, given the strong currents. Swimming hard, they made it to the mast. Slowly, Finn eased out of his rucksack and handed it to Fred. Fred awkwardly shouldered his way into it. Finn took several deep breaths, jack-knifed his body and dived down. He kicked hard and his body cut through the water until he neared the sea floor. There lay Sinbad, her white hull just visible in the gloom. Finn grabbed hold of the mast to stop himself from surfacing and tried to look around. It was hard in the sea depths to see much, but he felt his way around. Just as his lungs were beginning to protest, he gave a start of joy. Tethered to the back of the boat was the dinghy, outboard motor attached, looking in good condition - no holes - quite sound. Finn let go and kicked his way up. He broke the surface, gulped down some air.

'Fred! Fred, the dinghy's there, still attached, motor and all,' Finn gabbled breathlessly.

Fred beamed back at him. 'My father always keeps the tank full, and he also keeps two extra cans of fuel on board. If we can get them....'

'And detach the dinghy. I've got my Swiss army knife in there somewhere,' Finn pointed to the backpack. He delved around and withdrew it from a side-pocket. He handled it carefully. 'Birthday present from my parents,' he said. He flicked out the knife blade, took a few more deep breaths, stuck the handle in his mouth and dived down.

He found the rope, sawed at it with his knife, saw the dinghy give a judder as it was freed, but then.....nothing! It stayed locked in its underwater prison. Cursing silently, Finn moved round to the other side, and saw the twisted metal stanchion which normally held the dinghy aloft. He desperately needed air, but reached out and felt the clasp which should spring release the dinghy. It too was twisted. Finn fiddled with it, but nothing gave. With disappointment searing his lungs, he kicked for the surface and told Fred. Both boys gazed forlornly at the depths.

'I *won't* give up,' shouted Finn. 'There has to be a way. I'm going down again.'

Before Fred could say it was his turn and insist on going down, Finn had gulped in some air and dived down again. He headed straight for the metal stanchion and started heaving against it.

Something, instinct perhaps, made him turn. An enormous shark was hurtling towards him, mouth open, eyes implacable. Finn screamed, the sound escaping with bubbles from his throat.

Was this his end, he wondered? Well he wouldn't go without a fight. He held his knife at the ready and lunged. The shark did a quick shimmy, closed its mouth, but not around him. Finn kicked for the surface, but not before he had seen the shark's jaws close around the metal stanchion. He exploded above the surface, gulping for air, screaming. He just had time to see the look of horror on Fred's face before he was catapulted out of the sea and into space. He felt himself flying, then falling. He was too dazed to take in what was happening. Moments later, his world stilled. To his utter amazement, he found himself lying in the dinghy. He called to Fred, who was hauling himself over the edge.

'There's a shark down there!'

Fred turned white and flipped his legs into the dinghy with a moan of fear.

'It bit through the stanchion. It freed the dinghy. I thought it was going to kill me and it freed the dinghy!' Finn yelled. 'Look, there it is, swimming away.'

Finn pointed at a jagged fin, rapidly moving away towards open sea, almost as if its business was done.

'Amazing!' Fred managed to say. 'Rescued by a shark!'

Finn started to laugh and soon both boys were laughing hysterically.

'Now, all we need is some food, water and the extra fuel tank,' said Finn when the laughter had subsided. 'I'm going to swim down again.'

'What about the shark?' asked Fred

'I think he's a friend,' answered Finn, 'don't you?'

'You didn't exactly look pleased to see him when you came shooting out of the water.'

'No, well, I thought he'd been aiming his great mouth at me.'

'Maybe he had been,' argued Fred.

'No, I don't think so. Sharks have better aim than that. If he'd wanted me, he'd have got me.'

Finn stood up, took some deep breaths and dived over the edge of the boat.

Fred watched him, unease mounting the longer Finn stayed down. Fred peered anxiously into the water, but he could see nothing. Finn couldn't hold his breath for this long, could he? Fred was just about to dive in himself when there was a commotion in the water and Finn surfaced, grinning.

'Here, haul this up, will you?'

Fred reached down and pulled up an incredibly heavy petrol tank. Finn plopped himself down beside Fred and blew heavily.

'Now, rations,' he said.

'My turn,' said Fred.

Finn knew Fred wasn't much of a swimmer but the determination on his friend's face silenced him.

'Sure,' said Finn, affecting nonchalance. He watched as Fred took in a series of deep breaths then plunged over the side.

It took him three attempts. Finn watched him, as nervous as his mother might have been. Finally, on the third attempt, Fred surfaced with the dried rations that his father always kept on board. There were pots of noodles that you just had to add water to, juices, raisins, a few bars of chocolate and biscuits. Both boys opened a carton of apple juice and drank it in a few massive gulps. Then Finn went down for water. He came up with five water bottles in a net.

'I think that's it,' he said, catching his breath. He nodded to the engine.

'Give it a go?' he asked.

'Why not?' answered Fred.

Finn reached inside his rucksack and pulled out his Swiss army knife. On the handle was a compass. Fred said a silent prayer as Finn pulled the starter cord. The engine coughed, then started. The huge grin on Finn's face said it all as he steered the boat away from the island and headed due west.

The heat blazed down. The sun flashed back at them from a thousand waves, glinting and retreating all round them. The boys drank carefully, not sure how long their water was going to have to last. The boat bounced its way over the sea towards an endless, empty horizon. The motion was almost mesmerising and they both felt themselves nodding off.

'Whoo, Finn!'

Fred's yell caught Finn half asleep at the tiller.

'Whaah! What's up?' asked Finn, sitting up straight and giving himself a telling off for dozing.

'Look,' said Fred, eyes wide, pointing into the water beside the boat. Finn looked down. Cutting through the water, right next to the boat, touching the boat, was a fin.

'It's the shark,' said Finn, amazed. 'The same one.'

'Don't be silly, how could you poss-'

'See the nick in its fin? I noticed it before, when it swam off. I thought it was unusual then. I'm sure it's the same one we saw after the boat exploded by the fishermen's village,' said Finn.

'What's it doing?' asked Fred, almost in a whisper, as if afraid to attract the beast's attention.

'It seems to be guiding us. It's nudging the boat, see.' Finn consulted his compass and frowned.

'What?' demanded Fred.

'We're going north.'

Finn took his hand off the tiller and the boat shot on through the water, guided by the shark with the jagged fin.

'So what d'you think we should do?' asked Finn.

'How do *I* know?' asked Fred.

'How do *I* know?' responded Finn.

'I dunno. You always seem to.'

Finn gave a wry smile. 'That a polite way of telling me I'm a know-all?'

Fred grinned back.

'Well, he got us the boat in the first place. He seems to have a plan for us,' mused Finn.

'Yes, but is it a good one?'

'Time will tell. I don't think there's much we can do either way. I don't fancy making him angry, d'you?' asked Finn.

'Not particularly,' agreed Fred.

Jagged, as Finn had named the shark, not knowing that this was actually the shark's real name, guided the boys as the morning turned to afternoon and the shadow of the boat began to lengthen on the sea. The sun set in a blaze of crimson and night rolled in. The wind picked up and the boys shivered in the dark, with fear as much as cold. On they motored, inexorably cutting through the night, until lulled by the waves and exhausted, they both fell asleep.

Finn awoke as he felt a change in the atmosphere. He rubbed his eyes and tried to see through the blanket of darkness. There was something ahead. He took the boat off cruise control and slowed it down, peering over the side as he did so. Jagged was still there, doggedly guiding them.

'Fred, wake up,' said Finn, nudging his shoulder.

Fred sat up groggily.

'Look, there's an island,' said Finn, pointing through the darkness.

As they got closer to the island, the contours slowly became visible. Finn began to shake. He had seen this island before, in his nightmare. Only then it had been a kind of dark daylight and he had seen the slithering thing winding itself around the cage in which his parents were held.

☙ Chapter Twenty Six ☙

GEORGIE AWOKE WITH A grunt of shock as she felt a kick in her ribs. She sat up groggily in the darkness and rubbed her eyes. Dagmar was standing by her, smiling slyly.

'Rise and shine. Time to pass through.'

'Get away from me, you dog,' spat Georgie.

'Or what?' jeered Dagmar.

'You'll see.'

'Shut up and hurry up. You don't want to miss the porthole again. Father would be displeased and, believe me, you do not want that.'

'What porthole? What are you on about?' asked Georgie.

'The passage through to the Dark Kingdom. You missed it last night. You go into the sea,' hissed Dagmar, 'just off this island. Then, at midnight, the porthole opens in the middle of a whirlpool and you hold your breath and you get sucked down deep into the sea, into the other world. The Dark World.'

Georgie felt as if she couldn't breathe. The sea, going down, through it....she shuddered. And then, if she survived that, arriving in the Dark World, a world of evil and horror. This was her last chance of escape, she knew that. She'd agonised with herself all day over whether or not she should try to escape. She thought of her bedroom back home. Could she escape there with an astral leap? She'd only ever managed fifteen feet before, but she felt a new power. It seemed to vibrate within her. She felt that she just might manage to transport herself home. But even if she could, should she? The Dark World, however terrifyingly evil it might be, could be where she would find her father. In her mind, she pictured the faces of her mother and of her father. She felt herself veering back and forth between them. Then she decided, once and for all. She would go willingly to the Dark World, meet whatever waited there for her, as long as there was a chance, any chance, that she might see her father again.

She jumped as a shout rang out in the darkness.

'It's Father. C'mon. Let's go,' ordered Dagmar.

'Wait. I have to pee.'

Dagmar grimaced. 'Hurry up,' he muttered.

Georgie waited until he had walked out of the cave then she took off her lifejacket, got out her felt pen and scribbled down all that he had told her in a message to Finn and Fred, who, she hoped more than ever, were alive and would find her.

'Enough. Move it!' yelled Dagmar.

'I'm coming,' shouted Georgie. She ran out of the cave and quickly stashed the lifejacket further down the beach behind a rock where she hoped Dagmar would not see it.

Dagmar's father loomed out of the darkness. 'Take her into the water,' he said to his son.

Dagmar dragged Georgie off. Ivan Drax walked to the cave, quickly checked it, then, disappointed, started to make his way back to the shore. The lifejacket, hidden cleverly, but not quite cleverly enough, caught his eye. He picked it up, read the message and smiled before tucking it back where Georgie had left it. If the boys were alive, they would walk right into his trap.

Georgie waded out into the water. Her heart was racing with fear. She tried to breathe deeply, to prepare for going under, but all her instincts screamed out against it. Mr Gusting was blowing out his huge chest and taking in loud gulps of breath. He looked like a human bellows.

Mr Drax was wading out through the water. He beckoned Dagmar to him, bent to his ear and had a whispered conversation. Dagmar gave a gleeful smile then waded back to the shore.

Drax joined Georgie and Mr Gusting. He started to breathe hard too, consulting his watch. Then he grabbed Georgie by the wrist. Gusting grabbed her other wrist. Drax started a countdown.

'Ten, nine, eight...'

The water stared to swirl round and round. It quickly became a whirlpool. Georgie could feel it sucking her legs down. She ferociously trod water, desperate to stay afloat.

'Three, two...' incanted Drax.

Georgie, her throat constricting with terror, tried to force in one more breath before Drax yelled out 'ONE!' and the whirlpool accelerated like a washing machine on a spin cycle.

Georgie saw one last glimpse of the gibbous moon floating in the dark sky and then she was dragged under, going down, down, down. She felt an awful squeezing then a sense of fall, as if from a great height and from all that was good and whole and true. The despair that washed over her was almost overwhelming.

She was running out of air. With just seconds left, and no warning, she fell from the water into air. She gulped in a few desperate breaths and then once again fell into water. Still Gusting and Drax kept up their deadly grip on her wrists and it occurred to her that perhaps this was all just an elaborate way of drowning her. She kicked out desperately, but then to her surprise so did both men. Her head broke the surface. She sucked in more breaths and gazed rapidly around her.

She seemed to be in some kind of giant air bubble underneath the sea. Above her was a grey sky and above that she could see the dark sea swirling nauseatingly. What invisible barrier held the sea at bay she wondered?

She treaded water in what looked like another sea, the colour of gunmetal, with foamy waves that stank of effluent washing listlessly onto a grey sand shore.

Low in the dull sky there was another moon, but unlike the one from her world this one didn't glow like a pearl. It too was a kind of decaying grey, the pockmarks of craters and mountains like blemishes on an ugly face. The light it cast was thin, sickly and oppressive. Her chest hurt to breathe the air it lit. The sea itself seemed to moan, as if ill, but after a few moments Georgie realised it wasn't the sea, but a background dirge of low despairing noises, some human, some animal, calling out their misery in what seemed like a different sound register. Each moan sounded to Georgie like a footstep towards death. She found herself shuddering uncontrollably.

Gusting turned to her with a grim smile.

'Welcome to the Dark World.'

He kicked for the shore, dragging her after him. 'And now for a real treat. You're about to meet the Dark Djinn.'

Georgie fought down her terror.

'I think I'd rather have a chocolate chip cookie, if it's all the same to you,' she managed to say.

'Yes, very funny,' muttered Gusting, yanking her arm. 'Piece of advice, don't try any quips on him. He's not nice like me.'

Drax led her and Gusting into a huge cave. The sea sloshed listlessly against one wall while they walked along a passageway leading into the lair. Long stalactites dripped viscous black fluid from the ceiling a hundred feet above them. Wraiths of smoke curled round the walls of the cave. They seemed to move independently and there was no sign of a fire. One curlicue of brown smoke passed right by Georgie, so close she could taste the acrid tang. It seemed to be circling her. The hair on the nape of her neck stood up. Before her eyes, the smoke condensed into the form of a bird. Georgie shrieked. The bird let out a matching screech of mockery, then flew up and perched on a ledge. From there it watched her with malevolent eyes.

'Djinn like playing their little games,' mused Mr Gusting. 'Better get used to it.'

More wraiths of smoke curled up to Georgie. She convulsed with pain as the smoke seemed to pass through her. It felt like she was being stabbed by a dozen blunt knives. Soon there were so many swirling smoke wraiths that she could hardly see. The smoke djinn flew up to the ledges and metamorphosised into birds with long, hooked beaks and small vicious eyes. They were all staring with rapt attention at the sea that flowed into the cave.

Georgie had Finn's description in her mind, but that didn't prepare her for what lay ahead. The sea appeared to gather itself and shake and then from the grey depths a form began to rise. First came the head, a huge head of what might once have been a man. The face turned to gaze upon her. Georgie forced herself to meet its eyes. The brow was high, the nose long and straight. There was a vestige of aristocratic grandeur to the face, but it was ruined by the limp grey skin that hung in folds, by the suppurating yellow eyes, by the weeping sores at the corners of the Djinn's mouth. Eyes still on Georgie, Hydrus hauled himself half out of the water to lie on the sandy shore at the back of the cave.

He had the head, shoulders and arms of a man but then his torso sloped down to become a bloated, grey, obscenely writhing serpent.

Just looking at the creature made Georgie feel ill, but she found she couldn't look away. However repulsive Hydrus should have been, there was something captivating about him too.

His eyes remained locked onto Georgie's. A ThoughtThief, she realised.

She tried to think of nothing but grey sand. The creature spat with annoyance, watched the gob of saliva dissipate in the water then turned back to Georgie.

'Where is the boy?' Hydrus's voice oozed menace.

'What boy?'

The Djinn convulsed and a wave of sludgy sea splashed over Georgie. She rubbed it violently off her mouth.

'Lie to me, blank your thoughts and I will devise a particularly unpleasant end for you. Co-operate, however, and there is always room in my world for a helper at my side.'

'I'd sooner die,' said Georgie.

The Djinn smiled. 'That can be arranged.' He turned to Drax. 'Bring them. I might just have found a way to hurry them up.'

Georgie dragged her gaze away from Hydrus and stared at the mouth of the cave, at an escape that she now knew was impossible. The power she had felt before had been killed by the evil, despair and sickness that hung in the air like a miasma. She wanted to cry, she wanted to scream, she wanted more than she could ever have thought possible to return to the safe haven of the Pink Prison. She almost laughed. What a stupid name for her home. Now she knew what prison was; that sense of sheer helplessness, when there was NOTHING you could do to change your fate, no choice, no free will, where no-one cared if you lived or died. An anonymous prison in the heart of an evil empire, with no-one coming to rescue you, with a war brewing between her world and the world of her captors. There were no rules to protect you, no phone call to a lawyer. This place was beyond civilisation. She had never felt so alone. Words she had thought she knew the meaning of..... Freedom. Justice. Home. She had not known. No-one could know the true meaning until they had lost them. She thought of her mother and her sisters, of her lost father, of Finn and Fred with a yearning that was stronger than any pain she had ever felt. That yearning, it could cut you to bits.

But she did have a choice. A small voice in her spoke up. You have your mind, your sanity. It would be so easy to flip into madness. That, she decided with every ounce of force in her being, she would *not* do. She would hang on to her hope that her father was here, somewhere. If she was to have any chance of finding him and getting him out of here, she would have to use all her cleverness and calmness and then some.

She heard a shuffling sound coming from some way off. She turned and her eyes shot open in amazement.

'Uncle Will! Aunt Vicky!' With a yell of joy she ran towards Finn's parents. They opened their arms and grabbed her tight. Georgie's tears came now. She wept uncontrollably. Finn's parents just held her, determined, sad eyes meeting over her shuddering body.

A slow handclap broke them up.

'Aaaah, so touching, so very, very touching,' intoned the Djinn in a voice dripping with sarcasm 'But time is short! The full moon is the day after tomorrow. Then we shall launch the battle to end all battles. You two dabblers have until then to come up with my remedy.'

Finn's mother spoke. 'We're working on it. And we are almost finished. We just have a few more tests to make.'

'Almost finished!' The Djinn spat again and the effort of that produced a hacking cough that seemed to shake the whole beach. Georgie sincerely hoped that whatever he had was not contagious.

'As you can see, I am sick, getting sicker and the battle is imminent. I must recover my health and all of my powers by then. You are running out of time. But, good news. Your niece, I feel, will encourage you, no? Your little scene demonstrates you are fond of her and she of you. I think, perhaps, for the sake of her own health, you will have a cure ready by tomorrow. If not, the kraken gets a nice juicy meal.'

'The kraken,' said Vicky. 'Please do summon one so that we can make your cure. Kraken juice is the answer. I am sure of it.'

'For my cure? Are you mad? It is pure poison. It will kill me not cure me,' roared the Djinn, snake body lashing the foul water.

'No, wait. In small quantities, mixed with our other remedies it will cure you. It is the principle of homeopathy. A tiny bit of what ails you, packaged correctly, can effect a cure,' insisted Vicky.

The Djinn looked pensive. Georgie could see how desperate he was for a cure.

'I'll summon the kraken. At the very least, she can size up your niece for a snack,' decreed Hydrus and he laughed, a great roiling roar that gave way to another hacking cough.

When he could speak again, Hydrus summoned Drax. Georgie strained to hear his words. She studied his mouth, could just make out the movement of his lips and what he was saying: 'I need the boy. Find him. Spare nothing and no-one.' Georgie's heart leapt. Was Finn alive? Could he and Fred have survived the storm? The Dark Djinn seemed to believe they were alive. Surely, he would have known if Finn and Fred were dead.

She could see Drax nod.

'If he is not here by tomorrow, then your own son will die in his place.'

'I will find him,' Drax replied, his words full of determination, but fear too.

Georgie felt she was going to vomit. *Die in his place*.... so if by some miracle Finn had survived the shipwreck, the Djinn was going to kill him anyway. The message she had written on her lifejacket for Finn, giving him instructions to follow her, would lead him to his death.

Chapter Twenty Seven

FINN AND FRED USED the last of their strength to haul the dinghy onto the shore. They collapsed on the rough sand and got their breath back.

'I wish we could hide the dingy somewhere,' said Finn.

'You think there's someone around?' asked Fred. 'It looks totally deserted to me.'

'I don't know. Something feels funny. I thought this was the place I'd seen in my nightmare, but it's not quite. It's different, but it feels the same.'

'D'you think it's Bone Island?' asked Fred.

Finn shook his head.

'I don't think this is Hydrus's lair, but it feels evil.'

'I think we're both a bit spooked,' replied Fred. 'Can we hide the boat in the morning? I need to sleep so badly.'

Finn did too. He ached with exhaustion worse than any 'flu. 'C'mon. Looks like there's a cave up there. Let's go and get some rest.'

Eyes watched from the darkness as the two boys made their weary way up to the cave.

'See, totally deserted,' said Fred, shining his torch round the inside of the cave. They had brought the thermal sleeping bags from the dinghy's emergency rations and they were glad of them. Inside the cave the temperature was several degrees lower than outside and there was a chill in the dank air. The boys drank some water, ate a few raisins, then wriggled into the sleeping bags. Within seconds they were fast asleep.

Dagmar was better rested and better trained than Finn or Fred. This was a war his family had been fighting for generations. He had been honed for the activities of war since birth. He felt some sympathy for the children of Sparta in ancient Greece, whom he had read, were left out on the mountainside overnight to cull the weak and condition the strong. Instead of parental love he had received training and although he had often resented it, tonight he was to silently thank his father.

Barefoot, he did his night patrol round the island. He didn't expect to see anything, he was sure the storm had killed Finn and Fred, but his father had told him to look out for them, to be on high alert, and so he was. He couldn't believe his luck when he saw the dinghy, just pulled up beyond the waterline and left there with no attempt at concealment. That was not a mistake that he would ever have made. He, his father and Gusting had dragged their own inflatable up onto the shore and hidden it behind some rocks, where he had single-handedly covered it in seaweed so that it was invisible to all but the most determined searcher.

He skirted back, away from the boat, dropped to the ground and did a leopard crawl up to the rock face that led to the cave. Then he stood and stalked silently through the night, keeping close to the rock walls for cover.

Outside the cave he paused and listened. He couldn't hear anything above the sound of the waves and he had to know. He tucked his head round to look. There in the gloom, gleaming a dull silver, he saw two thermal sleeping bags and inside them, his enemies.

He fingered the knife in his belt. It would be so easy just to kill them both now, but that was not his father's instruction. So he shrank back, stealthy as a moon shadow. He moved along the cliff wall until he found a hiding place affording him a good view of the cave mouth and he hunkered down to wait and watch.

Hours later, the rising sun woke Dagmar. He swore silently at his weakness that had allowed him to drift off to sleep, but the boys' dinghy was still there on the sand and they were, he hoped, still inside the cave. He stayed hidden behind the rocks and kept watch.

It was some hours before hunger and thirst woke the exhausted boys. Finn surfaced first and woke Fred as he rattled around in the ration pack.

'Some noodles,' he said, shaking one at Fred. 'Fancy them?'

'More than you could possibly imagine,' replied Fred.

'Have to add cold water though,' said Finn. 'Don't want to have a fire and risk anyone seeing the smoke.'

They ate quickly, too hungry to speak, then shared a chocolate bar.

'C'mon,' said Finn, getting to his feet and pacing agitatedly. 'Let's hide the dinghy, and then search the island.'

The sand was already warm underfoot as the two boys padded out of their cave. They passed within three yards of Dagmar, concealed behind some rocks, but all they saw was the brilliant sun glinting off the water and their dinghy.

It was hard, sweaty work hauling the dinghy up the beach and hiding it behind a rock, then going back to the shoreline and gathering up handfuls of seaweed and covering the dinghy from one end to the other.

'Right, now for the fun bit,' said Finn, taking a long swig of water.

'What're we looking for?' asked Fred, draining his own bottle.

'I dunno, but we were guided here by old Jagged, so I'm hoping there'll be something here that'll help us.'

The boys headed off down the beach. After about a quarter of a mile, the beach curved round. The boys followed it and after another ten minutes they were on the far side of the island.

It was Fred who spotted the lifejacket. Finn was constantly looking back over his shoulder. He could not throw off the sensation that there was someone watching.

'Finn, look!' yelled Fred.

Finn followed his gaze then ran up to the lifejacket. He grabbed it up, heart racing.

'Look, it's got writing on it.' Finn read quickly, then yelled with glee.

'She's still alive. She left us a message, she's still alive!' He yelled.

'That's awesome,' said Fred, feeling a great surge of happiness. Then he read the message.

'Whooa. That's bad,' he said.

'I know, but at least we know where to go to get her,' said Finn.

Fred looked awkward. 'You're not seriously suggesting we follow her, down through the whirlpool. At midnight.'

'To the Dark World,' she said. 'To the lair of the Dark Djinn himself. That's where we've been heading all along,' replied Finn. 'That's where my parents are.' He studied

Fred, saw his fear, knew that this bit was not Fred's battle. He thought quickly.

'Thing is, Fred, let's say by some miracle that I can rescue Georgie and my parents and then by another miracle get back here, what if the dinghy's gone? How would we ever get off this place? We might have to wait for weeks before any ships passed and we'd have the Dark Fighters on our tail. Someone will have to stay and guard the dinghy.'

Finn could see Fred attempting to conceal the relief that flooded his face.

'I guess that would be me,' said Fred hesitantly.

Finn smiled. 'Exactly. Right, let's see what else we can find.'

The boys walked on in silence, both of them lost in their thoughts.

Suddenly Fred tripped. He looked down at the sand.

'What the heck is that?' he asked, peering down at an old hoop of rope that was protruding from the sand.

'Just some old rope,' replied Finn. 'Come on.'

'No, wait,' said Fred. He sat down on the ground and began to pull at it.

'What're you doing?' asked Finn. 'It's just some old rope.'

'I want to see what's there,' answered Fred. 'Come one, help me.'

'All right. If you want,' said Finn.

Together they got down on hands and knees and pulled at the rope. It didn't move, so they hauled and dug at the sand with their fingers and then Fred pulled on the rope again. This time the rope came out of the sand. It brought with it a sand-covered bottle. Fred untied the rope from the neck of the bottle and started to clean the bottle on his t shirt.

The bottle was beautiful. It was made of intricate red glass, with scrolls and decorations carved on it.

Fred twisted it between his fingers. 'It's lovely,' he remarked.

'Really old-looking' replied Finn, taking a look. 'I wonder what it held.'

'Might still hold something,' said Fred. Carefully, he pulled out the cork that stoppered up the bottle. He held the bottle upside down and shook it, his palm open underneath to catch anything that fell out.

'Nothing,' he said.

'But it could hold something,' mused Finn, as an idea suddenly hit him with the force of a sledge hammer.

'How do you capture a djinn?' asked Finn. 'Remember what Mr Violet told us?'

Fred looked in disbelief at the bottle in his hands.

Finn grinned. 'Think the impossible. Mr Violet told us that too, didn't he? So I am. First thing I need is bait. Now, what do we know that Hydrus would really like to get his hands on?'

'Er, the Pearl of Wisdom,' suggetsed Fred.

'Precisely!' replied Finn.

'But where are we going to find ourselves a pearl?' Fred asked.

'These be pearling waters, me hearty,' said Finn, putting on a piratical voice. 'I'm going to dive down and find me a pearl, then, somehow, convince Hydrus that it's the Pearl of Wisdom.'

Fred fell silent for a while.

'So, whadya think?' asked Finn.

'I think it's a wicked plan,' said Fred. If it works, he thought to himself, praying for the sake of his friend that it would.

CHAPTER TWENTY EIGHT

THE BOYS CONTINUED ON round the island. They passed the Drax's boat, hidden forty feet from them, superbly camouflaged by Dagmar.

Finn's eyes were fixed on the sea.

What're you looking for?' asked Fred,

'Deeper water. It's all pretty shallow here, but back near our cave I seem to remember there's some deeper water. I went diving for pearls with my father once when we were sailing off the Philippines. Oysters like the deeper water, and the deeper down, the bigger the pearl. That's what the local guys said, so I reckon it'll be the same here.'

The boys retraced their steps to their cave, had a quick drink of water and stashed Georgie's lifejacket and the beautiful bottle.

They went to examine the darker water that Finn hoped might contain oysters. The water swirled at the base of a cliff.

'I'm going to scramble up and take a look,' said Finn.

'Be careful,' warned Fred.

'I will. Stop worrying.'

Someone has to, thought Fred as Finn scrambled up the cliff.

Finn found a ledge about twenty feet above the sea. He stood there, scrutinising the water as it lapped back and forth at the cliff wall. The sea was quite calm and the water was clear.

'I can see a long way down, but I can't see the bottom,' he called to Fred. 'I reckon it's about forty feet down. I need a rock,' he announced, climbing back down the cliff.

'How big and what for?' asked Fred.

Finn described the size with his hands. 'To make me descend faster.'

Finn jogged back to the cave for his backpack. He emptied it out and stuck his Swiss army knife inside his shorts pocket and velcroed the pocket shut. Meanwhile Fred had found a rock the size of a cat which he handed to Finn.

'Perfect,' said Finn, putting the rock in his backpack and shouldering it on. He climbed back onto the cliff and started to breathe deeply, taking in as much air as he could manage and then he dived into the sea.

Fred gulped back his own panic as his friend disappeared under the waves.

Finn kicked hard and helped by the stone he descended quickly. As he got deeper the visibility faded but he could still see reasonably well. Suddenly, his outstretched fingers touched the sea bed. He cast his eyes around, looking for the rough, grey oyster shells he hoped he would find.

There were lots of shells, but no oysters. He swam further along, searching, but still no oysters. He let out a slow stream of bubbles from his mouth, then flipped round and kicked as hard as he could for the surface. The stone slowed his ascent. He surfaced and gasped for breath. When he'd got his breath back he swum out further, another fifty meters or so, then he trod water for a while, taking in more deep breaths.

Fred watched from the beach, concern mounting. What if the current took Finn? What if there were unfriendly sharks?

Then Finn jacknifed down and disappeared underwater again. He kicked out and swam down, down, down. He felt his ears pop. With one hand he held his nose and blew, so that his ears equalised. Still he hadn't reached the sea bed, so he just kept kicking out, wondering how much further down he could go. He slowly let bubbles of breath escape from his lips. It was getting quite dark now, hard to see anything. Finn guessed he must have been well over fifty feet down. Finally, his fingers scraped against an underwater rock. Finn scrambled for a hand hold. He was down so deep he had to hang onto to something to stay down. His ears began to ache but he ignored it. With his free hand he felt around on the rough rock, trying to find any oysters that might have attached themselves to it. He cut his fingers on some sharp coral, but ignored the flash of pain and carried on searching, gently fingering the rock. He fervently hoped there were no anemones bristling with spines, or, worse, that no sharks would be attracted by the trail of blood gushing from his cut fingers.

Suddenly his fingers brushed something. He tried hard to see what it was, but the visibility was just too poor. It felt like a cluster of oyster shells, attached to each other and to the rock. Finn was sure of it. He needed to breathe, desperately, but he could not risk losing this. He would never find it again in the murkiness. Just one more minute, he told himself, trying to still his mind and his body.

He got out his knife and worked on prising the clutch of shells loose from the rock. They came free as Finn felt his head was going to explode. He shoved the clutch and his knife into his backpack and then kicked with all his strength for the surface. The stone was slowing him and he fumbled in his backpack, trying to get it out. Agonisingly slowly, he rose up. Finally, he got out the stone and dropped it. He rose faster then, but still not fast enough. He could feel his oxygen-deprived brain getting dizzy but the surface still glittered a long way above him. Just hold on, he said to himself, *hold on*. Up he went, foot by foot by foot. He felt the blackness of unconsciousness swirl around his brain. He shook his head violently, desperately fighting it.

On the beach, Fred was getting desperate. Finally he plunged into the water and started to swim as fast as he could to the point where he had last seen Finn. Faster, faster, he told himself. He kept willing Finn to appear but there was no sign of him. Please, please, please, let him be all right, he begged, doubting every moment that he would be. He had been under too long. Far too long. On swam Fred, forcing his limbs faster and faster, then, just as he was giving up all hope, there was a disturbance on the sea about ten meters away. Finn.

'*Finn!*' he yelled. '*Finn! Hang on. I'm coming.*'

Finn was lying in the water, eyes wild, gasping in breath after breath. Blood was pouring from his nose and pooling around him in the water.

Fred grabbed him. 'Finn, thank God! Come on, we've got to get back to shore. You're bleeding everywhere.'

Finn nodded weakly. He knew what Fred meant. Sharks. He tried to kick out but he was totally exhausted and his kicks were feeble. Beside him, Fred kicked harder than he ever had before. Foot by foot, Fred pulled his friend towards the shore.

When they got there, both boys just lay collapsed on the sand, sides heaving.

Chapter Twenty Nine

GEORGIE WAS LOCKED IN a cage on the beach with her aunt and uncle. The same cage that Finn had seen in his vision. Georgie wondered what to say to Finn's parents.

As if reading her mind, her aunt Vicky leaned down and whispered in her ear.

'Be careful what you say. They have spies everywhere, listening.'

As she spoke a scorpion scurried across their cage and out the other side. Her aunt watched and moved away.

'What's more, if they see us whispering they'll get suspicious and come and interrogate us.'

'How do we talk? I have to tell you!' insisted Georgie.

'We keep our eyes open and wait till we're sure there's no-one around. Best thing is to lie down, pretend to sleep and whisper quietly.'

All through the day there were scorpions and crabs scuttling around, or Gusting and Drax passing by, taking up a pose on a nearby rock. And other men, and women, the human part of the Dark Army. They would walk past, smirk at the cage and its inhabitants. Georgie wondered what they did back in their normal lives. Were they accountants, lawyers, teachers, passing unnoticed as they prepared to fight in a battle, which, if they won, would mark the beginning of the end of the world they had lived in? Were they parents, and if so, did their children know what they were? Or were they djinn, taking on human form for the pleasure of it?

The smoke djinn curled by for a while. Georgie smelt them coming.

'Lie still. Don't talk. Do nothing. They get bored very quickly,' whispered Aunt Vicky.

Georgie wanted to scream and lash out at the djinn, but she followed her aunt's advice and soon the wisps of smoke drifted away in search of better entertainment.

Finally when the dingy light thickened and darkness fell, the scorpions and the crabs scuttled away, their captors disappeared, the smoke djinn drifted off and the parade of Dark Fighters ceased. Georgie and her aunt and uncle lay down and pretended to sleep. The beating of the waves on the grey sand drowned their voices. Georgie took a deep breath and began to tell Vick and Will what had happened, from the beginning; meeting Fred, meeting Mr Violet, meeting Triton, their training, the bomb, their frantic escape on Fred's boat. Her voice was steady until she came to the last bit.

'Then there was the most humungous storm and the boat capsized and sank.' Her voice trembled but she forced herself to go on. 'There was no sign of Finn or Fred.'

She saw Vick close her eyes.

'But the Dark fighters are convinced the boys are alive,' insisted Georgie. 'They're searching for them.'

Her aunt opened her eyes again.

'Finn's alive. I know it. I can feel it.'

Will took his wife's hand and held it tight.

'Finn knew you were here,' said Georgie. 'He saw you in a vision. And that thing. The Dark Djinn.'

'Hydrus kidnapped us at sea,' her uncle began. 'We pretended to be on a research trip because we didn't want to alarm Finn and Bess, or you and your mother and sisters, but we were actually searching for your father. We didn't believe he and the boat just disappeared. We thought he had been kidnapped himself.'

Georgie's heart leapt. 'So my mother was right. He didn't just abandon us, or sink without trace. I was right, too,' she added. 'Is he here?' She asked quickly. 'I have this feeling that he is.'

Vick paused before she spoke and seemed to be gathering herself.

'Hydrus did kidnap Johnny. I think the idea was to lure us out here to search for him.'

'So where's my father now?' asked Georgie, hope turning to panic. She saw the awful grief in her aunt's eyes.

'I'm sorry, Georgie. So sorry,' said Aunt Vick, trying to hug Georgie to her. 'Your father is dead.'

Georgie pushed her off. 'No, no,' she moaned. 'He must be alive. He must be. Why would they kill him? What happened? Tell me, *tell me*,' yelled Georgie.

'We have to tell her, Vick,' said Will. Tears rolled down Vick's cheeks as she nodded.

'I overheard Gusting and Drax talking one day,' said Will, his voice taut with grief and anger. 'They said they were sick of Johnny trying to escape all the time, that he had become a liability. Then Gusting said he had found a prison from which your father would never be able to escape. I saw Gusting lead him off, over that mountain.' Will pointed to the hills extending back from the beach.

'I heard Gusting telling Drax what he had done to your father.' Will's voice broke and he struggled to speak.

'Gusting threw your father down a well.'

The awful images rushed through Georgie's head. So he broke his neck, or he drowned, or he starved to death, which was worse? Georgie felt as if she would implode with grief. She felt her aunt and her uncle holding her tight, stroking her face, saying her name, over and over, but all she could think of was, no, he's not dead. He cannot be. It is not possible. She knew that if she thought anything else, she would go mad. He was alive, she would believe it, and it would be true. A well, she thought, over the mountain, a well. That was the last thing she thought before exhaustion and shock hit her like a fist and she passed out.

Hours later, she woke. Will and Vick, flanking her, were instantly awake too.

Georgie just lay there, in the stinking dark. It took her a long time to speak, but finally she managed to talk.

'Why have they kept you two alive?'

'The Dark Djinn is sick,' answered Will. 'Djinns normally live for thousands of years, but he's dying. He and his kind have polluted the seas and now they are paying the price. We're marine biologists. We can cure sick marine animals. We're known to have saved the unsaveable before now. Hydrus wants us to cure him so that he can go and wage war with the Light Djinn and the Light Kingdom.'

Georgie nodded. 'Finn's part of that war. He's meant to fight the Dark Djinn,' she said. 'We have no idea how, and it sounds impossible, but it's all in this Prophesy. But why does the Dark Djinn want to find Finn? And why did he tell Drax that if they didn't find Finn, Drax's son, Dagmar, would die in his place.'

Finn's parents exchanged a glance.

'They say Finn is a Child of the Light,' answered Vick. 'We've heard talk of a Prophesy too. A different kind of Prophesy. The Dark Fighters believe that if they cut open Finn's vein and cut open Hydrus's vein, and let Finn bleed into him until he dies, then Finn will give Hydrus his life.'

'Not Finn too. My father, now Finn,' moaned Georgie.

'It's not going to happen,' said Vick, taking hold of Georgie's hand and gripping tight. 'We couldn't save your father, my brother, but we *will* save Finn.'

'How?' Georgie asked.

Vick smiled for the first time. 'We're going to kill the Dark Djinn ourselves. We're going to poison him.'

'How?' asked Georgie, eyes wide.

'Watch.'

Vick stood up and yelled out.

'Hellooooo. Hellllloooo. We need something over here.'

Drax marched up to them.

'What?' he demanded.

'We need the kraken juice,' answered Vick.

'It's Hydrus's only hope for a cure,' added Will.

Drax looked scornful. 'I'll talk to Hydrus.'

Ivan Drax walked over to the Dark Djinn's lair and called out softly to him.

'My Lord. May I speak with you, my Lord.'

There was a sloshing in the water and Hydrus emerged, eyes weeping yellow.

'What is it, Drax?' demanded the Dark Djinn.

'The humans want the kraken. They insist it is your only hope.'

Hydrus gazed at the dank ceiling of his cave. His body ached without cease. Every day the pain became worse. He needed the Cure more than ever.

'Homeopathy. It is used by Princes, by Seers…' he mused. 'Why not by Djinn?' he pondered. 'I have nothing to lose,' he decided.

'You don't trust them, do you?' asked Drax.

'Of course not,' spat Hydrus. 'I shall test their potions carefully, but there is something in this homeopathy. They would be insane to try to trick me. They lack the courage and the imagination, but, even if they did try, if you and the rest of my Dark Fighters have done their job properly, I shall have my insurance policy.'

Drax laughed. 'You mean Finn Kennedy.'

'Correct,' replied the Dark Djinn. 'Finn Kennedy and his blood.' He laughed a horrible gurgling sound that reached Finn's parents and Georgie and chilled their hearts.

Drax walked back to the cage.

'You shall have your kraken,' he told Finn's parents. He moved closer to the bars until they could see the flecks of red in the pupils of his eyes. 'But if you try any trickery, I personally will kill you.' He looked at Georgie. 'All of you.'

↪ CHAPTER THIRTY ↩

HYDRUS PREPARED HIMSELF TO summon the kraken. He swam out into the sea and then before Georgie's astonished eyes, metamorphosed into an enormous plume of smoke. The smoke billowed and poured up into the sky as if belching from some enormous inferno. Gradually it cleared and Georgie saw an island a hundred feet across. Then the island moved. Georgie gasped. It was Hydrus. Magnified, his sickness and his power were horrific.

With a lash of his enormous tail, Hydrus dived under the sea and emitted a deep, haunting call that vibrated the water for a hundred miles. Hydrus emerged from the sea and moved closer to the shore.

After about twenty minutes, a trail of bubbles popped up through the water. Then the sea seemed to suck and seethe. With a horrible slurping sound, an enormous head emerged above the waves. The kraken had risen from the deep.

Its head must have been forty feet round. It was green, covered in nodules, with two enormous, unblinking eyes which swivelled to survey its surroundings. It gazed upon the shore with the evil arrogance of an unrivalled predator.

Georgie noticed the sea writhing for hundreds of meters around it, alive with its lashing tentacles. The stench of the deep rose with it and Georgie wanted to gag.

Hydrus welcomed the kraken in some strange hissing language. The kraken responded in a series of creaks that sounded like something huge and metal groaning in the wind.

Hydrus turned to face the cage.

'You want the kraken's poison. Go and get it,' he boomed.

Drax walked over and unlocked the padlock.

'Good luck,' said Will to his wife. 'I still wish you'd let me go.'

'This is mine to do,' Vick replied.

'Yes I know, you can talk to the animals and I seem to rub them up the wrong way.'

Vick gave him a light smile. 'Be back in a minute.' She ruffled Georgie's hair and was gone.

Vick walked up to the water's edge. She ignored the massive presence of the Djinn and focused only on the kraken. She bowed to it. In response, one enormous tentacle whipped through the air. Georgie screamed with terror, but the kraken just let the tentacle hover above her aunt's head, as if contemplating what to do with her. In one quick move it could grab her aunt, crush her and drag her off to the deep, but Vick, if she felt that, betrayed no sign of it. She reached up and began stroking the tentacle.

Slowly, languorously, the kraken lowered its tentacle to the side so that the tip of it lay on the sand by Vick's feet.

Georgie felt like she was holding her breath. Vick seemed to be saying something to the beast, something so soft it was inaudible to the rest of them. From her bag Vick took out a series of sponges. One by one, she gave these to the kraken. The beast wrapped a tentacle round the sponge and squeezed, then unfurled the tentacle and dropped the sponge, laded with poison from its suckers, into an open plastic bag that Vick held out. Then it raised another of its enormous tentacles out of the water and through the air. It lifted the huge weight of its tentacle effortlessly.

The lore of mariners across the world told tales of kraken crushing ships. Looking at the power of the beast, Georgie could see how easy that would be. One by one the kraken offered all of its eight tentacles to Vick. When she had eight sponges dripping with poison, she bowed again and backed away. Only then could Georgie see the sweat coursing down her aunt's arms and the rapid breaths she was now allowing herself.

Drax locked Vick back in the cage. There was an enormous sucking sound as the kraken disappeared under the waves.

Smoke poured from Hydrus until he was invisible. As the smoke billowed away, Hydrus re-appeared, normal size again.

'Got what you need?' he thundered at Vick.

She nodded. 'Give us a day, a load of bottles, large and small, and you'll have your remedy.'

'A day is all you have, then I recall the kraken, this time not to help, but to kill.'

Chapter Thirty One

Finn and Fred sat in their cave, gazing at the clutch of oyster shells that Finn had retrieved. Finn's nose had finally stopped bleeding, and after a drink of water and a bite of chocolate he insisted he was feeling much better.

Finn got out his knife and handed it to Fred, who shook his head.

'No. You risked your life to dive for those shells. I think you should be the one to open them.'

'All right.' Finn took a deep breath. He had come quite close to drowning. If the shells were empty he would feel totally gutted. Finding a pearl was essential to his plan.

The oyster shells were all attached to each other. Finn prised them apart, then readied his knife to open the first one.

Fred watched, eyes round with hope. The shell split open with a click, then Finn clenched his fist in the air. A pearl gleamed in the shell. It was small, but it was a pearl.

'Fantastic!' yelled Fred. 'Well done.'

Finn prised the pearl free and handed it to Fred. 'This is for you. For saving my life.'

'Well, er, I didn't exactly-'

'Fred, I know what state I was in out there,' said Finn.

Fred took the pearl with a smile. 'Thank you.'

'No prob,' replied Finn. 'Now, let's see if there's one for Georgie.'

He opened another shell.

'Nothing,' he said, disappointed. He threw it away and worked on the next one.

'Yes!' Yelled Finn and Fred in unison. Another perfect pearl gleamed inside. Finn laid the shell carefully on the sand.

'Next.' He opened another shell, which was empty. The next held another small pearl about the same size as the first two.

'That's one for each of us,' said Fred.

Finn nodded. 'I want a big one now.' He looked at the last shell, and crossed his fingers.

This one was hard to open. The rough edges cut Finn as he struggled with it. He swore under his breath, sucked the blood from his fingers then tried again.

The shells split apart and Finn fell silent. Inside the shell, luminescent in its beauty, was a pearl. It was huge; over five times as large as the others. Fred and Finn stared, mesmerised by it.

Finn cut it free then rolled the pearl around his fingers for a few moments. 'It's so lovely,' he said. 'Shame to have to give it away, especially to the Dark Djinn.'

'All in a good cause,' replied Fred.

'Mm. Now, for stage two of the plan,' said Finn. 'Bung us your bottle.'

Fred retrieved the beautiful red glass bottle. He took the pearl from Finn, unstoppered the bottle and gently rolled in the pearl. It just passed through the neck of the bottle then settled at the bottom of the bottle.

'It looks enormous,' yelled Fred excitedly. 'It's the thick glass and the curve of the bottle. It acts like a magnifying glass.'

'A perfect pearl of wisdom, don't you think?' Finn said to Fred.

'Oh, I think so,' replied Fred. 'I've no idea what the real one looks like, but this'd fool me.'

'Let's hope it fools Hydrus,' replied Finn. 'Right, now we need to build a fire and dig out those chemicals Mr Violet gave me.'

'You're not worried anymore about someone being here and seeing the smoke?' asked Fred.

Finn looked pensive. 'I still have this odd feeling from time to time, that someone's around. But we've walked round the island and there's absolutely no sign of life, and we need to make a fire to carry out our plan so I think we'll just have to risk it. What do you reckon?' he asked Fred.

'I reckon we go for it,' replied Fred. 'I'll go and get some firewood,' he added.

'I need to get the first aid box from the dinghy. It is metal, isn't it?' Finn asked.

'I think so,' answered Fred, puzzled. 'But I'll get it. You stay here and rest.'

For once, Finn did as he was told. Despite what he had told Fred, he was still feeling rough and he wanted to conserve as much energy as possible for his passage through to the Dark Kingdom. He glanced at his watch. Midnight was only twelve hours away. Half a day to recover, he thought grimly.

Alone in the cave, he dug around in the side pocket of his rucksack and pulled out the two ziplock bags he had almost forgotten about. He remembered Mr Violet giving them to him and not wanting Finn to ask about them. He wondered what was so secret about them. He assumed now that they were the limestone and sodium carbonate needed, along with sand, to make glass, but he couldn't be sure. Perhaps they were totally different chemicals, explosive in some way. He'd have to be ultra careful.

Fred reappeared with the first aid box then dashed out again to collect firewood.

Finn fell upon the first aid box eagerly. It was metal. Perfect. Finn emptied out the contents and stored them safely.

Fred returned with an armful of driftwood which he arranged on the sand outside the cave.

'Give us the bottle,' he called to Finn.

Puzzled, Finn came out, handed over the bottle and watched as Fred held the bottle above the wood.

'Magnifying glass!' said Fred, pointing to the spotlight of sun that was playing over one patch of wood. Soon the wood started smoking and then a minute later a flame burst from the smoke.

'Fred, you're a genius!' remarked Finn.

Fred chuckled then blew gently on the flame. Soon the dry wood caught and the flames danced high into the air.

Finn pocketed the cork stopper then delicately laid the neck of the bottle in the outer part of the fire. Then he shook out the powders from the ziplock bags into the metal first aid box.

He added a handful of sand and played with the proportions of the three compounds until he thought he had it right.

'I'm sure Mr Violet said it was seventy five percent sand, ten percent limestone and fifteen percent sodium carbonate,' muttered Finn. 'But it could have been seventy five per cent sodium carbonate, ten per cent sand and fifteen per cent limestone,' he added, furiously scratching his head in confusion.

'Better make your mind up before the fire starts to die. There's not much firewood on this island,' said Fred. 'And I seem to remember it was seventy five sand, ten limestone and fifteen sodium carbonate,' he added.

'I think that's it,' said Finn, crossing his fingers. He fiddled with the mix a bit more then balanced the first aid tin in the hottest part of the fire. He yelped as the flames licked his fingers and withdrew his hand quickly.

'Let's make it hotter,' said Finn. He went back into the cave and returned with a bottle of surgical spirits from the first aid kit. He poured a bit of this into the fire. The flames leapt and roared back at him. 'Whoa!' exclaimed Fred, jumping backwards. 'Scorch my eyebrows why don't you?'

Finn laughed. 'Sorry mate!'

He got a long stick and tried stirring the mix in the first aid tin. It was staying resolutely solid and looked nothing like glass.

'Come on,' urged Finn. 'Come on. *Melt.*'

'Let's use the bottle again,' suggested Fred. 'Magnify the sun's rays onto the mixture.'

'Worth a go,' said Finn. He took off his t shirt and carefully wrapped it round his hand, then he gingerly reached close to the flames and pulled the bottle out. It was hot, but holdable. He held it above the mix, trying to focus the spotlight from the sun as sharply as possible.

After a while, the mix seemed to shrink slightly.

'Something's happening, Fred,' yelled Finn.

'Does seem to be,' replied Fred cautiously. 'Keep still, keep the spotlight in place.'

'Yessir,' replied Finn, trying to keep his hand steady. After five minutes more his muscles were screaming with effort but he didn't dare hand the bottle over to Fred. He didn't want to shift the spotlight even for a moment because he could see now, quite clearly, that the mixture was beginning to melt. When it was sludgy, he laid the bottle gently onto the sand and took a long thin branch from the unburnt pile. He dipped the end of the branch into the molten mix and then as the wood snapped into flame, quickly stuck it into the neck of the bottle and twisted it around to deposit a thin layer of molten glass onto the old glass. He kept doing this until the wood had burned down. He got another stick and did the same. By the time that stick had burnt down Finn reckoned he had narrowed the neck of the bottle just enough without making it obvious that the bottle had been tampered with.

He sank back on the sand. Fred sat beside him and together the two boys watched the fire die down as they waited for the bottle to cool. It took ages. Both of them burnt their fingers testing it, but finally it was cool enough to touch.

The boys gave it another half hour, just to be safe.

'Must have solidified by now,' said Fred.

'Hope so,' said Finn. 'Come on, let's test it.'

Fred held the bottle and very gently tilted it so that the pearl ran down to the neck of the bottle. Both boys held their breath. The pearl stayed put. The glass the boys had made had solidified inside the neck of the bottle and stopped the pearl from coming out.

'I think that makes the perfect present for a Dark Djinn, don't you?' said Fred.

'I think so,' replied Finn. He took his penknife, whittled the cork very slightly, then jammed it back in the bottle.

All he had to do now was wait for midnight to come.

Darkness fell and the minutes ticked by agonisingly slowly. At ten to twelve, Finn and Fred said their good byes.

'Good luck,' said Fred, giving Finn's arm an awkward pat. 'I'll see you soon, hey.'

'Good luck mate, and yes you will. I'll be back before you know it.'

Finn shouldered his backpack with the bottle and pearl inside, gave Fred a last wave, then waded into the sea. The moon was nearly full and it cast a path of silver out into the deep. Finn swam under the breaking waves and followed the moon-lit path until he was perhaps fifty metres off shore. He trod water, glancing at his watch and waiting.

His stomach clenched tight with nerves. He heard a low rumbling sound, then felt the water begin to swirl around his legs. He stared to breathe as deeply as he could. The water around him gathered speed and became a whirlpool. Finn felt the pressure sucking at him. His nervousness turned to sheer terror. There was no going back now, no escape. If he didn't drown on the way, he was headed for the Dark Kingdom, and Hydrus. He managed a few more desperate breaths and then he was pulled under.

CHAPTER THIRTY TWO

LOCKED IN THEIR CAGE, Georgie and her aunt and uncle were working non-stop on the potions. Georgie's job was to help mix and measure for her aunt.

'Gosh, there's so much of this stuff,' said Georgie. 'Enough for an army.'

'That's the idea. We want to give it to everyone down here, all the Dark Fighters.'

'Kill them all?'

'Hopefully, and if we don't have enough to kill them all, then enough to kill the Djinn and to knock out everyone else for a few hours. Then we escape.'

'Back through the porthole?'

'Exactly. You can only pass in or out at midnight, so we need to time it all perfectly too.'

'Then we get out and hope Finn and Fred haven't got in the other way.'

'Exactly.'

'What's uncle Will doing?' Georgie asked Vick quietly. He had been working away alone on the other side of the cage.

'He's working on an antidote to the kraken juice,' Vick whispered.

'Why do you need an antidote?'

'We're pretty sure the Djinn won't take the stuff unless he sees us take it first. So we have to make stomach liners and an antidote,' replied Vick.

'You're going to take it?' asked Georgie incredulously.

'What choice do I have? We've made seaweed paste. We'll eat that before we take the juice to reduce the stomach absorption of the juice, then we drink the kraken juice, then we secretly take the antidote.'

'What if it doesn't work?' asked Georgie.

'Then we die.'

Before Georgie could respond, there was a great rumbling sound that shook the sand.

Will looked up at the sky, then checked his watch. 'Midnight already. The porthole's opening.'

They saw in the sea hundreds of Dark Fighters. There were humans, sharks, huge birds with vicious curling beaks, stingrays, barracudas. Around them the waters bubbled and swirled as the whirlpool deepened and accelerated. Moments later, they were gone.

'Where are they all going?' asked Georgie.

'To fight the *Mother of all Battles* as Hydrus calls it. These lot are off to get into advance positions I'd say,' replied Will. 'But he's keeping his key fighters here, by the look of it and sending the foot soldiers.' For a few moments, the sea was quiet, but then the deep rumbling started again.

'Someone's coming through,' said Will.

They watched someone hurtle towards the limit of their sky, and then fall through space and land in the sea about twenty yards from shore. Then the person surfaced, gasping for breath.

Vick screamed. *'Finn, my God. Finn, it's you!'*

Finn rubbed the water from his eyes and stared in amazement. He saw an island looming up from the stinking water - an island which was a mirror image of the one above the sea. But this really was the island of his nightmares. There, grabbing the bars of a cage and calling to him, were his mother, his father and Georgie. Through all his terror, he looked at their faces in pure elation.

'Mum, Dad, Georgie!' he yelled, with what little of his breath he had recovered, then he was surrounded by a legion of Dark Fighters.

'It is him,' they murmured and hissed. 'It is the Boy. Call the Dark One now. Call the Commanders.'

Finn was dragged up the beach, away from the cries of his parents and Georgie, to a towering cave, lit by sickly-coloured green lamps with lumps all over them. One of the lamps moved and Finn realised it was a jellyfish, like one of the photospheres he had seen when he was with the Light Djinn. He looked around and slowly his eyes adjusted to the gloom. Wisps of smoke whirled by him, coiling around him and rising in spirals to the roof of the cave. Smoke without fire, movement without wind. What were they? Finn shuddered and then he saw, lying in the brackish water, the coiled serpent man. Enormous, repulsive and awful.

'Hello Finn Kennedy,' hissed Hydrus. 'I've waited a long time for this.'

It felt to Finn as if Hydrus's eyes were boring into his soul, slicing through flesh and bone to get there. So this is my enemy, he thought. This is who I have to beat. He heard in his head Mr Violet's voice. *Think the unthinkable.*

I will beat you, thought Finn. I will beat you. Finn forced himself to stand tall, to speak with a powerful voice.

'Waited for what?' he asked.

'To meet you, of course,' replied Hydrus.

'Why? What am I to you?'

The Dark Djinn smiled, revealing rows of rotting teeth. 'You are a cure.'

'What, me? I'm just a boy. How can I cure you?'

'Since you ask, I shall tell you. In two ways you could cure me. I shall let you go and join your parents. I can hear your mother still calling for you, weeping for you. So, you shall go to her with this message. Finish my remedy by tomorrow night, a remedy which will cure me, or else I shall follow the prophesied remedy.'

'What's that?' asked Finn, fear clenching his stomach.

'I shall cut your vein,' replied the Dark Djinn. He shot out his massive hand and snatched Finn's wrist, 'here, and cut my own in the same place and again further up my arm. My diseased blood shall flow out, while your blood, the blood of Light and health, shall flow into me.' The Djinn's voice had turned slow and dreamy and his eyes had become distant as if contemplating some long-held dream.

Finn's fear turned to terror. He yanked his wrist free from the Djinn's grasp and clenched his fists by his side to stop himself from shuddering. 'How much blood?' He managed to ask.

'Why, all of it, of course. You must die so I can live. A noble exchange, wouldn't you say?' The Djinn smiled and became brisk again.

'So, you'd better make sure your parents come up with my cure, hadn't you.'

Finn tried to still his wild and terrified thoughts. He *had* to stay calm. He *had* to think clearly,

'How do we know you won't kill me anyway?' he asked.

'You don't. You trust me,' replied Hydrus with a sneer.

Finn knew, whatever his parents did, the Djinn intended to kill him anyway.

'When does all this happen?' asked Finn. 'When exactly do you want the cure by?'

'Mmm, let me see. I need to sleep now, so very, very tired, and I need the morning to brief my Commanders, for you see, tomorrow night brings the full moon. That's when we go through, into the Light World, into your world, to fight the mother of all battles, to vanquish your world and inhabit it ourselves. No more skulking around in the darkness, no more stinking, stagnant waters and nuclear skies. We will have sun, air, light, and health. I will need all my strength, do you not agree, to lead this army, and all my wisdom, so, let's say sundown. Let's say six tomorrow. Your parents and you will present me with the cure then. Tell them to make enough for me, and for the Hundred.'

'Who are the Hundred?' asked Finn.

'They are the creatures of your nightmares. They are the darkest of the Dark Fighters, the most skilled in the ways of Evil. They are the black heart of my army.'

Finn gulped.

'Take him to his parents,' said the Djinn.

Rough hands encircled his wrists from behind. Finn wheeled round to see Drax and Gusting.

'You two,' spat Finn. 'I should have known.'

'Welcome to the Dark World,' said Drax with a twisted smile. Gusting gave a guffaw of laughter and together the two men dragged Finn away.

As Finn was led off, the Djinn watched him hungrily, like a starving man who had not eaten for a thousand years.

The cage door clicked open and Finn fell into his parents' arms. They embraced, the three of them, with laughter and tears and exclamations of joy that each had feared they would never feel again. Georgie watched them, her own cheeks wet, happy for them, crying for her own father, and her mother who seemed just as lost to her.

'George, c'mon,' said Finn, and pulled her into the circle.

When they were sure no-one was looking or listening, they all lay down side by side to talk. Finn gripped hold of Georgie's hand.

'Any news of your father? Is he here too?' he whispered.

Georgie stared unseeing out of the cage. She tried to speak but no words came.

'Finn,' said his father gently. 'It's bad news. The worst.'

Finn's hand clenched around Georgie's. She stayed immobile as a statue. Finn sensed she didn't want to be hugged, didn't want to or couldn't speak. He turned to his father.

'What happened?' he asked.

Will, his eyes burning with anger and grief, quickly told Finn how Gusting had taken Georgie's father over the hill and thrown him down a well about a month previously. Finn wanted to shout, to scream, to smash through the bars of his cage, to find Gusting and kill him with his bare hands. He had never felt such rage, such grief and all the while, Georgie lay there, unmoving, as if to move would be to drown in the grief that swirled around her.

Finn grabbed Georgie, pulled her to him. Tears coursed down his cheeks.

'Georgie. Georgie. I am so sorry. So sorry.'

Georgie still didn't move. While Finn and his mother cried silently, Georgie just looked out through the bars of the cage, refusing to accept their grief. Her father was not dead, so she would not cry. When her chance came, she would search for him and she would find him. Alive.

She made herself speak. 'What did Hydrus say to you?' she asked Finn, pulling away from him. 'And where's Fred?'

Finn looked questioningly at Georgie. She would not talk about her father. That was plain. Finn wiped his face, and, for Georgie's sake, banished the grief from his voice. Then he began to tell her and his parents what the Djinn had told him and filled them in on Fred's guarding the boat.

After that, his parents told Finn of the potions and their plan.

'So we have to kill Hydrus and knock out or kill the Hundred, every single one of them, before he tries to kill you,' said his father.

'And if that doesn't work, then we try my plan,' said Finn, and he carefully showed his parents and Georgie the bottle and the pearl inside it and told them his idea.

Finn's father let out a long breath. 'It's one heck of a plan,' he said. 'Let's call it plan B, if for any reason, plan A doesn't work.'

'And then, whatever plan works,' said Finn's mother, 'we all escape through the porthole at midnight.'

'Back to Bone Island where Fred will be waiting with the boat,' said Georgie in a very quiet voice.

'Correct,' the others intoned.

'Now, let's all try to get some sleep,' said Finn's mother. 'Goodness knows, we're going to need it.'

CHAPTER THIRTY THREE

THE SOUND OF DRUMS woke them, a low, rhythmic throbbing that echoed dully through the Dark World. Finn, his parents and Georgie got wearily to their feet and stood at the bars of the cage looking out towards the Djinn's cave. Sitting beside it, half-in half-out of the water, was an octopus, its myriad arms beating a line of drums. Smoke wreaths danced around its tentacles. More trails of smoke were flying through the air towards the octopus.

Finn shuddered. 'What are those things?' he asked his father.

'Djinn. In smoke form. They can materialise into whatever form they like.'

'They're horrible' replied Finn. 'They feel like evil ghosts.'

'Only worse,' said his mother.

'How can the potion work on them?' asked Finn.

'It can't,' answered his father. 'We have to hope they materialise and then take it.'

Georgie stared at the octopus. 'Why is it drumming?' she asked.

'The call to battle,' replied Will. He turned to the others. 'Right. This is our own call to battle. The potions are ready, the antidotes and the *cure*. Remember, the antidotes are in the small green bottles, the *cure* in the larger ones. I've buried four extra bottles of the antidote, just in case they search us, but I think we should each carry a bottle in case we can't get back to the cage for any reason. Try to hide it on you, as best you can.'

Vick reached out and took hold of Finn and Georgie's hands.

'All right? Are you two ready?'

They looked at each other, into eyes that had changed and darkened with all they had seen.

'Yes,' they both said in unison.

Finn checked the bottle in his backpack. The bottle was ready too.

Gusting brought them a tray of breakfast. Grey rice and some kind of slimy, inedible fish. A mug of tea each and some water. They ate and drank everything, save the fish, which smelled so rank they threw it as far from their cage as they could. It sweltered there all day, reeking at them.

The drums beat on, hour by endless hour. Waiting, just waiting, trying anything to kill time was agony. The minutes inched by to five thirty. Georgie watched the Dark Fighters arriving outside the Djinn's cave, some in the water, some on land. The Hundred, he had called them, the darkest and most evil of all his fighters. There were humans, and enormous snarling dogs, giant feral cats with merciless amber eyes, huge birds with vicious claws and beaks, ten foot scorpions with fatal tails poised, thirty foot sharks, sleek and sinister, and obscenely huge snakes, hissing and spitting as they slithered in. There were smoke djinn too, lashing the air with barely supressed excitement.

Finn's mother pulled out the jar of seaweed paste.

'Eat, all of you, as much as you can. Just in case he makes you two take the cure, you'd better line your stomachs like me and Will,' she said to Finn and Georgie.

'You too, Mum,' said Finn, grimacing as he tasted the first mouthful.

'I will,' she said, taking a scoop and swallowing it down. No one queried whether or not it would work. They had to believe it would. Georgie ate the seaweed, saying nothing.

The day gave way to the dull violet of twilight. The moon rose from beyond the water's edge. The full moon. Then came six o'clock and with it the summons from the Djinn. They looked at each other, the four of them, and embraced. It was horrible. Each of them wanted to cling on to the others, knowing this might be the last time.

'We won't die here tonight,' Finn's mother said in her strong, rich voice.

Don't make promises, thought Finn, that you can't keep, but he loved her for it, for her unshakeable faith, and it gave him just that little bit of extra courage so that when the gate of their prison clanged open, he walked out, head high.

Drax and Gusting led them towards the cave. Outside the cave mouth, in the water or beside it, was the black heart of the Dark Djinn's army; the Hundred. Inside the cave, lying in the shallows was the Dark Djinn, eyes gleaming, tail writhing in obscene enjoyment.

'So you come to me, bringing me my cure,' he boomed.

Finn's father stepped forward. 'I do.'

'Knowing that if you fail I shall bleed your son dry before your eyes.'

'This will cure you of your ills, I promise you that,' Finn's father said, meeting Hydrus's eyes with his own, steadfast gaze. If he felt fear, he showed none. He held out the large green bottle.

'I've made twenty bottles of this. For you and the Hundred.'

'You would make us all strong, cure us all?' jeered Hydrus.

'I thought that was what you wanted. This place has made you all sicken. You said find a cure so we did,' replied Will. It was essential to their plan that all the Dark Fighters take the *cure*.

'A good idea of mine, wasn't it? We will be all the stronger to vanquish the Light. Bring it to me,' commanded Hydrus.

Finn's father waded into the water. Wraiths of smoke curled through the air and spun round him.

'Wait!' commanded the Djinn. He turned to Drax. 'Search him.'

Finn could see his father stiffen, ever so slightly. The smoke djinn fled at Drax's approach. Finn's father paused and waited as Drax patted him down. In only moments Drax found the small green bottle. He held it up to the Dark Djinn.

'Ah, what have we here? Some treachery, perchance? Search the others,' shouted Hydrus before Will had a chance to respond.

Drax and Gusting searched them, more roughly than was necessary. Georgie spat in Gusting's face. He back-handed her with his fist, bloodying her nose.

'You cowardly scum,' said Vick, 'to strike a child.'

'Shut up, or you'll get one too,' jeered Gusting.

'You think I fear you?' asked Vick, her eyes defiant.

'Mum, leave it,' said Finn, as Gusting approached his mother, fists bunched.

'Got it,' announced Drax, holding aloft another small green bottle. Gusting unclenched his fists and got on with the search, unearthing the other two bottles.

The Dark Djinn looked at the bottles then back to Will.

'More of your cure?'

'Yes, very concentrated in format, which is why it's in the smaller bottles,' answered Will.

'Oh really. Is that a fact? Search their cage,' hissed Hydrus to Drax and Gusting.

Georgie and Finn and his parents waited, trying to act as if they had nothing to hide, hoping desperately that the other bottles of antidote would not be found.

Drax and Gusting returned minutes later with their haul of antidote. They laid it on the sand behind Will.

'Ah, four more bottles of the cure, eh?' taunted Hydrus.

'Yes,' replied Will.

'Well,' hissed the Djinn. 'Let's do a little experiment, shall we? I think the four of you should drink my bottle of *cure*, half of it anyway, just so I can see how effective it is.'

'But we're not ill,' protested Will.

'No, not yet, but let's see what it does for you anyway. Bring the girl first,' he instructed Gusting.

Gusting led Georgie before the Djinn. He opened the bottle, ordered Georgie to drink.

She looked from Gusting to the Djinn and back again. Her eyes blazed with hatred but her voice was deathly calm. 'Pop the cork then,' she said.

With a smile, Gusting removed the cork and handed her the cure. Georgie tilted back her head and took a swig. It tasted like sugar and coffee mixed with some other strange and bitter taste. Her uncle had added sugar and coffee, just to try to cover up the vicious burn of the kraken juice, but it still tasted rank. With all eyes on her she swallowed it with a smile and clasped the bottle out of sight, behind her back. She had plans for it. She turned to her uncle.

'Hey, you never said it tasted good too, Uncle Will.'

Will smiled at his niece, at her incredible bravery.

'You next,' the Djinn said to Vick. Gusting looked round for the first bottle, gave a grunt when he couldn't find it, then uncorked a fresh bottle and handed it to Finn's mother, who took a swig, smiled, and handed back the bottle.

'Now you,' said the Djinn to Will. 'Take a swig. Make it a big one.'

Will swigged, returned the bottle and smiled at the Djinn.

'Thanks,' he said. 'I needed that. I was shattered after working so hard to make it.'

'Is that right?' asked Hydrus with a sneer. 'Well, let's just watch all of you for a bit, see how you fare.'

'None for me?' asked Finn.

The Djinn shook his head. 'This is not how I foresee your death. I have other plans for you, as you should know.'

'This'll cure you,' said Finn.

The Dark Djinn noted the exact position of the moon in the sky, using it as his clock. 'I think ten minutes should do it. Poison kills quickly, after all.'

Finn's mother stretched. 'You know, I always had a painful elbow, too much hauling sails up and down, but I do believe it's getting better.'

'My mouth ulcer,' said Will, 'that's stopped stinging too.'

Georgie said nothing, she didn't want to overdo it, she just tried to act utterly relaxed, as if she had not just ingested a lethal poison. She wondered how much longer the seaweed would protect their stomachs. Was she imagining it, or was the burn starting?

The Djinn writhed irritably as the minutes ticked by.

'You're not dying,' he hissed.

'I told you,' said Will patiently. 'It's a cure. If it were poison, we'd have been long dead by now.'

The Djinn thought for a while, then gave an evil smile.

'I think what you need is the stuff in the small bottles. The concentrated stuff. Bring it,' he ordered Gusting. 'Drink a bottle each,' he ordered them, 'then we'll see.'

'Fine, whatever,' said Georgie. As Gusting handed her the bottle of antidote she could feel the tremble beginning in her fingers, feel the bile of vomit churning in her stomach from the poison. She took a deep breath, desperate to keep it down, then tilted back her head and drank the antidote as if it were nectar. She wouldn't die. Not here. Not now.

Gusting gave the other bottles to Finn's mother and then father. They drained the bottles, each hiding their relief. They waited, hoping, praying the antidote would kick in. Finn watched in agony. He could see the strain Georgie was trying to keep off her face. Her body was small and she had taken the first dose of the poison. It had been in her body the longest. Finn looked at his cousin with a fierce love. He could not bear her to die. Please, God, save her. Please, all that is good and Light, please save her. The minutes ticked by. The Djinn watched his captives curiously.

'Well,' he finally declared. 'It seems to work, or, at the very least, it does no harm. Bring me a bottle,' he ordered Drax. 'A whole one for me. Share the others out between the Hundred. Each fighter must have some.'

When Drax and Gusting were collecting up the cure, Finn's father apparently accidentally stepped back on the pile of antidote bottles, smashing them all. He hid his grin as the antidote drained away into the sand.

'You idiot,' shouted Gusting. 'You just wasted those bottles.'

'There's plenty more, don't worry,' replied Will.

'There'd better be,' shouted Gusting.

Yes, thought Will, agreeing with him for once, there'd better be.

Gusting marched up to Hydrus with a full bottle of the cure and proffered it with a bow. The Djinn took the bottle, drained it, then turned to watch his army take their doses. Drax took another bottle, knocked half of it back quickly, then passed it on.

Gusting was busy handing the other bottles round, mixing their contents with water to make them go further, handing them to the Dark Fighters, both human and animal, who were gathering like flies round honey. The wraiths of smoke circled him frenetically, then materialised into a menagerie of cats, dogs, birds and humans. Finn's father watched and gave a silent cheer. Gusting passed round bottles to them until they had all drunk. Then he walked up to the sea, waded out and poured a succession of bottles into the open mouths of the sharks and sea serpents and other Dark Fighters of the sea. Then he just emptied one into the water to catch any of the fish that hadn't had a dose. Laughing, he walked back on to the beach

'Here' said Georgie, calling to him. 'You forgot this one.' She handed him the bottle she had kept hidden, intending it especially for him. Gusting took it, glanced around then greedily drained it all himself. Georgie turned away so that Gusting would not see her smile of triumph. A bit of revenge for you, Dad, she thought to herself.

'Have you all taken the cure?' Hydrus yelled to the Hundred.

There were roars and shouts and hisses of assent.

'Excellent,' boomed the Djinn. 'And now, it's time for my second cure of the evening, in the form of some young and healthy blood,' he pointed his huge, bloated finger at Finn.

'You said you'd leave him alone,' screamed Finn's mother, 'if we gave you the cure.'

'I changed my mind. Djinn's prerogative,' said Hydrus, and roared with laughter as if he'd told a great joke.

'Come here,' he ordered Finn.

'Nooooo,' screamed Finn's mother. She and his father and Georgie raced towards Finn to protect him, but Dark Fighters quickly encircled them and held them back. Gusting and Drax grabbed the struggling Finn, who just had time to snatch the rucksack lying un-noticed at his feet before he was hauled off to Hydrus.

'What a night this is turning into, hey my saviour? Bet you didn't think it would end this way,' mused the Djinn.

'Wait,' said Finn. 'There's something I have. You might just like to see it.' It was time for plan B. The potion didn't seem to be working. If they were ever going to get out of this alive, then his plan had to work, and it had to work right now. He tried to keep the desperation from his eyes. He concentrated hard to blank his mind so that nobody could read his thoughts. 'Let me go,' he said to Drax and Gusting.

They looked to Hydrus who nodded. 'He's not going anywhere,' the Djinn said.

They released his arms and Finn carefully opened his backpack and drew out the glass bottle. He held it high above his head.

'What's in it?' demanded the Djinn. 'I see something inside.'

'Yes, you do. I believe it's something you've been looking for a very long time. Something very -'

'Oh shut up and get on with it before I just bite your neck. What is it?'

Finn was trying to drag it out. Keep talking; stay alive just a bit longer. The potion might just start to work.

The Djinn passed a hand over his eyes, as if in pain. Finn hid his smile and kept talking. *Work, work* he willed the potion.

'Something I found, in the sand. Very ancient. Unearthed on Bone Island by the storm.'

The Djinn massaged his temples, squinting violently.

'Give me the bottle,' he commanded.

'I think it's something only you should see,' said Finn. 'Might be tarnished by the wrong eyes.'

Finn took the bottle a few paces closer so that the Djinn could see what it contained.

'It's the Pearl,' said Hydrus in a hoarse whisper. 'The Pearl of Wisdom.'

'Finn smiled. 'Yes, it is.'

'Get back,' yelled the Djinn to the Hundred, who were clustering round to take a look. They hurried back to the cave mouth. Only Drax and Gusting stayed forward.

'Now. Give it to me. Give it to me,' hissed Hydrus

'Patience,' said Finn, 'or I'll smash the bottle and the Pearl with it.'

The Djinn screamed with fury. 'It's mine. I will have it. Give it to me now or I'll kill your mother.'

Finn looked into his eyes, knew he would. He was running out of time. The potion still hadn't kicked in. Hydrus had to fall for the trap. It was their only hope.

Trying to veil his thoughts, Finn took out the stopper and handed the bottle to Hydrus.

The Djinn grabbed it, eyes wide with wonder. He tipped up the bottle and tried to let the Pearl ease out. It would not pass through the neck of the bottle. The Djinn hissed in fury.

'What have you done to it?' he screamed at Finn. 'You have charmed it. It won't come out.'

Finn shrugged. 'I've done nothing,' he lied.

'If I smash the bottle I will smash the Pearl,' muttered the Djinn. 'It is so old, so fragile. I cannot risk it.' He gazed at the bottle, eyes narrow with lust. 'I must have it. I will-' he winced suddenly, as if in pain. He shook himself, as if the pain were a mere inconvenience he could shrug off. Finn watched, heart racing as the Djinn's eyes clouded for a moment. The cure! It seemed to be working. Hydrus started muttering again, and his words became slurred, but Finn heard him say to himself: 'There is only one thing for it.'

Drax, watching, saw what the Djinn was proposing and tried to shout. He struggled to form the words, but his throat would not obey. His jaw seemed to be clenched. He saw the terrible danger, summoned all his will, tried to yell out a warning.

'Iiiit's a traaaaaaaaa-' was all he could say in barely a whisper. His failed cry took all his strength and he found himself fighting desperately for breath. By his side, Gusting tried to move. He too, found his jaw locking, and he struggled for breath. He saw the danger, felt it suddenly in every pore and he forced his failing body forward, arms outstretched. He seemed to move in slow motion.

The ranks of Dark Fighters outside the immediate circle could not see what was going on, could not perceive the terrible danger, could not protect the Djinn from his own yearning, from his drug-induced vulnerability. His brain was beginning to shut down. His warrior's instincts were dulled. His vision was blinded by his passion for the Pearl. That was all he saw, gleaming, luring him on and in. Just to hold it, to possess it and all the wisdom of the Light would be his. He had waited a thousand years for this and he would not be denied.

Finn's eyes were fixed on the Djinn. Hydrus let out a huge, fetid breath and began to shrink. Finn watched his head shrink; the huge, bloated snake-like body emerged from the water as the Djinn became smaller and smaller and smaller until he was just inches long. Then he wriggled into the bottle. In an instant Finn leapt forward and stoppered up the bottle, trapping the Djinn inside.

Finn had trapped Hydrus. The plan had worked! Both plans had worked! He couldn't quite believe it. He looked at his parents and Georgie in amazement as all around them the Dark Fighters fell to the sand.

CHAPTER THIRTY FOUR

ON BONE ISLAND, FRED woke at dawn. He hurried down to the water's edge to check for any signs of Finn. The night before, he had watched Finn disappear into the whirlpool in the sea with a mixture of terror and despair. He should have been with him, whatever Finn had said about guarding the boat, but he was not sure he could have waded into the water and waited for it to suck him down. He shuddered now, hours after Finn had gone, wondering where his friend was, if he had really passed through into another world or if his drowned body was floating around somewhere.

He couldn't see any sign of a body, and he took comfort in that. He would just have to stay here and keep lookout. He headed back to the cave. The hours dragged by. The sun rose high in the sky. Fred drank some water and ate another pot of dried noodles. He was beginning to get sick of them, but there was nothing else to eat, save dried fruit. He wondered how long he would have to wait. Perhaps he should try and catch a fish? But what with? If he could find a stick, sharpen one end on the penknife he had found in the raft's emergency kit then perhaps he could spear one.

He stuck his nose out of the cave, glancing up and down nervously, before heading off down the beach. It was freaking him out, being alone in this place. It wasn't like some dream tropical island with gentle palms waving in the breeze. It was sand, rock and the unrelenting glare of the sun bouncing off the hard blue waves. It had a bad feeling about it, as if evil had been done here and some trace of it remained.

Fred shook himself. *'Come on. Get it together,'* he told himself, wondering what true terrors Finn was encountering at that moment, and if he had found his parents and Georgie.

He headed off down the beach and quickly found a stick he thought might work. He took out his penknife and was sharpening it when he looked up sharply at a sound behind him. He just had time to see the looming body of Dagmar Drax, swinging a plank of wood at his head, when the plank made contact. He felt a sickening thud, then nothing.

When he came to some time later, he found himself lying on the sand with his hands tied together behind his back. He groaned and tried to shift position. The afternoon sun was blazing down on him and he could feel his skin was already burnt. His head throbbed, his mouth was parched and he could hardly see out of his right eye after the blow from Dagmar's plank. He peered around for Dagmar and was rewarded with a kick in the back.

'Who said you could move?' drawled his enemy.

Fred had never truly hated anyone before, but he did now. He truly, totally understood the meaning of hate. And he was terrified. He was completely at Dagmar's mercy and the other boy knew it. Fred decided the best thing was to say nothing.

'Huh, silent treatment. That the best you can do?' demanded Dagmar, but he didn't kick him again so Fred reckoned silence was the best strategy for now. He tried to force his aching head to think. There must be some way out of this. He just had to stay calm and figure it out.

He watched Dagmar checking his watch out of the corner of his eye. He seemed to be mulling over something.

'Right then,' he said decisively. 'Time to go. Get up.'

Fred struggled to his knees. Getting up with your hands tied behind your back was hard and he twice stumbled and fell over before he managed it. Dagmar watched him and laughed. Finally he was up, and he'd done what he intended. Concealed in his hands was a sharp stone he'd managed to grab.

'Just one thing I have to do before we go. Your knife should do the trick,' said Dagmar, with a sickly grin.

Fred tried to keep his breathing even. Dagmar nudged him forward and he walked ahead of him, trying not to imagine the knife in Dagmar's hands. His shoulder-blades twitched.

Dagmar marched him to the dinghy that he and Finn had camouflaged so carefully, Fred had thought.

'You did quite a good job,' Dagmar remarked conversationally. 'But I saw you and your buddy hiding it. I had you covered,' he said smugly.

He swept off the seaweed with a few brisk strokes, then raised the penknife and with grunts of enjoyment he stabbed the dinghy. Over and over he stabbed it, eyes gleaming, smiling as the air hissed out. Then he turned to Fred.

'If by any remote miracle your friend escapes alive from the Dark Kingdom, which I very much doubt since the Djinn is planning to feast on his blood, then he will die on this island. No way off. That's why it's called Bone Island. Full of the bones of the dead.' Dagmar laughed. Fred felt despair twist like a knife in his gut. Finn, Finn, he thought desperately.

'Right, job done. Time for us to leave,' said Dagmar briskly. Fred stared at the ruined boat and refused to move. Dagmar took the penknife and jabbed it at Fred's back, drawing blood. Fred flinched, felt the pain, felt the blood begin to ooze, but all he could think of was Finn arriving back on the island to find it deserted, to find that Fred had gone and the boat had been destroyed.

When Dagmar jabbed him again, he moved. I need just one chance, he thought. Dagmar marched him round to the other side of the island and up to some rocks. Concealed behind them was another boat, a powerful inflatable. Dagmar cleared off the seaweed and began to drag the boat down to towards the sea.

'I can give you a hand if you untie me,' said Fred, watching the other boy struggle.

'You think I'm stupid,' replied Dagmar.

Yes, actually, thought Fred.

With a lot of heaving and cursing, Dagmar got the boat into the water.

'Get in,' he ordered Fred.

'Where are we going?' asked Fred.

'Later.'

Fred refused to move. He was rewarded with another jab of the penkife in his back, harder than the last one. This time he felt the blood gush out.

'Dead or alive, what'll it be?' asked Dagmar.

Fred turned and saw murder in Dagmar's eyes. He got into the boat.

Dagmar pushed the boat out further, let down the engine and cranked the starter. The engine fired up first time and they shot off into the darker water and away from the island.

'So, er, where're we going?' Fred asked again. He sat with his back pressed hard against the side of the boat to stop the bleeding.

Dagmar smiled. 'To see an old friend of yours.'

Fred looked puzzled.

'Mr Violet. Remember him?' taunted Dagmar.

'Of course. He helped us. He trained us. Why would you take me to him?'

'Because he's a Dark Fighter, that's why.'

Fred felt sick. 'No he's not. He's a Light Fighter. One of the best.' Fred refused to believe Dagmar. It was unthinkable that Mr Violet would betray them.

'He *was* a Light Fighter,' corrected Dagmar. 'But the Dark One was clever. He had plans for him. Thought he might come in useful. So, one day when Violet was swimming in the sea, Hydrus metamorphosed into a shark. Bit off half Violet's leg. Drank his blood and ate his bone, left some of his own saliva in Violet's body.' Dagmar looked wistful. 'Once the Djinn has bitten you, you're his. He can see into your mind, and he can control you. Only Hydrus was clever. He didn't control Violet at first. He let him rise up the ranks in the Light Fighter army, until he became a Commander and he was sent to teach you lot. Hydrus let him train you for a bit, then he started to control him and there was not a thing Violet could do about it. Oh he tried, he struggled, but he couldn't change his nature. He couldn't even tell the Light Djinn that he had been forced to change sides. He was, and is, totally under Hydrus's control.' Dagmar grinned. 'Brilliant, huh?'

'So that's why Hydrus let him live?' mused Fred. 'He said to us that he was amazed the shark let him live.'

'He let him live to become his agent when he needed one.'

'But why did Hydrus need him now?' Asked Fred.

'Because he needed your friend Finn to pass through the porthole voluntarily. You can't be forced through. You have to want to get in, or we'd have just kidnapped him and taken him through ourselves. Violet's job was to train and encourage Finn, to make sure he would try to get through. The Dark Djinn had Finn's parents as bait too. Worked a treat.'

'But how did he get Finn's parents there? They couldn't have wanted to pass through either.'

'They didn't, until we told them we'd kill their blessed son if they didn't pass through.'

'And now you're going to kill him anyway,' said Fred, biting back his rage.

'Not me, unfortunately. I'm guarding Bone Island. Hydrus will be the one to kill Finn.' Dagmar glanced at his watch. 'Not long till sundown. Then the full moon will rise, and that will be the end of Finn Kennedy.'

Not if I can help it, thought Fred.

'But why are we going to see Mr Violet anyway?' Fred asked. 'You said you're meant to be standing guard.'

Dagmar smiled. 'I am, and part of that means reporting anything strange. I need to tell him that I saw Finn diving around under water, then the two of you fiddling round with a bottle on a fire. Looked downright suspicious to me.'

'We were cooking fish,' said Fred, thinking quickly. 'Finn dived down for some shellfish, then we cooked them.'

Dagmar eyed him suspiciously. 'Maybe. Maybe you were making some kind of weapon to use against Hydrus. Mr Violet will decide. He can Look into your mind and find out the truth, and then he can communicate that to Hydrus.'

'The truth is that we were hungry and ate some fish,' repeated Fred, desperate now to find a way to stop Dagmar ever getting near Mr Violet. He knew he couldn't block his thoughts from Mr Violet, and if Mr Violet saw what he and Finn had done, then Finn's only hope of vanquishing the Djinn would be destroyed, and Finn, Georgie and Finn's parents would all be killed.

The boat sped on, leaving the island miles behind. Fred tried to memorise their route, in case he somehow managed to get control of the boat and return this way, but it was impossible. There were no landmarks.

Fred began to fidget. 'Can't you untie me?' he pleaded with Dagmar. 'It is so uncomfortable like this, and I'm not exactly going to jump overboard and swim off, am I? Nor could I possibly be any threat to you,' he added.

Dagmar gave a grunt of laughter. 'No, you couldn't possibly be a threat to me, you pathetic wimp. But tough. You stay tied up.'

Fred groaned silently. He would have to come up with a better plan that that.

Around them the sea was becalmed, as if listening and waiting. Clouds blew in and the sky changed to a sinister luminous grey tinged with an almost nuclear orange glow cast by the setting sun. As the darkness crept around them, the full moon rose. Almost as if they had been waiting, the waves grew choppier and the boat pitched and tossed.

The waves grew bigger still, and with nothing to hold onto and unable to brace himself, Fred repeatedly crashed around in the boat. He waited for the boat to bounce over a particularly big wave, then crashed apparently accidentally into Dagmar.

'Ow!' yelled Dagmar, rubbing his shin where Fred's knee had rammed it.

'Gosh, sorry,' apologised Fred.

'You idiot,' shouted Dagmar.

'I can't help it,' said Fred. 'The sea's so rough.'

Dagmar turned to study him. He saw a miserable, exhausted-looking boy with severe sunburn, blood still oozing down his back from the penknife jabs, a scrape above one eye from where he had crashed into the side of the boat and severe bruising on the other eye from the plank-blow.

He got out the penknife and advanced on him. He grabbed Fred and turned him around. With a quick flick, the penknife cut through the rope and Fred was free. Fred kept the elation from his eyes and concentrated on continuing to look miserable. It wasn't too hard.

'Don't try anything,' warned Dagmar.

Fred nodded weakly.

Just then the engine gave a spluttery cough and Dagmar turned to take a look at it. Fred watched him lean over the edge of the boat. He didn't give himself a chance to think, he just lunged at Dagmar with all his might, ramming his two hands into his back, sending him straight over the side.

Dagmar flailed in the water, screamed with rage and reached out for the boat but it was already out of range. Fred grabbed the tiller and steered it further away.

'Help me,' shouted Dagmar.

Fred just kept steering the boat away.

'You can't just leave me here, abandon me. I'll drown,' screamed Dagmar. 'I'll die.'

'Maybe one of your Dark Fighters will come,' shouted Fred. Just as he had spoken the words, he saw movement beneath the waves, then the water erupted and a dolphin leapt into the air then arched gracefully back into the sea. Fred watched it. It seemed to be heading directly for Dagmar.

Fred had thought the dolphins were all Light Fighters, but now it looked like Dagmar was going to be saved. Perhaps the dolphin would let him grab its fin and race back to the boat with him, or take him back to the island where Dagmar would lie in wait for Fred to return. Fred had to get the boat back to Bone Island, but he knew he could not take on Dagmar in a hand to hand fight and win.

Delphine screamed through the water, picking up speed. She aimed at the boy; the murderer who had harpooned her mate, Dauphin. She had been there and watched her mate bleed to death in the sea, and she had sworn her revenge. She had followed the boy ever since, watching, waiting for her chance. Just ten feet away now. She gathered all her strength, leapt from the water, looked into the boy's eyes, and then she rammed her snout full into the boy's face. Delphine hardly felt a thing. The boy was dead on impact.

Fred watched as the dolphin swam away, leaving Dagmar's body lying face down on the waves.

CHAPTER THIRTY FIVE

GEORGIE WATCHED FINN TRAP the Dark Djinn in the bottle. She watched the Dark Fighters fall. But she knew it wasn't the end. While Finn and his parents embraced, she slipped away. She knew they wouldn't help her search for her father. They were convinced he was dead. But she wasn't. She would not give up, even if she had to hunt for him on her own. This was her last and only chance and she was not going to let anyone stop her, not even Finn and his parents.

She stepped nimbly over the bodies of the Dark Fighters. They could be dead or just unconscious. She didn't know and she didn't care, apart from the danger of their waking and capturing her if they weren't dead. She rounded the far side of the Dark Djinn's cave, getting out of sight. She reckoned she had perhaps a minute before Finn and his parents noticed she was gone and came looking for her. She could only hope they would head down the coast in the other direction, and give her more time.

She hurried up the rough hill in the direction her uncle had pointed when he told her that her father had been led away. There was no grass and the grey stones were crumbling from the rock. She stumbled a few times, cutting her shins, but she didn't notice. She rushed on as fast as she could go.

Soon her breathing was ragged. The antidote had neutralised the poison, but not before the poison had already done some damage. She could still feel the vomit swirling around her stomach, but she refused to stop. She had just this one chance.

She got to the top of the hill and looked down. A rough valley stretched out before her. On the hill that sloped down towards it, there were a number of tin shacks and what looked like a rudimentary mine. Her pulse quickened. Perhaps there was a well there, or a mine shaft, maybe they meant a mine shaft. She hurried down, falling repeatedly in her haste and lacerating her legs.

Five minutes later, she got to the mine. It was not a shaft, but a cave dug into the hillside. It was boarded up, but badly. The boards hung loose. Georgie hauled at them, ripping several out to make a space big enough to squeeze through. Inside it was pitch dark. She got down on her hands and knees and inched forward. If she weren't careful, she would end up falling down a mine shaft herself. She fluttered her hands over the rough ground before her. Her heart lurched when her fingers found nothing but space. Here was the shaft. She stopped and abandoning caution, called out:

'Daddy, Daddy, are you there?'

Her words echoed back and reverberated around the walls, like a hundred daughters calling their lost fathers. She waited, but when the echoes abated, there was nothing, no answering call. She tried again and again, until her head felt as if it were going to explode with all the echoes. He's not here, she thought. He must be somewhere else, in a well, *not* a mine.

She inched back out of the darkness onto the hillside. Clustered around the mine was a group of shacks. She threw open the doors and peered into the gloom. Nothing. She searched each one, and each one was empty. Back outside she slumped against the door for a moment. She would not give up. She would simply go on searching until she found her father. She hurried on down to the valley. The night was dark but the full moon cast a silvery pall.

She walked past cairns of stones that seemed to mark graves. She passed by, face set, not allowing herself to wonder who was buried there. Where was the well? *Where* was it? She walked on through the dark night. Clouds scudded over the dirty moon, erasing what little light there was. No stars twinkled here. Without the moonlight, she might walk within yards of a well and not see it.

Suddenly she tripped in the darkness, went flying and landed on her chest. She lay there, winded, struggling for breath. Then she began to vomit up the poison and her fear and her dashed hopes. Everything bad inside her seemed to be coming up. She struggled to her knees, retching. Finally, the spasms subsided and she slowly pushed herself upright. She needed water, God, she needed water. She pushed her hair from her face and as she struggled to her feet the clouds blew away from the moon, and there, perhaps twenty feet in front of her, loomed the dark shape of a well.

Could it be? Could it be? She hardly dared hope. She ran towards it, slumped down against it.

'*Please*,' she said out loud, '*please* let him be here, let him be alive.'

'Hello?' came a feeble voice. 'Who's there?'

Spasms ran up and down her arms. Could it be? Could it really be her father? She hardly dared say the word. She leaned over the side and called softly down. 'Daddy?' and the voice came back up,

'Georgie? Georgina? Is that you?'

She laughed and sobbed with joy, the tears steamed down her face like a torrent. 'Daddy, it *is* me! I'm here to get you out.'

There was a winch, but instead of a bucket, there was a big basket.

She let down the basket; felt the tautness on the rope as her father climbed in. She braced her feet against the side of the well, leaned back and hauled with all her strength. The basket hardly moved. It was all she could do to hold his weight. She tried to crank the winch but it just moved a few inches, then the strain of holding him was too great and the basket swung back down inside the well. Georgie slumped back against the walls of the well for a moment. She tried to think. She could go back and get Finn and his parents. They could easily pull her father out, but what if the Dark Fighters had come round? She would never get back here. And she knew too, she could not leave her father, not now that she'd found him. She would just somehow have to pull him out. She got up and leaned over the edge.

'Daddy, you're going to have to grab the sides, take some of your weight.'

'O.K. Let's give it a go.'

Georgie braced herself again and began to crank. This time it was a bit easier. The wheel turned, inch by inch. She hauled on the winch, coiled in more rope. She wondered how deep the well was. Her arms and shoulders began to burn. Still she cranked the winch. Her muscles felt like they were on fire. Every sinew screamed for her to let go, but with every ounce of will she clung on, turning the winch. Another foot, then another. The pain was almost unbearable, but still she turned. Sweat burned her eyes and made her hands slippery. No, please no, she thought. Do not let go.

'Daddy,' she yelled. 'I'm not sure how much longer I can hold this. Can you climb onto the walls? Grip onto something.'

'I'll try. Just get me a bit higher. I think I can see a ledge.'

The sweat slicked her hands. Georgie gripped tighter till the rope dug grooves into her skin. She pulled him up one more foot, then another. The rope was cutting the skin from her hands. She tried to grip tighter, but the rope began to slip.

'Daddy, it's going!' she screamed, 'Climb onto the wall. Grip on. Now, do it!'

Her flesh gave up. The rope ripped away from her grip and the winch unwound madly.

'Daddy!' she screamed.

'I'm on the wall,' he said, voice weak. 'I'll try to climb up.'

Georgie hung over the edge, straining to see in the darkness. She wondered how long he could hang on, how long he had been down in this prison, how weak he was. Then she could see the top of his head, inching upwards. His arms were shaking, but up he came, painstakingly slowly, until she could almost touch his fingers. Up came his hand and gripped onto hers. She braced herself. Up came the other hand, gripped the top of the well and then with a lunge, his leg. He got his leg up, and over, then he slipped over the edge and onto the ground. Georgie threw herself on him. Her father held her so tight she could feel his heart pounding through his ribs like hers.

❧ Chapter Thirty Six ❧

FINN AND HIS PARENTS searched frantically for Georgie.

'Did someone take her?' asked Vick. 'I didn't see anyone, did you?' she repeatedly asked Finn and his father.

Both shook their heads. 'All the Dark Fighters drank the potion. And fell,' said Will.

'Maybe one didn't,' Vick said. 'God, I'll never forgive myself.'

'We'll just go on searching,' said Will. 'We'll find her.'

'What'll we do with him?' Finn asked, pointing to the bottle containing the Dark Djinn.

'Take him with us, in your backpack,' replied his father.

'Should we kill him?' asked Finn.

His father shook his head. 'He's the perfect hostage. We'll keep him alive. He might be useful.'

Finn didn't like the idea of having a Dark Djinn on his back, however small and drugged he might be, but he knew his father was right, so he carefully placed the bottle containing the Djinn in his backpack, tightened the straps and eased it gently onto his back.

'How long have we got?' asked Finn.

His father glanced at his watch. 'Two hours till midnight, till we can pass back through the porthole.'

Finn knew what he was thinking: *I hope the potion lasts that long.*

'Let's go and get Georgie,' he said.

Finn gathered up several small, sharp rocks. He gave one each to his parents and pocketed a couple himself. If he came face to face with a Dark Fighter he wanted to have some kind of weapon. Hurriedly, they searched along the beach. They searched on the mountainside, on either side of the Djinn's cave. They climbed to the top of the hillside and gazed down the other side. The moon was covered by thick clouds now and they saw nothing.

'Maybe she got disorientated and went deeper into the cave,' suggested Vick.

'Possibly,' replied Will. 'Let's go look.'

Together they ran back down the hillside and searched the cave.

There was no sign of Georgie.

The minutes seemed to race by now.

'What's the time?' Finn asked his father.

'Eleven forty five.'

'Oh, no,' came his mother's voice. 'Look, they're beginning to stir.' Finn looked to the heaps of bodies lying on the beach. Some of them were tossing and turning, as if trying to drag themselves from their drug-fuelled stupor.

Georgie, Georgie, Finn felt like screaming. *Where are you?*

CHAPTER THIRTY SEVEN

FRED TURNED THE BOAT around and headed back in the direction he and Dagmar had come from. After about ten minutes, he wasn't sure if he was going in a straight line. The movement of the waves made it impossible to hold the tiller on a rigid course. How was he going to get back to Bone Island? He didn't have time to try the hit and miss approach. If he were going to be there by the time Finn came back through the porthole, he had to find it first time.

He almost jumped out of his skin at a loud splash just alongside the boat. He peered over the side, but saw nothing. Then a dolphin leapt out of the water and disappeared back under the sea again. It was the same one that had killed Dagmar, he was sure of it. There it was again, leaping out of the sea just off to the right. Fred smiled. It was a beautiful sight, and he owed the dolphin, big time. He kept his hand on the tiller, craning his neck to watch the creature cavorting in the water. Then it came back, swam right towards him.

Oh God. Perhaps it had come to capsize the boat, thought Fred. Perhaps it's no friend at all. The dolphin got closer, leaping from the water just feet from the boat.

It didn't make any attempt to capsize the boat, but it did seem angry. Its tail lashed the air and the splashes were like slaps against the sea. Fred watched it, puzzled, until an idea finally broke through.

'You want me to follow you?' he asked, 'Is that it? You want me to follow you?' he yelled above the roar of the motor.

In answer, the dolphin shot off to the right and kept up a course, leaping and diving, ahead of him. Fred followed. Every so often, the dolphin would pause, look round as if to check he was still following, then it would take off again. They kept their course, minute by minute. Fred checked his watch. Quarter to twelve. He groaned. Fifteen minutes to get to Bone Island and the light of the full moon showed nothing but endless sea.

❦ Chapter Thirty Eight ❧

G EORGIE AND HER FATHER struggled up the side of the mountain. They fell repeatedly in the darkness on the rough ground. Georgie could see the lacerations on her father's pale skin. He was so pale, like a ghost, and so thin.

'How long have you been in there?' she asked.

'A month,' he answered. 'I kept trying to escape. I got out of most of the places they rigged for me, so they decided to finish me off, threw me down the well. What they didn't know was that there was enough water at the bottom to cushion my fall. I went in feet first, thank God, so I survived the fall.'

Georgie blew out a breath. She couldn't imagine how awful it must have been, trapped in that dark, dank hole.

'How did you survive for a month?' she asked. 'What did you eat and drink?'

'I could drink the water. It wasn't exactly pleasant tasting, but it did the trick, and also what Drax and his mate Gusting didn't know was that there was a side passage just above the water line. It was about twenty feet long. I could lie there, and sleep. There were mushrooms growing, and a kind of sea grass. I ate that, and some slugs, and there were a couple of birds' nests just above me too. I kept pinching the eggs and the birds just kept on laying, so I had two or three eggs a day. Every day I tried to escape, but the walls at the bottom of the well are like marble. No handholds, nothing. Just the one small ledge where the birds nested and nothing besides that.'

'Well, you did escape, and now we have to get off the island. Finn and his parents are down on the beach. We'll catch up with them, then all of us will go through the porthole.' If they made it in time, she thought, glancing at her watch. Only fifteen minutes left to get to the top of the mountain and down the other side. They'd never make it at this rate.

'What about the Dark Fighters?' asked her father.

'Uncle Will and Aunt Vick made a potion. They all drank it. Finn got the Djinn to shrink himself and crawl into a bottle and-'

Her father startled her by laughing. 'Aah, that really is something to cheer a man up. Trapping the Djinn in a bottle. Let him befriend claustrophobia.' He laughed again and his pace quickened.

They got to the top. Georgie checked her watch. Seven minutes to twelve.

'Daddy, we have to run now, really run.'

He stretched out his hand. 'Here, hold on to me.'

She gripped his hand and together they hurled themselves desperately down the mountain, towards an escape which ticked away from them with every second.

CHAPTER THIRTY NINE

'What's that noise?' Finn asked. 'Listen!'

His parents paused. 'On the mountain, look,' cried his mother. 'Someone running.'

'Sounds like an army running.' Will strained to see in the dark. 'Reinforcements. The Dark Fighters are coming.' Will fell to his knees. 'Get down you two.'

Finn and his mother crouched down.

'No, wait,' said Finn, jumping up again.

'It's Georgie and Uncle Johnny. He's alive! She found him!'

Finn wanted to yell and scream with joy, and then he wanted to yell at them to run faster, faster, time was running out.

'He's alive!' Tears streamed down Vick's cheeks and she and Will and Finn started to run towards her brother and Georgie. They all groaned when they saw father and daughter take a tumble. It seemed to take them ages to get up and start running again, but then they hit the plain and Finn and his parents reached them.

'You're alive, you're alive, thank God,' cried Vick. 'Oh Georgie, you *found* him!'

There was no time to stop, to embrace, they just had to keep going.

'Two minutes,' said Will. They all grabbed hands and ran. They left the hard ground of the plain and hit the soft sand.

They could see the bodies of the Dark Fighters strewn over the sand. Some of them, perhaps the greediest ones, were clearly dead. Foam and vomit lay pooled around their mouths and their open eyes stared unseeing at the night. Others were in varying states of unconsciousness. From some there were groans and thrashing limbs as the poison wore off. Finn and his parents had to dodge and jump over them.

Suddenly Finn went flying. One of the Dark Fighters had woken up and grabbed his ankle. Finn saw with horror that it was Mr Drax. Finn felt a moment of paralysed terror as he looked into the other man's eyes, which blazed with hatred. Drax began to pull Finn closer to him. Finn reached for his sharp stone and stabbed Drax's hand with all his might. The man screamed out a curse into the night and let go, but his screaming woke others. All around them, the Dark Fighters began to stir. Some, including Drax, were pushing themselves groggily to their feet.

Will handed off two and they had to dodge others. The seconds roared by, time wasted dodging. The soft sand of the beach felt like treacle, sucking at their feet, slowing them down even more.

'Thirty seconds,' rasped Will. 'Get in the water. Swim.'

Some of the Dark Fighters were stumbling after them now. They could hear their breaths and curses, but there was no time to turn, no time to stop and defend themselves, they just had to go on.

They plunged into the sea. Georgie felt as if all her strength was gone, but the water was like a slap in the face and she kicked out wildly. Finn grabbed her hand and pulled her. Finn's mother grabbed her other hand. Will pulled Johnny along, lashing his arms through the water.

They saw the whirlpool forming, ten feet ahead. They all lunged for it. Georgie's hand slipped from Finn's at the last moment, but he turned and grabbed her, then kicked out with all his strength and dug his arms into the water. His mother did the same and together they pulled her into the circle. They all joined hands. Around them the water bubbled and swirled and accelerated into the vortex.

'Take a huge breath,' Will managed to yell, and then they were all sucked under.

Georgie felt the water like bands of steel around her chest. She had only managed a small breath and soon she felt that running out. As the seconds passed and they barrelled up through the enormous weight of water, she saw colours in her head, like fireworks exploding, and then she began to feel dizzy. It wasn't all bad, apart from the pain in her chest. Bit like just drifting off to sleep.... sleep, so nice, just to rest a bit, even her thoughts seemed to go to sleep. She could see them sliding away, everything was sliding away........ aaah, something was pinching her. She opened her eyes and looked into Finn's. He looked desperate, pleading, and pinched her again. Just leave me alone, she wanted to say, just let me go, drift off, but then someone else pinched her. Her father. FATHER. The voice in her head said, *hang on, just hang on, you will not drown here*, and then she felt a sensation like being shot out of a rocket and the next thing she knew, they had all exploded up and out of the water.

Air, air, breathe. Air, it had never tasted sweeter. Georgie took breath after hungry breath and then she began to laugh. 'We made it, we made it,' she managed to say, tears of laughter and release teeming down her cheeks. The water bubbling around them subsided and calmed.

'And no-one else made it through,' said Will. 'The potion lasted just long enough.'

'Thank you kraken,' said Vick.

They all kicked out for the shore, then collapsed with relief on the sand.

Finn took a brief rest then pushed himself up.

'Fred should be here somewhere, with the boat. There's a cave just over there,' Finn pointed it out to his father.

'Let's go,' said Will.

'Fred'll probably be there, fast asleep,' said Finn. The first whispers of doubt began to creep into his mind. He had expected Fred to be there, on the beach, waiting.

The cave was empty. There was no sign of Fred.

'I'll just go and check the boat,' said Finn, trying to keep the fear from his voice.

He headed down the beach to the pile of rocks where they had hidden the boat. Finn could see the seaweed strewn around. Then he saw the boat cut to ribbons.

He sunk down onto the sand in despair. *Oh Fred, Fred. What's happened to you?* He didn't want to go back to the others, tell them his friend was most likely dead and that their only means of escape from the island was shredded. Wearily, he got to his feet. He had no choice.

He started to head back up to the cave when a faint sound drifted across the sea to him. He stopped, straining his ears to hear. They were still ringing with the after effects of going through the porthole, and for a moment he thought his ears were playing tricks on him, but then the sound came again, stronger. A boat, with a high powered engine.

He ran back to the cave.

'Fred's not here. Boat's shredded, but someone's coming from the sea,' he said. They sank back into the shadows and waited.

CHAPTER FORTY

FRED CHECKED HIS WATCH. Ten minutes past twelve. 'Please God, let them have made it, please, please let me see them again,' he prayed out loud. He approached the island at speed then eased back the throttle and coasted in close to shore. He didn't want to leave the boat, he had no idea what would be waiting for him, but he could see no sign of Finn.

He had no choice, he thought, but to call out. If there were any Dark Fighters there, they would already have heard him arrive. A power boat was not exactly discreet.

'Finn,' he called out urgently, 'Finn, are you there?'

Fred watched as dark shadows emerged from the cave. Then a cloud shrouded the moon and he could see nothing, save the rough outline of shapes moving. There seemed to be an awful lot of them. He kept his hand on the tiller, ready to swing the boat round and accelerate away. His heart pounded as the shapes drew closer, hope mixing with fear. Then the moon emerged from the clouds and lit up Finn's beaming face.

'You made it!' yelled Fred, punching the air. 'You made it. It's awesome, it's fantastic!' Fred felt himself bubbling over with joy.

'It's a flipping miracle, mate,' said Finn, grinning ear to ear. 'And you made it too,' he added, taking in his friend's battered face with its cut and black eye. But he was alive. Fred was alive.

Finn felt dizzy with a mixture of worry and happiness. 'What took you so long?' he joked

Fred let out a peal of laughter.

'Glad to see you haven't lost your sense of humour,' he replied, then his face turned sombre. 'C'mon, everyone get in.'

Vick leapt up and pulled herself in so she could help haul in the others. Will stayed in the sea, heaving everyone up and into the boat. Then he took one last look at Bone Island, and jumped in himself.

Inside the boat there was much embracing and laughing. Georgie grabbed Fred in a bear hug. She released him and said, her voice tremulous:

'Fred, I'd like to introduce you to my father.'

A thin, white-faced man with a shock of unruly red hair and a grave smile came forward.

Georgie gazed up adoringly into his eyes.

'Daddy, this is Fred.'

Fred shook hands with Georgie's father.

For a moment, emotion threatened to silence him, but then he remembered his manners.

'Pleased to meet you,' he said.

Georgie's father smiled. 'I can't begin to tell you how pleased I am to meet *you*, Fred,' he replied.

Then Finn came forward. 'Fred, I'd like to introduce you to my parents.'

Will shook Fred warmly by the hand. Vick couldn't contain herself. She grabbed Fred in a huge hug and squeezed him tight. Fred grinned, shy but delighted. He couldn't quite believe that they were all there, together.

'How'd you get the black eye?' Finn asked Fred when his mother had finally released Fred.

'Later. I think we need to get out of here,' Fred said decisively, 'and first I want to hear exactly what happened and how you escaped from the Dark Djinn.'

Finn chuckled. 'We haven't quite escaped from him.'

'Whaddayou mean?' asked Fred nervously.

Finn took off his backpack and slowly and carefully pulled out the bottle containing the shrunken Djinn. Holding it tightly with both hands, he stretched it out to show Fred.

Fred looked down at the bottle where a slimy looking snake-man was writhing in what looked like sheer fury.

'It worked,' yelled Fred elated. 'Your plan worked.'

'Plan A and Plan B,' replied Finn.

'He looks disgusting,' said Fred.

'You should have seen him full size,' said Finn. 'Terrifying.'

Fred rubbed his eyes in amazement as if they were still deceiving him.

'Right. I want to hear everything. Plan A, Plan B. The lot.'

Finn carefully put the bottle containing the Dark Djinn back into his backpack.

'Er, sorry to interrupt,' said Vick, but where are we going now?'

'Home,' said Fred. 'Back to Dubai.'

'How?' she asked. 'There are no maps, no charts for where we are.'

Fred smiled and gestured at the water.

'We have something better than charts. We have our own personal guide.'

As if to introduce herself, Delphine leapt gracefully from the water, cast her friendly eyes over all of them, and plunged back into the sea. Then with a swish of her tail, she was off, leaping from the water in front of them to guide them, but, just as much to show them how joyful she was that they had escaped, that they had captured that thing in the bottle.

'Cool,' replied Finn, admiring the display. 'How did you get yourself a guide, and, er, not to mention, a new boat?'

Fred began to tell them about Dagmar and Mr Violet. Finn and Georgie could hardly believe that Mr Violet had changed sides.

'Dagmar said Mr Violet hadn't wanted to, but that Hydrus controlled him, because of the bite,' explained Fred.

'How awful,' said Georgie, overwhelmed with pity.

Finn thought of his friend, and what he had been forced to become and he felt like smashing the bottle and the Dark Djinn with it. But perhaps Hydrus would be freed by that. Finn didn't know. He would give the bottle to Triton and let him decide what to do.

'Did Dagmar give you that black eye?' asked Georgie.

Fred nodded.

'What I'd give to get my hands on him,' muttered Finn.

'Don't worry about him. He won't bother anyone again,' said Fred.

'Why? What happened?' demanded Georgie. 'You make it sound like he's dead. Did you kill him?'

'Not exactly. That dolphin did.'

Fred told them what had happened.

'We'd never have got off Bone Island if it weren't for you, Fred,' said Finn, looking awestruck by what Fred had done.

Georgie gave Fred a huge hug. 'You saved our lives,' she said. Her father and Finn's parents nodded.

Fred looked embarrassed.

'What're friends for?' he asked with a grin, and they all laughed with joy.

☙ Chapter Forty One ☙

THE TWINS HEARD IT first, the pre-dawn ringing of the doorbell. They pushed themselves bleary-eyed from bed.

'Better get Mummy,' said Cordelia, looking scared.

They met her in the hallway. She had been woken too.

'Who is it?' asked Cressida.

Camelia shook her head. 'No idea, but they sound determined,' she added, as the door bell rang again.

Her heart was thudding against her chest. Ever since Georgie and Finn had gone missing, she feared the ring of the bell, telling her it was over, that bodies had been found. *Stop it*, she said silently to herself. *Just hold it together.*

'Come on girls,' she said, taking each by the hand. She somehow felt they all had to go together. They opened the door to the cool night. No birds sang, there was no sound save the dreadful ringing of the bell. The three of them walked towards the garden gate.

Her nerve failed. 'Who is it?' she called out.

'It's us,' yelled Georgie. 'Open up, Mummy. It's us!'

Camelia ran for the gate, unlocked it and threw it open. She took in her missing daughter, her missing husband, then Finn, her sister, her brother-in-law, and a happy-looking boy with dark tousled hair, a cut face and a black eye. She held out her arms and Georgie fell into them. Then her husband came forward, and the twins screamed with joy and launched themselves at Georgie and their father and the five of them just held onto each other, laughing and crying. Camelia pulled herself away and grabbed hold of Finn and his parents.

'Everyone's home,' she said, quietly as if she didn't dare believe it.

'And we have an extra member of the family too, I see,' she added, looking at Fred.

Fred grinned. 'I'm Fred,' he said, shaking her hand. 'Pleased to meet you.'

'And I am pleased to meet you, Fred,' replied Camelia, pressing a gentle kiss on his cheek.

With tears of joy glistening in her eyes Camelia led them all inside.

'Right, now for the biggest breakfast in history,' said Georgie, envisaging a mountain of pancakes.

'Sit down,' said her mother. 'I think it's about time I cooked something for you, don't you?' Then her eyes went to her husband. 'And for you my love.'

Johnny came over and gripped Camellia's hand tight.

'They all said you'd just run off, abandoned us,' she told him. 'I never believed it for a second.'

'It nearly broke me,' he replied, 'being away from you. Knowing people would say that to you.'

'But you didn't break. You're here now, and you can tell the twins and me what happened.'

They ate and they talked and then, exhausted, they all fell into bed. They had agreed that they'd take Fred home to his parents after he'd had a sleep. He didn't want to leave his friends yet, and he wasn't sure if he was ready to face his parents, exhausted as he was.

Finn watched Fred sleeping. The whole house was sleeping, apart from him. He couldn't stand having that thing in the house, writhing in its bottle. Mind made up, he shouldered his rucksack, grabbed a chocolate chip cookie and slipped out into the garden just as the first rays of dawn were brightening the sky.

CHAPTER FORTY TWO

FINN HEADED THROUGH THE empty streets. The occasional car whizzed by. He felt as if he was being scrutinised, a young boy, alone so early in the morning. He ran the last few streets to the beach, and was relieved when he saw the beach was deserted. In his head, he called to Triton. *Come please, I need you. Triton, please come.*

He walked to the water's edge, sat down and waited. He placed his rucksack beside him, but kept the Djinn inside. The water was calm, the waves unfurled in little ripples along the sand. There was just the softest of breezes stirring his hair.

He kept willing the good Djinn to appear, studying the waves, searching for his form. Then suddenly, the air beside him shuddered with a hidden energy, and Mr Violet appeared.

'Mr Violet!' exclaimed Finn, jumping violently. 'What are you doing here?'

Mr Violet smiled. The smile cut deep grooves in a face that looked as if it had aged ten years in a matter of days. The deep blue eyes were haunted and there was a flicker of something alien in them. Finn felt pity and a terrible sense of loss for what Mr Violet had been; a friend and a mentor who had given him the idea of how to trap Hydrus and some of the tools with which to do it, both physical and mental.

'Came by astral travel, of course,' replied Mr Violet, jolting Finn out of his reverie. 'Triton sent me. He's on his way, bit delayed. Well done Finn,' he said, his voice rich with warmth. 'You did it! You should be proud.'

Finn muttered an acknowledgement.

'So, would you like to hand him over to me? I can see you don't like having him so near. Neither would I,' Mr Violet continued when Finn said nothing, 'but duty calls and all that.'

Finn got to his feet, picked up his rucksack and began to walk off down the beach.

'Finn, Finn, don't be like that,' crooned Mr Violet. 'The others been telling you nonsense, have they, silly stuff about me? You know better than to believe them. Who helped you? Who taught you? Who sent you on your way?'

Finn paused, then wheeled round to face him.

'You, of course.'

'Yes, that's right. I did be-'

Finn cut him off. 'Because Hydrus wanted me. They couldn't kidnap me, could they, the Dark Fighters? Couldn't force me through the porthole, so your job was to persuade me to go through so that I could be sacrificed there to Hydrus, so that he might heal himself with my blood.

Mr Violet's face contorted with what looked like agony. He struggled for words.

'I did what I had to do. I had no choice. Finn, I tried, oh how I tried, but he's inside me. He controls me. Now come on, please hand him over. Let's not make this any more difficult than it needs to be.'

Finn looked at his former friend standing before him, ruined. He felt another terrible flash of pity, then he hardened his heart,

'Never. You'll just free him.'

Mr Violet doubled over. 'Freedom, freedom,' he wailed in a voice that wasn't his own. 'He just wants freedom.'

Suddenly Mr Violet began to retch, vomiting up bile. When he had finished, he straightened up and Finn saw Hydrus in the hatred blazing from his eyes.

'Hand him over,' he hissed.

Finn shook his head. 'I will never hand him over,' he repeated.

Mr Violet doubled up in agony again. Smoke poured from his body. Finn coughed violently as the acrid stench burnt his throat. The smoke billowed and cleared and revealed a hideous sight. The lower part of Mr Violet's body had become a serpent, just like the Dark Djinn.

The serpent writhed and hissed. 'You are just a foolish boy who knows nothing of the Light and the Dark, of compromise and statesmanship, of strategy and war. You too could have my power. You too could straddle the worlds of Light and Dark, as I do. My very name is of the twilight. I have Light and Dark in me and the power of each.'

'You can't be both,' said Finn, moving away. 'You've been forced into Darkness, you have lost the Light.'

The snake hissed as if branded by the word. 'Soooooo be it.' It writhed and slithered round with alarming speed so that it lay between Finn and the beach. Then it moved towards Finn, forcing him into the sea.

'Hand him over, then you can go. I don't need to hurt you.'

'No,' shouted Finn, desperately trying to think of a way out of this.

Triton, he called in his mind. *Triton I need you. Now.*

'Then I will drown you and take him and then I will free him,' hissed Mr Violet.

He moved closer, backing Finn deeper into the sea. The water lapped at Finn's backpack and the waves began to grow rougher. Finn struggled to stay on his feet. His heart raced as terror pulsed through his body. Then he saw movement on the beach. He tried not to show it in his eyes as he watched Georgie and Fred moving stealthily closer. He saw them stop by a rowing boat where a big fishing net lay drying. He watched them pick it up and approach.

A wave broke behind Finn, throwing him off his feet. Finn began to feel a sick dread. To have come so far, won so much, only to lose now. It was unbearable. Mr Violet laughed.

'Come on Finn, boy. You're wasting time. He's in his element now. Your backpack's wet. He'll be commanding the waves to rear up and engulf you. Better give him to me now.' He reached out a hand towards Finn, who lurched backwards, out of reach, just as Georgie and Fred flung the fishing net in the air, up and onto Mr Violet. He let out a scream as the weights fell into the sea, trapping him in the net.

'Boy am I glad to see you two,' said Finn. He grabbed a weight and swung it round Mr Violet's body, encasing him more tightly in the net. The man writhed and lashed, screaming his curses at the sky. The three children struggled to hold the net. Then, in the water, another shape appeared. With a great splashing rainbow of water it emerged from the waves.

'Triton,' yelled Finn.

Mr Violet fell silent and stopped thrashing. The three children towed him onto the sand and knotted the nets around the end of his tail so he was completely trussed up. Finn couldn't bear to look at him.

'Thought you could do it all without us, did you?' said Georgie angrily to Finn.

'Sorry,' said Finn to her and Fred. 'I should have known better.'

'You're a pretty good team,' said Triton, smiling at them. 'You couldn't have done any better than you did. It is a miracle you got out, all of you.'

'Still doesn't seem real,' said Finn.

'What's real?' asked Triton with a chuckle.

'Nothing and everything,' said Fred.

'Pretty much. Now, would you like to lighten your load a bit?' the Djinn asked Finn.

'Would I ever!' Finn took off his rucksack and pulled out the bottle. He took one last look at the writhing creature that had haunted both his nightmares and his waking hours and handed him over. The Djinn held the bottle in one huge hand. He turned his mesmeric eyes on his ancient adversary who writhed and spat in impotent rage.

'Hello Hydrus,' said Triton, in a voice as cold as pity.

Hydrus fell still, as if frozen. Triton raised his arms and the bottle up to the sun. He stayed like that for a while, unmoving, and then he lowered his hands and turned his gaze back upon Finn, Georgie and Fred.

'What will you do with him?' Finn asked.

'Keep him in his bottle. Lock him in a cave somewhere,' answered Triton.

'You can't kill him?' asked Fred.

Sadly, the Djinn shook his head. 'You can't kill evil, merely contain it. If I killed him, someone else would spring up in his place. Better to have a weakened, imprisoned Djinn of the Night than a vibrant one.'

'And him?' asked Finn, darting a glance at Mr Violet.

The Light Djinn's eyes filled with compassion. 'My old, dear friend, Ulysses. Why didn't you tell me?' he asked.

Mr Violet squirmed and moaned. He would not look at Triton and it seemed to Finn that his eyes were full of shame.

After what seemed like an enormous struggle, he spoke. In his eyes Finn saw again the vestige of the old Mr Violet he had known. The spark of humour, the intelligence, the wisdom, and the sadness. Finally, Finn understood the sorrow that had always haunted Mr Violet's eyes.

'I tried, many times I tried, but the words would not come. You could have done nothing for me, Triton. Once I was bitten by him, I was his. The only cure is death. We both know that.'

'Is that what you want?' asked Triton, with infinite sadness.

Mr Violet bowed his head. 'It is.'

'As you will. But not here, not now.'

Triton turned his head and called out to the sea. Two dolphins emerged.

'It's my friend,' yelled Fred. 'My guide.'

'Delphine,' said the Light Djinn. 'You did her a favour.'

'And she me. Us,' replied Fred. He rushed into the water, stroked the dolphin's gleaming body. The dolphin lowered her head and seemed to nuzzle him. Fred smiled with pure joy.

'Take him to the Cave of Light,' said Triton, pointing to Mr Violet. 'Be gentle.' The dolphins bowed in the water. Delphine and the other dolphin took hold of the net in their mouths and swam off into the sea, dragging Mr Violet with them.

Georgie watched them go, tears coursing down her cheeks.

'I liked him' she said simply. 'I really liked him.'

'I loved him as a brother,' replied the Light Djinn. 'And now I must respect his wishes while he is still able to express what he truly feels. With each day that passes, he will become more like his master, and for the man that Mr Violet once was, that would be torture. It was terrible for him to be compelled to do what he did do.'

'He told me how to capture Hydrus in a bottle,' said Finn. 'It was really strange. He must have been under Hydrus's control at the time, because he did this weird thing, sort of hummed, then projected his voice to the other side of the room, I guess so that Hydrus wouldn't be aware of what he was telling me.'

'If Hydrus had known that Ulysses had told you that, it is not likely that you would have succeeded in capturing him,' agreed Triton. 'At least not in that way.'

'We should thank him,' said Finn, gazing out to sea, his face tight with emotion.

'I will thank him, on your behalf and mine, when I see him for the last time,' replied Triton quietly. 'But now, the ones to be thanked are you. Finn, Fred and Georgie,' said the Sea Djinn, turning his burnished, beautiful face to each of them, one by one, 'I thank you, on behalf of my Kingdom and yours.' He reached into a pouch and took out three pendants. Hanging from thin leather straps were pieces of glass, green and radiant as the sea.

'Sea glass. Hundreds of years old and smooth as stone,' intoned Triton. 'This glass has the light of good in it. No-one evil can wear it. If you ever see it on another, then he or she has been part of this fight too. It will protect you too, from the Dark Ones.'

With a bow, the Sea Djinn slipped a pendant over each of their necks. It was warm against their skin. It seemed to glow.

'It's not over then, is it?' asked Finn.

The Sea Djinn shook his head. 'The sea war is done, at least until the Dark Djinn dies a death which will take him hundreds of years, maybe thousands. I'll make sure to keep him alive for as long as possible. Without a strong, free leader to organise them, his supporters won't fight, and there can only be one leader, so if we keep him imprisoned and alive, we paralyse his army. It will languish. But not so the other armies. Earth, Air and Fire. Those armies are mobilising. Those battles still need to be fought.'

'But our battle is over,' stated Georgie.

'It is,' replied the Sea Djinn. 'Go home to your families. Live, and enjoy life,' he said, before bowing again and swimming away. Only Finn read his mind, heard the words said silently. It is over. *FOR NOW.*

THE END

Grammatical and Historical Note

Scholars will know that djinn is the plural and djinni the singular. I have invoked artistic license to spell both the same as I think it sounds better. There are alternate spellings - jinn (plural) and jinni (singular) and of course, the English but sometimes cliched-sounding genie.

Djinn are alluded to in both Christianity and Islam. The Holy Qur'an describes how Allah created two parallel species of creature; man and djinn, the one from clay, the other from fire. According to the Holy Qur'an, djinn are supernatural spirits below the level of angels (who were created from light) and demons.

Djinn can be good or evil. They can be visible or invisible and can shape shift, assuming human, animal and inanimate forms.

According to the Arabian Nights, Solomon was reputed to have mastered djinn, imprisoning them in sealed jars and throwing them into the sea.

Early Islamic belief suggested that shooting stars were darts thrown at djinn by angels, on whom they were attempting to eavesdrop.

Djinn are altogether rather wondrous creatures. Look out for them! Cunning humans who know the right charms, like Solomon, are said to be able to control them.

Acknowledgements

First I would like to thank my children for teaching me to think as a child again and for showing me how to see magic where it shimmers and lurks.

I need to thank Dubai's gorgeous beaches for hypnotising the plot into my head.

I would like to thank my publisher, Isobel Abulhoul, for her entrepreneurial spirit, dynamism and support, and Jane Hodges, also of Jerboa, for coming to dinner that night and for all her subsequent support.

And I would like to thank my husband, Rupert Wise, for patiently and dynamically reading aloud several drafts over many weeks in many different locations to me and our children so that I could see and hear what worked and what didn't from their reactions. Their support and appreciation made all the writing and re-writing an absolute joy.

Photo by Stu Williamson

Linda Davies read Politics, Philosophy and Economics at Oxford University and then worked for seven years as an investment banker in New York and London. She then escaped banking to write bestselling novels. She lived for three years in Peru before returning to London. She now lives in Dubai with her husband and three children. In an eerily prophetic case of fact following fiction, in October/ November 2005, just after she had woven the theme of kidnap at sea into the Sea Djinn, she and her husband were kidnapped at sea by the Iranian navy and held captive for two weeks. Happily they were released and with considerably greater insight, she completed her novel. Sea Djinn is her first novel for children.